FIRES' ASTONISHMENT

Geraldine McCaughrean was born in Enfield, North London, in 1951. She gained a degree in Education from Christ Church College, Canterbury, working subsequently in magazine publishing and journalism for twelve years until she became a freelance writer. Her children's books have won the Whitbread Children's Award, the Guardian Children's Fiction Prize and the prestigious Carnegie Medal. She has also written drama for radio. She is married, with a daughter.

GERALDINE McCAUGHREAN

Fires' Astonishment

Minerva

A Minerva Paperback
FIRES' ASTONISHMENT

First published in Great Britain 1990
by Martin Secker & Warburg Ltd
This Minerva edition published 1991
by Mandarin Paperbacks
Michelin House, 81 Fulham Road, London SW3 6RB

Minerva is an imprint of the Octopus Publishing Group,
a division of Reed International Books Limited

Copyright © Geraldine McCaughrean 1990

A CIP catalogue record for this title
is available from the British Library
ISBN 0 7493 9120 0

Printed and bound in Great Britain
by Cox & Wyman Ltd, Reading, Berks

Saint Patrick's Breastplate

Today I put on
the sinews of the sky
flames of the sun
moon's glitter
fires' astonishment
lightning's strike
the power of the wind
ocean's trench
ungiving ground
solid rock

I call these powers to take my side
against every pitiless power
that seeks to stray my soul and body
against the chants of false prophets
against dark deeds of the gentiles
against the wrong-thinking of heretics
against sterile idolatry
against the spells of women, smiths and druids
against every mote of evil in man's body and soul.

for Giles Gordon

1

Remembered People

What a journey that had been, after the King's wedding! All that snow on the highways, and two bouts of plague to skirt around. And yet Leo had not minded it. Poignant melancholy had kept him warm all the way home. He had so much in common with the poor King Henry.

Poor Henry. Hadn't they both taken English wives? And hadn't they both been widowed and obliged to remarry? (No, the King had been obliged to remarry: Leo, for some reason he could no longer recall, had done so of his own free will.)

Poor Henry. His only son and heir was dead – drowned in the cold, disestablishing, disinheriting sea. The grief had been there at the Royal Wedding, like a pit in the centre of the cathedral, paled round with smug barons and their rudely healthy sons. 'I should have taken my boy along,' thought Leo.

Poor Henry. No man of his age should have still to be chafing for sparks to light his posterity, still trying to get an heir. What desperate loving there would be for the new Queen. Poor Henry.

Leo's melancholy had warmed him on the homeward ride. Secure in the possession of a grown son, a half-grown daughter and a pregnant second wife, he felt he had the right to pity the King. And to feel pity for a man was tantamount to having the better of him. To feel pity for a king – well, it swelled the breast of a mere feud-lord.

Then he got home to find he had almost everything in common with the King. His children were gone, too.

'Where have they gone? Why have they gone? Did no one think to keep them till I came home?' he had demanded to know. But all he got by way of reply were smiling faces and congratulations. There was to be no pity for Leo.

'God blessed you, sir. God's truly blessed you – to plant a saint in your line. And what a match for your daughter, sir! A French princeling!'

He remembered thinking, 'They didn't grin when they told the King his son was gone.' That was the moment he had begun to feel disaffected from the King. Leo did not want a saint in the family. Just then it mattered not a whit to him whether his grandchildren were princelings: he wanted his children more than grandchildren. Grandchildren were for old men.

Lord God, how he missed those children! He could remember looking furtively into all the rooms, hoping to catch them out in a lie – hoping to find Elshender and Frideswide hiding from him for a joke.

Better to have your son plainly drowned than gone of his own free will, and God knew where. Better not to have had a daughter at all than to come home and find all those years of loving had been poured into a little boat and shipped abroad for ever.

The King had a married brother: a nephew could always succeed him. Why, then, had the barons bothered to shovel such quantities of pity into that bleak wedding ceremony? There was no call for it. Henry need not ratch for sparks at all to light his posterity, unless he chose. And if Henry chose to ratch, the Queen could not gainsay him, Leo supposed. The damned King had the power of command, whereas Leo had long since been banished to the outer darkness of the marriage bed – to the place of wailing and gnashing of teeth.

'Stop grinding your teeth,' said his wife, abandoning the bed as if his waking made it untenable for her. 'Must I be forever telling you?'

'I was thinking about the children.'

'Still?'

Leo laughed miserably. His wife was wholly practical. She never wasted energy on chagrin or sentimental reflection. He could have understood it better if she needed to ration her energy: as it was, she had so much more than he did.

'I miss them,' he persisted.

'Did you expect them to stay at home all their lives?'

'Of course not.' Had he? No, but he was not prepared for them to have disappeared so abruptly down such dark and separate tunnels. 'I can't picture them, you see. If I could picture where they sleep, where they eat – what they see when they look out of their windows . . .'

'What then?'

'Well . . . I might not miss them so much. I was away for a year in Wales with Rufus. I didn't miss them at all then – not in the least! I want to go and see Frideswide.'

'Must we have all this again?' said his wife. Her features seemed to have grouped defensively round her nose, like the occupants of a castle falling back to the protection of the keep. 'You can't go abroad with the countryside in such a state of – '

'Insanity.'

' – flux.'

'Elshender, then. I want to go and find Elshender.'

3

'My dear, if your heart's set on it, I can't stop you looking.'

'Excellent!' Leo clapped his big hands together. The air exploded between his palms. A pigeon flew off the roof, and his manservant, who slept across the threshold, stood up with the door-hanging draped around his shoulders. 'Prepare for a trip, Mann. Gwyne and I are going to find Elshender.'

'Praise be to God,' said Mann, who was deaf.

'Please don't involve me,' said the Lady. 'I won't come. I was with the boy when he had his Calling. I know his thoughts. He'll refuse to see you. The Order may refuse to let you see him. I couldn't bear to see you humiliated. I won't go.'

He tried to turn his surprise into a look of disappointment. Like a cold draught in the small of his back, Gwyne always seemed to stay close, however much she disliked his company. It was one of her many acts of heroism.

'Don't mistake me,' said Gwyne, holding up her hand. 'I know exactly how you feel. I know just how deeply Elshender has hurt you. It was irresponsible – no question. Perhaps if you had been here you could have stopped him going . . . I don't know. He was odd before, but afterwards – I doubt if you could have influenced him. You mustn't blame yourself.'

'Oh. No.' Not for the first time, he was startled by that turn in the conversation. He did not blame himself. Ought he to blame himself? No, it was useless: he blamed Elshender for disappearing overnight into a monastery – not even leaving word which monastery. And chiefly he blamed God. God, he thought, should at least have waited until the boy's father was at home.

And Gwyne ought to have waited to send his little daughter away to a foreign marriage. With a girl of fourteen was such haste really necessary? A child needed more than a stepmother's blessing on her head. Mawkish tears welled up in Leo's eyes. As for Elshender, God should definitely have waited until the householder was at home before commandeering his heir.

'Tell me again about the Vision,' he said, catching hold of her wrist with a certain amount of spite, to make her sit down on the bed beside him.

Her eyes became glazed. Although she often found him too stupid to waste words on, this one extraordinary story she showed no unwillingness to recount over and over again, in every detail. And, standing half-in, half-out of the doorway, Mann was tireless in eavesdropping.

'There was a noise like a hayrick blowing against the house, and when I looked out, all manner of stars and tongues of fire were buffeting the wall and flying off and whirling up. I thought the thatch would burn for sure. Elshender came to my room out of purest fear – he was always a rabbit of a boy, of course . . .

'I held his hand. It was cold like a corpse, and he was breathing very fast through his mouth, like this – *ahaa, ahaa, ahaa*. And all the time this constellation kept washing over the house, as if it would tear it to shreds and scatter us.

'Elshender reached out his hand and caught a piece of fire – or it fell into his hand, I don't know. But it didn't seem to burn him. No, he had it against his belly, low down – like so – and he clutched it there. And all the time he was staring up into the sky. *I must be pure*, he kept saying. *I must be pure, Mother. Don't you see how the clouds are shaped into a map? It's a sign, Mother, where I must go!*'

'And him always so cold with you!' murmured Leo.

The Lady Gwyne gave this a moment's thought. 'Yes, he

5

was always a nasty child. But that night he was altogether different. Changed. Next morning he had me burn all his velvets and woollens, and he wrapped himself in a yard of hessian and said I was never to call him by his name again, nor were any ever to go looking for him. But he'd devote his life to prayer and hardship, and help save his country from the powers of evil.'

'Why not give 'em to the serfs?' muttered Mann unconsciously loud. 'Such a waste of velvets.' And he shuffled away down the steps dragging his buckled feet.

'And yet no one else saw it,' murmured Leo.

'Frideswide saw it. She could tell you if she were here. Otherwise – the village scum – would their coarse minds really comprehend such a thing?'

'No, no. That must be it.'

She stroked his hand – such an unfamiliar gesture that he snatched it away. 'You do understand, husband? I would have gone with Frideswide to France, but with the child new in me, and you away at the Wedding, and Elshender gone on his Calling . . .'

Leo hastened to reassure her. He felt suddenly cheered by the mention of her pregnancy. Perhaps Providence had, after all, allowed for this turn of events. Gwyne would give birth to a boy, and Leo would live long enough to see him grow to an age for responsibility. Then hang Elshender for a thankless heir. Yes: he was, after all, still one step ahead of the poor King.

Still, he would go and find Elshender, even so, and thicken his ear for leaving home without a word to his father.

Some way away, Elshender woke up, dreaming of his father,

and turned over. The great weight of his body almost crushed the air out of his lungs. He flung his hips back into their first position, and waited for the feeling of panic to subside. He wondered if his legs were chilled or cramped into numbness. To keep his mind from a similar atrophy, he recited his daily catechism of remembered names:

'I am Elshender, and Leo is my father;

> Elfleda my love;
> Frideswide my sister;
> Jesus Christ my Lord –
> *and Gwyne belongs to the Devil.'*

Then he slept again, so as to escape his belly's insistence that he was hungry.

2

ANSELM AND ALBAN

'It's been seen again.'

Leo's brother, having sat on the bed, the window-seat and the press, sat down on the travelling chest and got in the way.

Mann was impressed by the news. He had been on his way out of the room, but stopped in the corridor to listen. Leo was not impressed.

'You're a fool, Anselm. It hasn't escaped me that every time I want to set off to see Elshender, you tell me about another sighting. I don't know why you do it, but you always do.'

'I don't think it can be ignored, that's all.'

'Well I do. It's sheerest nonsense.'

Anselm plucked the selvedge of his cloak across and held it in his teeth. He looked like a child clenching its blanket. His big shoulders wilted. He gazed, baffled, at the manservant who kept jerking his head and flicking his hands as if to signal encouragement. Mann wanted him to talk about the sighting. But when the cloak dropped down on to his chest, he had changed the subject. 'You ought to see Elfleda, you know. It's a bad political move to visit Elshender before you've made some sort of reparation to his betrothed. He cast her off.'

'Reparation? She's still marriageable, isn't she? The circumstances are . . . extraordinary. She isn't making an issue of it, surely?'

'She isn't,' said Anselm. 'But she could. Her father could.'

'A God-fearing girl ought to be willing to lose her betrothed to the Almighty. Besides . . . she's still marriageable.'

'Are you sure about that? They saw a lot of each other.'

'Have a care, brother. My boy wasn't any kind of a goat!'

Anselm wrapped both fists in his cloak and sat hunched obstinately on the chest.

"Bout the sighting, sir,' whispered Mann, hanging into the room like a church gargoyle. 'Been seen agin, has'm, sir?'

But Anselm was engrossed in his own thoughts. Leo picked his way round him. He could think of no offence in the world he had done Anselm, but one look at his brother in this mood was enough to make Leo depressed and guilty. He waved Mann away to the courtyard. The superstitious peasant could at least be ordered out of the room, unlike the brother.

Anselm suddenly stood up. His enormous bulk filled the room: his clothes washed over the furniture. Leo took two involuntary steps back and looked up at him, hoping that, after a morning's nervous lurking, Anselm was about to go.

'Well if you won't take any action about these sightings, I suppose I'll have to.'

'Absolutely not,' said Leo indecisively. 'Don't pander to these ignorant scaremongers. Where's your common sense? You know it's foolery.'

'Oh yes, I know . . . Well, in that case,' said Anselm, wringing his cloak between both hands, 'I may go over and ask for Elfleda.'

'You what?'

'Yes. Well. You said it. She's still marriageable. If your lunatic son has bolted for good, the way's open for someone else. Maybe. We'll see. Give my regards to the boy if you see him. No need to mention my intentions, though. It might unsettle him.' With his usual nervous difficulty in negotiating the small door, Anselm left.

Having finally learned the reason for his brother's visit, Leo had no chance to say a word in response. 'Good God,' he said repeatedly. 'Good God. Good God!' He ran to the window, thinking he should call down something appropriate – a blessing, perhaps. His brother had come there to consult him about marrying Elshender's cast-off fiancée, and instead they had talked about sightings and reparation.

But down in the yard, Mann was at Anselm's stirrup, asking questions, asking about the sighting. 'Mann! Shut your mouth and get back here!' shouted Leo furiously, and his brother rode off, unblessed.

'What did that big buffoon want?' asked Gwyne, sliding into the room like a green afternoon shadow.

'The dear old charlatan! He wants to marry Elfleda! Would you believe such a thing? It took a while to get it out of him, but he wants to marry Elfleda!'

Gwyne laid a sudden hand over her belly, protectively. 'At his age. The opportunist. Well then, what of it?'

'It will placate her father . . . Or it might be just the jolt my boy needs to fetch him home. A rival! I don't suppose he gave thought to her marrying with another man . . . least of all his uncle.' Leo snickered to himself. He did not mind riding any distance to find Elshender now: he had something to say. Logic made a poor weapon in an argument with a boy summoned by angels, but to enlist jealousy . . . Emotional over-reaction had always been a family weakness.

'I'm afraid I have bad news for you,' said his wife. 'A messenger's come from Elshender.'

'*Where? Who?* Send him to me! Who is it?'

'Someone – no one. A religious. Elshender's gone on pilgrimage to the Holy Land. *Think of me as dead*, he said.'

'Damn him. Curse him. Damn him. If I had him here to kick . . .' He kicked the chest instead, until it blossomned like a peony, splitting down its seams and spilling folds of tightly packed red cloth. 'Curse him. Let him go. Time's not for wasting on madmen . . . bastard saints.'

'He was always a nasty child,' said Gwyne.

'And you can hold your tongue, woman!'

Nevertheless, she sent for the monk. When he arrived, Leo wished she had not. He had nothing much to ask the mud-matted boy whose tonsure was dark with stubble and whose shoulders rose up like barrows round his monolithic head. He was the embodiment of terror – surely a man who observed the Jesuitical practice of contemplating each night the contents of his own coffin.

'Where are you from?' asked Leo.

'The North Country, sir.'

'Nowhere more precise? No particular bivouac on the long climb to Heaven?'

'Excuse me, sir? You'll have to forgive me my slowness . . .'

'No, little brother. God has to forgive you that. I only have to struggle with impatience . . . I've failed. *Where are you from?*'

'Northumberland, sir. The abbey of Saint Front.'

'That's better. And is my son there?'

'Nobody of your family name has been admitted . . .'

'Is my son Elshender there?'

'No, sir. He was. But now he's not. He's gone on pilgrimage. To the Holy Land. I believe that's the message I'm called on to give you.'

Leo sat down heavily on the bed and stretched out on the

11

covers, suddenly overwhelmed with weariness. The monk began backing towards the door. 'How did he seem?' asked Leo.

'I'm sure he's in health, sir.' This clearly sounded inadequate. 'Saddened by the world's sin, I suppose,' he added.

'I suppose so,' Leo sneered. 'Most of us are, at seventeen. It gives way to despair after a while. Did anyone go with him?'

'With him, sir?'

'With him, sir. To the Holy Land, sir.'

'Yes, sir. No, sir. A handful of monks.'

'It's not a good time of year for a sea crossing.'

'Ah, but with God's . . . you know.'

'Yes, yes. Did he tell you anything about his Calling?'

'Oh no, sir!' The monk stared at Leo for a moment, then shut his mouth with a snap. His eyes bulged a little, and blue veins flickered in his throat.

'What's your name?'

'Name, sir? Names don't . . . Brother Alban, sir. Sir. Please believe me when I say that your son isn't . . . shouldn't . . . give you any cause for grief.'

Leo pulled the covers over his head and asked peremptorily for a blessing. The monk's arm lifted without conviction and, when he saw that the man's eyes were covered, he shuffled out of the room.

The Lady Gwyne's white hand took hold of his hood and pulled back on it so sharply that the cord closed his wind-pipe. She hurried him, coughing and rubbing his neck, along the corridor and down the spiral stairs. She was accustomed to their dips and flaws; he was not. She rushed him down them, her knees and feet clipping him from behind, so that he only kept from falling by sliding his hands down the sharp bricks.

12

At the foot of the stairs she trod on the back of his habit; he was hobbled like a horse.

'I'm sorry, madam,' he said. 'So clumsy,' and picked himself up. Still she towered over him, fully a hand taller, and heavy with alabaster flesh.

'I saw you. You didn't bless my husband.'

He rocked from foot to foot and twisted the rope of his belt. 'No madam. I told you. Grace, you see. I'm not in a state of Grace, you see.'

'Did he believe what you told him?'

'Oh. I suppose so. I'm afraid I'm not the best man you could have chosen. For telling a lie.' He smiled, and the grin hung on his face like a quoit shied at a peg, that almost at once falls off.

He toyed with the possibility that this white bluff of a woman was shielding her husband from bad news. Perhaps the son, the unheard-of Elshender, had met with an accident or died somehow shamefully. 'I feel bound to say that the gentleman, your husband, may go to Saint Front himself, checking . . . Such a long trip . . . Such a disappointment to find . . .'

'My husband will go nowhere. He is always packing. He likes to pack. He likes to think of travelling: it broadens his mind. But he has more important business to keep him here. The countryside hereabouts is in uproar. Perhaps you've heard.'

Brother Alban had not heard. He did not want to hear. He did not want to know about these people. He wished he had gone without bread for a week rather than have asked alms at the door of this particular manor. He wanted to pull his ignorance over his head like a cowl, and continue his long walk. Every time he stopped *en route*, the past caught up with

13

him, like a pebble caught in the hem of his habit. It came as no surprise for this ambush of a woman to have fallen on him and dragged him into her dingy castle and had him memorise some bogus piece of news.

It was no more than the priesthood had done when he was fourteen.

His stomach rumbled.

'Did you hear what I said?'

'Yes, madam. Uproar locally, madam. If I can be of any . . .'

'You can. Come with me.'

She took hold of his hand and led him through the ground floor rooms. One after another, room after room; up a step, down three; through one door, through another; past a servant, past a petitioning serf. Their eyes did not leave the floor until Lady Gwyne was past, then bored into the monk's back. Over a carpet, over a rug – and never once did she let go of his hand, even though their pulses were knocking together like people trying to pass in a doorway. Up stairs, up a spiral precipice all draped in the front of his habit which he kept treading into and tripping up – and still she kept hold of his hand, a hand that for fifteen years had touched nothing but earth, food, water and the dead.

He thought, 'She knows, of course. She sees through me and she knows what I am.'

Of course, the hoop of fire had gone – that magic aura that kept lay people from touching him, a monk. They could reach him now. Men in inns could throw their arms round him and bully him with lewdnesses. Dogs could leap up and tear mouthfuls out of him. Beggars could nudge at him with imploring stumps. Women could catch hold of his hand and drag him through their dingy manor-houses. His habit was

14

not even worn out yet; he had not even been forced to put on lay clothes. And yet already they could grab hold of his excommunicated flesh. His halo of fire had gone. He trembled violently, feeling the loss of his sheltered life like a canary-bird turned out of its cage.

'I need a creature. Alban, did you say your name was?' She took a handful of coins from a purse hanging hidden in the folds of a bed-curtain, and wrapped his hand round them, folding the fingers across his palm. 'Now you are my creature, Alban.'

The monk stared at the money in his palm.

'A situation has arisen locally. An Unquiet. Rumours. At Worm Head, for instance. The local man of God has done what he can, but now it's for you to speak.'

'You want me to calm the people?' Brother Alban followed her face as she paced about the room examining the palms of her hands as though she were reading her own fortune. He was mesmerised by the puckering and smoothing of her red mouth while it disdained to speak. 'Is it a fit of superstition, then, that's taken hold? I own I'm not a superstitious man.'

Lady Gwyne sniffed. 'Why should you think it interests me what you are? Besides, you aren't any manner of a man. You're a monk. Never tell me again what you think. Is that understood?'

'Pardon me, madam.'

'The world is full of rational monks these days. Ha! What a contradiction that is! A rational monk . . . I would prefer the rumours to be believed. Do you understand?'

'To be believed, madam. What rumours?'

'Of the dragon, boy. The dragon.'

Such a spasm of laughter shook the monk that he dropped

the money he was so unaccustomed to holding, and had to crawl around the lady's feet picking it up. His blue jaw wagged, equally unaccustomed to holding a laugh, and he bit his tongue.

She jerked the thong round his neck, so that the metal leg of his crucifix stabbed him in the throat. 'You *can* persuade the scum that the dragon exists, can't you?' she whispered, almost tenderly. 'I don't have to find another creature for such a simple task, do I? I mean, those scruples of yours about lying – nobody's asking you to lie. You see, it's perfectly true. The dragon does exist.'

Brother Alban got up and smoothed the Moorish rug whose silver fringe was washing up against the stone wall like water. He was so glad to be mistaken for a monk, so glad that the secret of his excommunication was intact, so glad to submit to the soothing discipline of obedience again, that he was ready to obey this his new owner to the very last syllable.

Outside in the yard, he even put on the breastplate of Saint Patrick – a kind of doggerel reflex from the past. Formerly he had chanted the prayer each day of his obedient life – to arm his soul with holy words. He put on *the sinews of the sky, fires' astonishment, the strike of lightning, ocean's trench, ungiving ground, solid rock* . . . But the armour was not his. He was no longer entitled to the magic of the words. They refused to shield him. He remained a little lone man made of nothing more than flesh and hair and bone; unhaloed and vulnerable. A piece of animate clay, no more.

THE LADY'S MAN

The hide flaps fell back across the master's window, and Mann hesitated, his eyes on the house, his hand still holding Anselm's stirrup. 'But is it true?' he said for the tenth time.

'Are you so eager to see a dragon, then?' Anselm asked him mockingly.

Mann spat. 'Things've got to be done. If it's true.'

'So you and I shall form an army, shall we, and hunt it down?' Anselm tried to extricate his boot gently from the old man's rooty hands.

'Foh, master, no good you making a joke of it. Things've got to be done.' He was still repeating this as Anselm rode out of the gate.

The frost that had sealed the earth as he rode in had turned to steam now – a white vapour loath to shift or disperse, so that the ground looked like a bubbling cauldron. At the end of the short day, the moisture would settle back and congeal like a white scum of fat. While it steamed, the savour of spring was mouth-watering.

The contours of the land channelled him down towards the sea, hanging in folds like a cloak from the collar of white chalk at Worm Head. At the Head the wind was so blustery that it stole all sound from the seagulls, from under the horse's hoofs and out of the leather tack. It left only the sensation of his cloak cracking and his horse staggering a little as he hurried on down into the arms of Worm Bay. A spring tide was stuffing sea water enthusiastically but clumsily up the estuary, leaving patches of sand bare but swamping dry roots and bushes. A fluke of wind had flexed the sea round the promontory and swelled the basin where the fishing boats were moored. From up on the slopes they looked like dogs straining to get free.

On the opposite headland, in a deep hollow behind the cliff, stood Elfleda's home – a long building whose shape was obscured by a fungus of outbuildings. A scalding trickle of adrenalin ran down from Anselm's stomach, as he remembered what he was doing there, and he hurried his horse down to the harbour to defer the dreadful climax of arriving.

At various stages of mental and physical decay, the oldest inhabitants of the village sat propped in doorways. The rest were sitting out in the open round three black cauldrons, among the trestles where, in the right course of things, they gutted the fish. The black legs of the cauldrons jostled for warmth over the same strung-out heap of embers. Listless even to the extent of ignoring him, the villagers sat with bowls in their laps and birds around their feet, looking out to sea. Children stared down into the cooking-pots, their heads erased by the steam.

'Too rough to fish?' said Anselm cheerfully, and a woman who was winkling out a last mussel threw down the shell in disgust.

'What fish?'

Anselm, whose thoughts were entirely up in the cliff-top house, nodded and stared out to sea like everyone else, holding his cloak edge between his teeth. He was not there in spirit, but he could not quite bring himself to go.

'No fish,' said one of the children, looking up out of the steam. Her eyebrows were wet with fishy condensation.

'Ah,' said Anselm. He knew nothing about fish.

But there truly were no fish. There had not been one now for eighteen days. Not one muddy flounder, not one spiny gurnard, not one slimy conger eel. White in the pot, bubbled into the semblance of swimming, were a dozen crabs, a handful of barnacles, mussels and some whelks. Communally scavenged, they were for communal eating: one meal a day of broth in which shale and sand and sea shells hung in gritty suspension. The old women in the doorways looked at the salt slops brought them and rolled white eyes at their children and asked if they were to go mad drinking sea water.

The little children, having grown tired of asking after the fish and getting no reply, had taken on the only active role, grubbing for shellfish and crabs, while their parents, too horrified at this unmerited supernatural punishment, sat and stared at the sea. And the sea, glutted and swollen in its springs, made mouths at them.

They sat and they waited, to see if it was the end of the world. They asked the priest, but he did not know. He said, 'You know my needs are small: a little mackerel, perhaps – or a sole will suffice.' He thought the fishing was bad and that they were hoarding for themselves. But this was not a shortage. There were no fish.

So they watched the blow-hole, and listened for its instructions, and hoped that in time they would deduce the syntax of its speech. That is what they were watching now. And that was what Anselm was watching, without realising it, for his eyes were resting on the base of the cliffs, while his thoughts climbed strenuously towards the house in the hollow.

The tide was almost full. There was a noise like some tubercular sea monster hawking up phlegm. There was a

19

pause – one long, dire, apocalyptic hoot that made the fisherwomen pull up their knees – and then a deafening, racketing geyser of water, solid and sinewy, poured into the sky. It dissolved into a plume of white foam, and the wind caught it and drew the veil of spray across the face of the sea. When it fell, the bar across the bay mouth was flattened. It lay like a barn floor, hard and shiny, and a winnowed chaff of silver water rattled down on it.

Anselm was spellbound. The villagers turned on him expressions of belligerent pride, as if to say, 'Well? Can you match such an omen of doom?'

Six waves shouldered their way into the bay and lost impetus in the oval lee of the cliffs. The seventh howled its way up the blow-hole and stood so brightly white in the air that after it had fallen the cockade of it stayed on the retina. 'God's breath! I've never seen the like,' said Anselm, as drifting spray fell on his face. He wiped it on to his finger-tips and looked at them as if the water should have some different quality, some elasticity to make it mould into such a shape.

''Snot the first time,' said an old woman, her face so reddened with varicose blood vessels that she looked apoplectic. 'Each time there's high-water springs with an east wind following, the cliff speaks. It speaks grief and graves. Grief and graves, that's what. 'Twas so last time. 'Twill be so again.'

'What happened last time, then?' said Anselm, biting back a snicker of embarrassment.

The woman ran her eyes up the estuary, up the cliffs, up the fetlock and withers of Anselm's horse, and said with a great spreading of hands, 'Well, the floods, man!'

Anselm plucked at his cloak. 'What's that? Astounding. Amazing! Oh freak of nature! High-water spring tides, an onshore wind and you got *floods*? Truly, God had a hand in that.' And he gave a great woof of laughter that made him look and sound like an Irish wolfhound. He reined his horse back on to the path.

The woman's husband thumped his knees and shrieked with laughter. The more his wife slapped at his shoulders, the more he laughed. The children joined in out of confusion, and their parents joined in out of nervous relief. The noise of their laughing followed Anselm up the hill like a cheer. He felt most heartened. Even the blow-hole hooted with mirth.

The joke took him all the way to the top of the slope without a qualm. He did not hear the old oracle of Worm Head crush a mussel between her jaws and say, 'Bloody gentlemen.'

Anselm got off his horse, trying to occupy his mind with possible reasons for the shortage of fish, and so keep himself from sweating. But his thoughts returned one by one to Elfleda, like homing pigeons.

Young as she was, and many as the years had been in his life before she was born, he could not remember a time when he had not wanted Elfleda. And now he was going to ask for her. Sweat swamped the small of his back.

Earnestly, he greeted de Rochfoll with, 'I hear there are no fish in the bay. Most awkward for you in Lent, I suppose.'

De Rochfoll glowered at him. The old man's look of malice meant nothing. His eyes were milky with cataracts, and he relied chiefly on smell to tell Anselm from his horse. 'Leo's son's a cow-pat.'

'It's Anselm, sir. Leo's brother.'

'I know that. I can tell that, can't I? Come in. Come in. It's the turn of the tide.'

Rain fell like an adze out of the massed clouds, and continued long after the tide had crawled away and left the blow-hole silent. As Anselm stood by the fire and tried not to look about for Elfleda or listen for her footsteps, he remarked on the blow-hole to de Rochfoll. 'A remarkable trick of nature.'

But nobody had told the old man about it. He could not understand what Anselm was trying to describe. For him, the sea was a grey gap in the fence of blurred green and brown that surrounded his house. He was content to go as far as the stables each day, leaning on the shoulder of a boy, or to be put into a cart and taken to church or to market. But as for the sea, it was just a colour he associated with the coldest draughts, the loudest clatter of wind against the house.

Anselm cursed himself for not thinking in advance of a reason for calling on de Rochfoll. He had thought it was a simple matter of getting together the courage and having the one conversation. De Rochfoll sat in his chair, drumming the arms and talking about wheatmould, hunting, dog-breeding, Lenten food. 'What a civil old gentleman,' thought Anselm with a pang of grateful affection, and went on chatting inconsequentially and fumbling with a coin that had got into the lining of his jacket.

'Well?' said de Rochfoll suddenly, raspingly. 'Has Leo heard from that mooncalf son of his?'

'What?' said Anselm, startled. 'Oh. No.'

Like a clover-blown cow stuck with a pin, de Rochfoll deflated in the chair. His hands dangled over the arms and twitched. 'You've not come from Leo, then?'

'No. No, I'm just . . . a visit . . . being sociable. I thought I'd come over and . . .'

'Kind thought. Kind thought, yes. Don't see many people –

especially now. I remember one year. My wife was alive then. There were scores of saucy boys paying court to the Elf. Day and night. Day and night. Different now. Different. Have some dinner.'

He led the way through to the dining area on the far side of the hearth. Only then did Anselm see that the old man had interrupted his meal to entertain him. But thinking he had come on Leo's business, de Rochfoll had not been going to offer him food.

A mess of cold meats was thrust at him by a gauche, slovenly, stunted boy. It was Anselm's guess that servants were chosen for the height of their shoulders in relation to de Rochfoll's outstretched hand. He was a man of average build, but he moved around his household like the blinded Cyclops among his tick-ridden sheep.

'And how's Elfleda?' asked Anselm, examining his food closely.

To which de Rochfoll said in reply, 'Done much hunting, sir? I've not been out on a horse this twelvemonth past. Too many trees, you know. 'Sides. Can't tell a boar from a bear, eh?'

'Yes, sir. I mean, I fear it must have lost its pleasure for you, sir.'

As the curtain at the foot of the stairs was drawn back, the rings clattered on the pole like a birdscarer, and Elfleda, like the bird, fluttered to the table. She carried her head down, and her hair was so tangled that it met over her nose and mouth in brown strands – as if someone had scribbled on her face with charcoal. The serving-boy jumped out of her way more quickly than deference required. Elfleda took in the presence of Anselm the moment she entered, and instead of sitting down

23

at table, picked up a morsel of chicken murmuring, 'Forgive me, gentlemen,' and ran back up the stairs.

'Was that Elfleda?' said Anselm. The long anticipation, the sudden arrival, and the sudden flurry of unexpected movement had brought him to his feet like a pointer. There was sweat between his ribs and an absolute determination in him to ask what he had come to ask. 'I was wanting to speak on the matter . . .'

'I'm glad her mother's dead,' said de Rochfoll. 'And how *is* that dear brother of yours, Leo the liar?'

Anselm hesitated, then eased himself back into his chair, hating himself. 'He's troubled by a dragon,' he said. 'You must have heard about the dragon.'

'Dragon? Is it dragons now? I know that kind of vision. Sent by God? It's sent by too much gin and Rhenish. The man's a pickled gherkin.'

'It's not Leo who's seen it. The way I guess it, some ill-advised priest chanced to mention the Last Days . . .'

'Why? What's happened in the last days?'

'No, sir. The Last Days. I mean the absolutely Last Days. The beast of Satan walking on the earth.'

'Dog vomit,' said de Rochfoll.

'Um, anyway. Someone saw it.'

'Saw what?'

'Saw the beast of Satan walking on the earth, sir. Now everybody's seeing it. At least everyone knows some man who has a cousin whose mother believes she has seen it.'

'Pickled gherkins,' said de Rochfoll, and belched to add emphasis to his spleen.

'Yes, sir . . . But it's occupying Leo's time, that's all I meant to say. It's giving him trouble.'

'Good. I dare say he believes in it.'

'Oh I dare swear not, sir.'

De Rochfoll laughed snarlingly, maliciously. 'That pig's ear believes what he chooses. Visions. Heavenly summonses. Dragons . . . He probably believed that first wife of his didn't lie astray to get that goblin son of theirs.'

'You don't mean that, sir,' said Anselm, moving round the table to put the old man's wine within reach as he choked on his fury.

De Rochfoll panted and gasped. The spittle rattled in the loose pouches of his cheeks, and his beard shook. He hawked and spat and wagged his head. 'No, I don't blame her. I blame that mad bullock your brother and that cow-pat son of his. Don't they know what they've done to this house? I'm the last de Rochfoll. There'll be no more after me. No one will take the Elf now.'

'I will,' said Anselm.

Standing up behind de Rochfoll to bang his back as he coughed, Anselm suddenly felt the great bulk of his physique. No need to beg. He did not have to beg. There now, it was said.

De Rochfoll half turned in his chair and patted the hand resting on his shoulder. 'That's kind,' he said chokingly. 'That's . . . truly . . . kind. You really shouldn't be so . . . That's womanish kind of you, Anselm. But of course you shan't. I wouldn't let you.'

'But I *want* to, sir.'

'No, no.' The old man shook his head and smiled. 'Take my advice, lad. Don't go doing penance for another's sin. That's no reason to make a marriage.'

'No, truly! I *want* to marry her, de Rochfoll! That's what I came here for!' shouted Anselm.

The wide, grinning old face closed up as though a cord had

been drawn tight round it. The eyes puckered. The mouth suddenly had no lips. 'So your brother's finally seen his duty, has he? And you're the reparation, are you? The sacrificial goat, eh?' He tugged his lower lip with finger and thumb, trying to see the subterfuge, the trick. 'It's good,' he said. 'I don't know what it makes of you, 'Selm, but it's good reparation. Brother for son, eh?' Then intuition cracked his face and he wrapped a fist in Anselm's belt. 'Are you *fancy*? Are you *gelded*? Can you get children, or what?'

Anselm was speechless, appalled. He pulled his belt away with such force that the old man nearly fell out of his chair, then he strode round the hearth and came back clutching his cloak to his chest. 'Pox on you, Rochfoll! I'm a man as much as another . . . I'm as much a man as . . . pox on you, Rochfoll! What else would I do with your daughter?'

'Well then!' The blind old man beamed at him. 'It's a contract!' Misjudging Anselm's position in the room, he contracted the settle to marry his daughter. For him, the restoration of his family honour was so unexpected, so complete, that any settle in the land that could offer such satisfaction was welcome as a son-in-law.

The smart quickly went out of the wound to Anselm's pride. Insults could not make him foolish to the fact that he had what he had come for – for whatever reason he had been given it. 'And you won't miss her too much?' he asked, with what casual good grace he could summon. 'She must be a second pair of eyes for you.'

'There's my boys,' said de Rochfoll, and the serving-boy was there, under his arm in a second, with a smirk and the impudent offer of a filthy hand for Anselm to shake, and afterwards a quick, indecent gesture of the forearm.

26

'No call to wait,' de Rochfoll was saying. 'As soon as you like.'

'Tomorrow, then. A sevendays. Whenever you choose, sir. But not beyond a fortnight, I pray.'

The old man began to flutter and tremble with gratification, and Anselm saw the topic of a dowry hover on his lips. Perhaps he was wondering if he could make Leo's family pay another forfeit for the broken engagement between Elfleda and Elshender. But the matter skirted away again, for fear of rupturing the euphoria. Instead the father said, 'You must speak to the Elf herself now. You'll want to see her and tell her.'

Anselm would much rather have talked about the dowry. He did not want *that*.

Disappointment as sharp as if de Rochfoll had shut the door in his face overwhelmed him. Never during all the stoical preparation he had made for being refused had he pictured himself speaking to Elfleda herself. Her feelings he had pushed to the back of his mind, telling himself that in time she could be persuaded to believe in this second-best marriage. But what if she had the power to sway her father's mercenary heart, begging him not to sell her to this ageing, overgrown oaf? No. No. The contract had been made. The old man would not let his unfortunate daughter's feelings stand in its way.

'Elf! Elfleda! Go and get her, boy. Tell her our visitor wants to speak with her.' De Rochfoll dropped clumsily into his chair and smiled to himself. In his blindness, he had lost the trick of hiding his pleasures and pains.

The boy came back with word that Elfleda would receive the visitor, but in her own room, where the draughts were fewer.

27

'Show me the lady's room,' said Anselm to the boy, though he had long since calculated exactly where it must lie.

Elfleda sat on the pillow of her bed, a permanent structure carved into a crossbeam of the floor below and hung about with curtains. Her knees were clutched up against her chest, and she was wearing her cloak, so that he could take in no detail of her clothing. Hair that had been dark brown at his last visit was white at the temples. Her eyelids were red and flaked with dry skin, and the lashes crusted with yellow by some slight infection. An area of psoriasis across her chin and in the creases from her nose to the corners of her mouth gave her the muzzled look of a ferret. Hollow in the cheek and hollow under the eye, she put one hand up in front of her face the moment he ducked into the room.

Shocked by the horse-like bigness of his body, Anselm was still more shocked to see the smallness of her. Her wrists were no more than the hipped stems of dead roses.

'Madam, you're not well.'

'I'm quite fit, sir,' she said, 'I promise you.'

'I am glad. Such a long time since I've taken pleasure in the seeing of you. When was the last time, I wonder?'

'At my betrothal to Elshender. You were kind enough to promise a bullock and a cow.'

'Ah. Yes. Yes.' Anselm had exhausted his conversation and destroyed his hopes. He leaned his forehead against the roof so that he was propped against it like a ladder. 'Your father and I . . .' he said. And he could hear de Rochfoll shuffling about at the foot of the stairs.

'I heard what you both said.'

It was a relief. Anselm opened one eye, but the beam he was

resting against was spidery, and her face too was webbed across with hair. He could only see her straighten her back and lower her legs over the side of the bed. Contract or no, he knew he could not hold her to a marriage when she spoke her revulsion for him.

'I am indebted to you, Anselm, for the compliment you pay me,' she said, as if it were a formula whose meaningless words had been learned along with her catechism.

'But?'

'And I am agreeable to the marriage, if it can take place at once. Please persuade my father to bring it about quickly. Today. Is that possible?'

Anselm opened his mouth to reply, but nothing came of it. His sinuses were swollen with tears, and his bowels had melted. He dared not smile: the ferocity of it might frighten her off her perch – make her flutter away through the window crevice to some inaccessible roost.

Besides, there was not the smallest trace of joy in Elfleda.

Not very far away – within earshot of the blow-hole, and without shelter from the torrential downpour – Elshender lay and watched the shafts of rain spatter him with mud as they landed like javelins. He found it of some interest that the shock of the icy drops hitting him high in the back was much greater than low down, at the base of his spine, and that round his rib-cage he could feel the course of every drop as it trickled round his chest and swelled the mire beneath his belly. He thought, from an itching, that parasites had probably invaded his genitals. But then perhaps it was an omen.

With a sucking 'shuck', he pulled his face out of the mud and looked up. A cow had wandered into his restricted line of vision. If it had not been for the cow, he would have held good to his intention of dying.

4

THE CATTLE THIEF

Leo looked at the woman in front of him and realised that he did not know what she had just said.

'Try to show an interest,' said Gwyne's voice loudly from behind him. The words rang round the cold, bare room. 'Do try to show interest.' Angrily, he determined to take issue with her later. She surely did not realise it, but in her lust for efficiency she was forever adopting that mother/son inflection: Do wake up; Do pay attention; Do wipe your nose. He would not take issue with her later, but he knew that he should.

'Tell me again, in your own words. Take your time. Precisely what did you see?' As the widow began again, he tried to chafe his right ankle between his left foot and the chair-leg to stop the spangling sensation. But it continued to feel as if he had trodden in nettles. The widow's eyes wandered unintentionally to this crossing and uncrossing of legs.

She was about thirty. Leo remembered that her husband had died the year before of anthrax, along with most of his cows. It had caused a stir – rumours of plague, some ostracism of the woman herself. A drizzling child sat on her hip, watching the rain-water spill in under the door. Leo began to watch it, too.

'Are you listening, Leo?' said his wife.

'Yes.'

'Well there's only one left now, lordship, and she won't give

31

milk. Two gone out of three. I won't live, lordship. It'll be the end of me. And I'm only one. There's others.'

'Was there any sign of blood?'

'Blood, sir?'

'Blood. Or chewed-up skin, or horns, or hoofs or burned patches?'

'No, sir. It ate the lot, sir.'

Leo sighed and shook his head. He felt helpless. His determination did not match the widow's. 'Your cows have wandered off, woman. That's the sum of it. Go home and look for them.'

The widow grasped her child's thigh and hitched it higher on her body. But she remained standing, two steps down from Leo's dais, doggedly refusing to go. 'Them were good cows,' she said.

'I'm not disparaging your cows, woman. But if you really think they've been eaten by the Great Beast Satan, and that even at this very minute the End of the World is rushing down on us, with bloody moons and the dead raised up and no more sea and such – should we in fact be talking about cows? Should we be so petty? Should we not in fact be praying and fasting and making ready for Judgement?' He followed this up with a laugh, but the widow scowled and stood firm while his words percolated through her grubby head. One or two lodged on the way.

'I can't be praying all the time,' she said sulkily. 'Life goes on . . .'

'Precisely!'

'. . . for now. The children got to be fed, for now. I got to go on thinking of cows and such. And I won't live on one cow. Not me and the children.'

'But what do you want me to *do*, for God's sake?'

'Kill it. She wants you to kill it.'

Leo screwed himself round in his chair and scowled at his wife. Had she no sense of humour? Gwyne was smiling gently at the widow. 'The good dame is frightened, Leo. Please do try not to be heartless. The good woman has suffered a loss. Try to understand her view of it.'

'*But there is no dragon!*' he shouted.

The widow shielded her infant's head against the noise. 'Where are my cows, then, lordship?'

Leo sniffed long and furiously.

'My husband will investigate the matter,' said Gwyne. 'You may go home now.' The widow curtsied at once and hurried towards the door.

'Oh, no. Oh, no.' Leo got up with much waving of arms and melodramatic wagging of his head. 'If I'm answerable for the cows now, I'd better start searching, hadn't I? A cowherd now, am I? Or a dragon-slayer? I know where your cows are, you ignorant woman.'

'Where, master? Tell us!' The widow stared.

'Oh, no. Let us not put off our responsibilities. Such weighty matters mustn't fall on the shoulders of inferior men! Let me undertake *in person* to find them. Look, didn't I wake this very morning craving the lot of the merry cowherd?'

'A tantrum, Leo?' whispered Gwyne frostily, loudly. 'So early in the day.'

He stamped out to the stables, the rain waking the widow's child into full cry, the woman splashing after him through the puddles. Seeing the scantiness of her clothing, he at once regretted his outburst, for it meant trailing her and her child across the rainy heath, instead of simply letting her shelter in the sheds until the rain eased off.

She would not hear of staying behind. Whether to prove him wrong or to find her benighted cows, she was prepared to walk beside his horse all the way to her hut. So he gave her a horse. And by then his wife had dressed herself against the weather and was coming too. He was cornered.

'Think of our babe,' he muttered at her. 'This is foolishness.'

'I agree,' said Gwyne, arching her neck.

'I forbid you to put the child at risk.'

But his theatrical gesture had taken on a momentum of its own. They all set off on horseback to look for a pair of lost cows four miles away. And the closer they got to the scene of the disappearance, the more impelled Leo felt to justify himself.

'This dragon madness – I don't know how it got started, but there's some with sense to see it for nonsense, and there's some can turn that nonsense to their advantage. Do you understand?'

'Um,' said the woman.

'I mean your *neighbours*, woman. What better time to thieve cattle than when a poxy dragon will carry off the blame? That's where your cows are, dame. In the next-door herd!'

The widow chafed her child's blue hands between her own thoughtfully. She had never sat in a saddle before, and rocked in it more than she needed so as to hear it creak. But she did listen. And she did have the shreds of an intelligence. He pitied her as he pictured her struggling with the idea of the End of the World. He tried to imagine how frightened he would be if he had been fed from birth on black bread and superstition. But he quickly turned to the more present problem: what to do if the cows were not easily found?

'Of course your beasts may be butchered by now,' he told her.

34

The nearest house to the widow's belonged to a pig-man. There were pigs under the trees, pigs eating a row of raised turnips, pigs in the doorway of the hut, and a big old sow, trussed front and back, covered in a welter of piglets. There was a riven carcase hanging from the outside eaves, and a tank of brawn cooking inside the door.

At the sight of Leo, Gwyne and the widow, the pig-man came slithering down the hillside on the sides of his bare feet, gathering a raft of twigs and wet vegetation as he came. His face was smeared with mud and he was as wet as if he had been in the river fully clothed. His trousers were made of a blanket tied round each ankle and round the waist, so that the chaps hung open and dripped. He seized hold of Leo's stirrup and banged his forehead twice, three times against it. 'It's had me pigs, master! It's had six o' me pigs!'

'Damn,' said Leo. He glanced at Gwyne, but her revulsion at the smell of pig hid any other expression. Though she was not shivering as he was, her wet clothes had stuck to the incipient swell of her belly, and he was frightened for the baby. They said the sight and smell of a pig could affect the unborn. But that too was just superstition. 'Where were the pigs taken from?' he asked the pig-man.

'Over yonder! Blood all over!' He was like a mongrel, leaping and yelping round the horse.

One ordure-covered furlong past the hut, the sparse grass was treacly brown. Blood from the jugular of a pig had spurted fifteen feet and left a straight stain – almost as straight as the cart-tracks that led up to the stain, and almost as plain as the print of donkey-hoofs in the mud.

The widow with the child pointed them out to the pig-man scornfully. 'Be you blind and stupid both? Your good neighbours has took 'vantage of you, you gob o' yellow. Dragon? Foh fah, y'dolt.'

The pig-man looked from widow to master, and fell in behind the horses as they moved off along the cart tracks. The peculiar, triumphant procession empressed two foresters at the lodge at the end of the Royal Chase – because they had axes and a log-rolling spike.

They left the child at the lodge, along with Gwyne silently rubbing her sides in front of the fire, the bad smell persisting in her face.

The cart tracks led to a hutless campsite. Not neighbours but outlaw didicois had visited the widow and pig-man. Their thieves' camp was in a soggy hollow, surrounded by beech trees. As the procession approached, the heavy tassles of the spring trees bobbed as rain gathered in them and dripped away. Like lanterns they were fittingly cheerful over Leo's head as he prepared, with some pleasure, to be proved right.

The cart lay overturned outside the trees, its axle broken, they supposed, by one too many stolen pigs. The rain gullied down into a central quagmire, but the dead tree in which the fire had been lit still smouldered. A dozen sheep-fleeces, rolled inside out, had been crammed into the branch junctions of a tree. From one of the branches hung two split pigs, the lights puddled in repellent heaps underneath. A piece of canvas was stretched between two bramble bushes to make a shelter, and there was a smell of burned flesh.

As they glimpsed this over the rim of the hollow, and dismounted, there was a great tossing and fracture of branches that made them all start. A cow broke from the bushes and lunged clumsily up the slope only to slither back down on its hocks.

'Mine, lordship!' cried the widow, inadvertently grasping Leo's arm in her delight. She looked across at the pig-man and laughed at him: 'Dragon! Foh fah, y'ninny!'

'Are the pigs yours?' Leo asked the pig-man.

'Look at 'em. Killed with na' but a scrap of flesh on,' said the man, and clumped his forehead with the heel of his hand.

The loose cow righted itself at the foot of the slope and, trotting across the mire, shouldered up against the brambles. The canvas shelter sagged and pulled taut again, showering a catch of rain-water out of its folds, and loosing an appalling crescendo of screaming from inside.

"Way! 'Way! Get off! Nah! Please! God! God! God!'

Leo stood still. The pig-man lost his footing and slid back down the slope they had climbed. The two foresters swung their weapons in both hands. But the widow picked up her skirts and ran down a staircase of tree-roots and rabbit-holes and mud towards the canvas awning.

A man of about her own age and griminess was shuffling himself, feet first and still screaming, out of the tent in an attempt to get away from the cow. He saw the cow, he saw the woman, and he saw the man on the brink of the hollow. But he went on flapping his hands ineffectually, and his eyes went on gaping round the hollow. 'Where is it? Where is it?'

The widow stepped astride the man (whose right leg seemed to be worn back to front) and began hitting him in the face with her fists and demanding, 'Where's the other? Where's me other cow?' Her fists hit him on every word, and each time he caught hold of her fists, she twisted them free and hit him again.

'Stop! Stop it!' called Leo. 'Let him speak.'

But the didicoi did not speak. He only sobbed, and clung to

the widow's legs with his pulpy face buried in her skirts. He was afraid of the daylight.

His leg had been broken, and his fellows had abandoned him when they fled. He had dragged himself under the canvas as the darkest cover he could find. And he had lain still for perhaps two, perhaps four, perhaps six hours, crying into an uncured fleece. Every turning leaf, every drop of rain on the canvas, every fly finding its way towards the pigs' lights had fallen into his ear like hot lead.

And then the cow had shouldered up against the tent, trodden on his broken leg. And terror had come down on him like the temple on Samson, crushing his sanity to a pulp. The woman with the fists was powerless to rouse him from his nightmare: the pillar of fire among the trees, the rattle of hoofs and horns falling through the leafy canopy, the squealing of pigs as they tried to climb out of the hollow and rolled back on top of him – on to his legs – the quicksand of pain that had stopped him moving out of that place, out of the path of its shadow, out of its reach.

It overtook him on the ground. It passed him on the ground. It touched him as it passed. And then the silence, and then the cow brushing against the tent.

'So your friends saw us coming, did they?' asked Leo, bending down to straighten the man's leg. The widow was holding the didicoi's head now, squeezing the mud out of his hair and rocking him against her knees as she made the shushing noises that soothe babies to sleep.

The vagrant looked around him out of unfocused, darting eyes.

"Twill come back, won't it?' he grizzled, and his jaws chattered. "Twill come back for me.'

'What will?' said Leo gently.

"Twill come back for me. The dragon will, won't it, sir?'

'Damn you,' said Leo, and let the broken leg drop out of his hands.

Brother Alban had been at his friary since he was fourteen. His father was a ferryman on the Tyne. Only as a little boy, when he had been collecting fares all day on the crossing, had Alban held the sum of money he now had in his purse, given him by Gwyne to make him her creature. They were no riches, but the coins were enough to breach the only vow he had ever found easy to keep. Poverty was not a discipline for such as Alban; it was a foregone conclusion.

He had had a possession once. A shawl his father had brought home as a sailor, from Portugal, and given to Alban's mother on their wedding day. She gave it him when she was dying. But that had been destroyed. His abbot had insisted on its destruction. He had ordered Alban to destroy it as an act of obedience to the vow of poverty.

Feeling the purse of money bang against his groin, Alban thought the abbot had probably been right. Given the long years of possessionlessness, he could see how easy poverty had become. He had lusted so fiercely to preserve that shawl that he recollected even now the heat from the flames as it burned. But he could feel no link of ownership whatsoever with the coins at his waist. It was irrelevant that the abbot owned his grandfather's brewery and six pairs of boots: he had been right to make Alban destroy the shawl.

Though Alban had lost the trick of ownership, it did not prevent him from feeling owned. Even if Gwyne had not sent her brutish, spiteful horsemaster to accompany Alban, he would still have felt bound to do just as she told him. He tried to explain this to the horsemaster, a man called Bruno. But Bruno only looked at him and said that thieving came as naturally to priests as dogs did to bitches.

Bruno's nose was so Roman that it might have been chipped off by a slip of the chisel, or suffered collision with a wall. And he seemed to resent the fact that Alban, though not a man built to Olympian proportions, was a head taller than him. He had supplied Alban with a horse which, at every third stride, dropped a shoulder, fit to pitch its rider out of the saddle.

Obedient to Gwyne's commands, they rode up to the cliffs, to the village at Worm Head. The latest reported sighting of the dragon had been close by the sea. Because of the rumours, there was already a priest in the village – a spiritual comforter sent by the Prior of Saint Bede's to put down superstition; to quell any pagan stirrings. A whipper-in, it might have been said; a lad born in the village.

The 'lad' was forty and greatly revered among the villagers, who held him as a mascot. On holy days in the past, urged by his old mother to walk her from end to end of the village, this bright, confident man called Paul had collected an entourage, a train of neighbours, asking him for news and advice. They lobbed cut flowers into his cowl; and lots were drawn to decide which boat would offer him a day's fishing. He ate lemon sole and oysters. He was the nearest thing the village had to their own madonna.

Paul was affectionately amused by his home villagers. A serious sin was unrecorded among them. The wind was too piercing, the sea too demanding, the damp too crippling, the wealth too communal for the Devil to get a foothold at Worm Head. Even old Mother Occult had been cheated out of her

40

niche when all her symbols and ceremonies had been made over to Christianity. Now the sea and the boats were blessed rather than overcast with spells. In return, God gifted fish to the fishermen, instead of the fish having to be conjured into the nets. Over the generations, there had been a very amicable change of management – the old spirits letting their tenure lapse, the new God dancing in over the water.

When Paul heard tell of the dragon and the blow-hole, he hurried to Worm Bay feeling nothing but sadness that he would have to reprove his sheep for silliness when silliness was, after all, such a natural characteristic of sheep. Waiting in his mother's hut for the afternoon rain to stop, he realised that silliness had stampeded into stupidity. He was glad to see another religious arrive on horseback, out of the drenching storm – especially one sent from the manor-house in the company of one of Lord Leo's own serving-men.

'Come in. Come in and get dry.' He startled Alban and his horse as he jumped out of the doorway across a puddle, and grabbed the bridle. 'Come on both of you. Get in out of this filth.'

The horsemaster dismounted at once and pulled Alban out of the saddle, for quickness. He knew just where to grip an arm so that the blood stopped and the muscles pulled up short.

Alban jibbered at the sudden appearance of a priest. He felt his disguise gape. He felt certain, as he peeled off his hood, that his secret was laid as bare as his stubbly tonsure. As he went to duck through the door, the fingers again gripped his biceps.

'Wouldn't go ahead of me, scum, would you? Not ever, would you, scum?'

'I beg your pardon, Bruno.' Alban stumbled into the slatted

41

darkness of the hut. Already the local priest was reaching out a mug of hot wine, which Alban handed at once to the horsemaster. The priest's old mother sat in a corner, pulled an unwilling dog into her arms and plucked at its ears uneasily. The rain stopped pattering on the roof almost at once, but the trickling of it under the back wall continued. 'Get your clothes off, lad,' she said sharply to Alban, and watched with yellow eyes until the newcomers submitted to hospitality and peeled off their clothing. Alban sat amid the white arms and legs he so rarely saw, and Bruno, who had stripped entirely naked, reclined Romanesque by the central fire, head on hand, and sniggered.

'This is excellent,' said Brother Paul. 'You can help me. You're Lord Leo's man, aren't you? And you, too?'

'The Lady Gwyne asked me to . . .' Alban let the sentence taper off, since this cleric seemed to know already that he was an owned man.

'I saw the brands on the horses,' said Paul, looking pleased with himself. 'Yes, excellent. You can help me. The Prior would be most unhappy to see the state of things hereabouts. Which house are you from, boy?'

'Me? I'm . . . I . . .'

'He's a new chaplain for the Lady Gwyne,' said Bruno.

'I guessed as much. But which house raised . . . Oh.' Paul interrupted himself, crestfallen. It had just occurred to him that the Lady of the manor had chosen a North Country man in preference to any at Saint Bede's. The Prior really would be most unhappy.

'Got a bite to eat, have you Mother?' demanded Bruno.

The old woman rolled her pale eyes and shook her head at him and mouthed, 'No fish! No fish!'

42

'That's an odd thing, don't you think?' said Brother Paul, pausing most effectively to gather everyone's attention. 'No fish for twelve days. Not a scad, not an eel, not a single fish. Of course the winds are freak, the tides are freak. But you can see how these poor simple folk might fret.' To hear him, he might have been born between sheets, a hundred miles inland.

'And the sea talks,' said his mother, glowering at the back of his neck.

'Dear Ma.' Paul smiled round at the visitors. 'A rock fault. A high tide. Water pushed through.' He spread his hands. 'A blow-hole. Indeed, I hope you'll both stay and hear it on the midnight tide. It won't last another day 'fore the moon wanes too far. Stay and hear it tonight.'

'I'd like to,' said Alban.

'The Lady Gwyne wants to hear about the dragon,' said Bruno, stretching himself like a cat.

Brother Paul gave a loud and skilful laugh, signifying at once good humour and superior knowledge. 'It's time I went to speak to the folk on that very subject. Come and join me when your clothes are dry.' After he went outside, they could hear him, like Christ on the shores of Galilee, paternally calling people out of their houses on to the draughty waterfront. 'Come along now! Who's going to tell me about this – what is it? – this *dragon* – ha ha!'

From among the shuffling feet and uneasy muttering, a woman's voice, snatched into rags by the wind, demanded to know what kept the nets empty of fish.

'Well, it's no dragon, that's certain, ha ha! Offshore currents,' said Brother Paul emphatically. 'They've gone deep. As soon as the neap comes, they'll be back, you mark me. And where will you be then? Eh? Hiding in your houses? Making

43

yourself little heathen images? Or paying some witch to burn cow dung in your yards, ha ha! Children! What are we come to? The Prior asks me, *How are the folk at Worm Head bearing up under this trial Our Lord has sent to test them? Are they brave as Job? Are they faithful like Elijah? Are they praying?* He said to me, *Paul, go and tell these folk that I want to hear their prayers up here, up here at the priory. Bring word to me, for sweet Jesu's sake, that no devil has whispered in their ears of spirits and demons, as others have down-country!* I try to put his mind at rest. God knows, I've even lied for you folk. *My kith and kindred wouldn't pay heed to gossip! My kith and kin are Christian folk.* Was I wrong? Tell me, was I wrong?'

Bruno picked up Alban's wet habit and threw it at him. 'Get out there and put a stop to him, like you were told.'

But as Alban stooped to pick up his belt, Bruno tugged it out of reach and put his hands over the leather purse. 'I'll take care of this.'

Flapping and shapeless in his unbelted habit, Alban ran down to the sea front, his shoulders heaped round his ears, his backbone hunched and obedient to misery.

5

A Prophet without Honour

As Alban got there, the villagers were turning away, buffeted by Paul's cheery condescension and without words enough to question.

Seeing a man of the church coming, some of them broke off the path, frowning – a little resentful of God for nagging them all on empty stomachs.

Alban caught hold of a sleeve that flapped by him. 'Have you asked about the dragon?'

The man looked startled and glanced back over his shoulder at Brother Paul, beatific arms flailing on the shore.

'They do say it's been seen again round here,' said Alban. 'Ask him about it.'

The man pulled his sleeve away, and ran and whispered in another's ear. Alban could see that they did not want to confront Paul face to face. The first glanced up at the sky and screwed up his face as if he was about to duck underwater. He was mustering courage. 'The dragon ain't a trick o' tide!' he shouted, without turning to face the village priest.

'Who said that?' Brother Paul cupped his hand to his ear. 'Was it one of you spoke? Or was it Satan himself? What's this babbling of dragons? Are you poor, jack-o-green heathens to believe in monsters? Couldn't your mothers lie straight in their beds? Were you all born simple?'

'Maybe 'tis the Great Beast Satan,' shouted another voice.

'Maybe 'tis the End of the World!' The villagers ran back to Paul, pressing round him, baying for an answer.

'How dare you, you ignorant children! What Latin do you have? What do such as you know about the Beast Satan? Satan's a serpent, isn't he? Watch and pray, my dear folk. Watch and pray! When the world ends, I'll tell you what will be seen. Shall I? Shall I tell you how the end of the world will come?' He had them, like Saint Patrick's snake, under a forked stick. They could not move. Their terror had no room to squirm. He spread his arms and pointed up at the sky. 'You'll see the clouds part and a million angels carrying Our Lord Jesu down to the Earth to gather up his people. And in His right hand He'll have a pitchfork to toss the sinners into the Fiery Pit!' All eyes rose to the evening clouds, piled fleece upon fleece above a blazing sunset.

'And the Antichrist?' said Alban.

He almost expected the hissing of the sea to swallow his voice. But there it stood in the air. And there were Brother Paul's eyes rummaging the crowd for the dissenter's face. 'What about the Antichrist?' Alban repeated, a little louder. 'The beast revealed to Saint John when the Lord showed the Final Things of this world. The seven-headed dragon . . .'

'Seven heads, foh!' snorted the priest. 'Does it have seven heads now?' But he dared not snatch at Holy Writ, for his scripture had been poor always, and this outsider might taunt him with it if he guessed.

The effect on the crowd was devastating. It grew sibilant with whispers. 'Seven heads! It has seven heads!'

'*What has*, in the name of blasphemy? What has?' shouted Brother Paul. 'I charge you, on peril of your souls – has any one of you seen a beast with seven heads?'

'Don't know,' said a woman. 'None here's seen the beast. 'Tis said it's big and huge and breathing fire and all's dead that's in its way. Seven heads. It likely has!'

'Or the Beast from the Sea?' said Alban. 'It's written that the Antichrist will trust its power to a lesser beast from the sea, and the people of the world will fall down and worship the sea dragon – all but those with the name of the Saviour written on their foreheads!'

'Get down, Paul, and give's a blessing! Give us something to fight it off's!'

'No! There *is* no dragon, you stupid woman! It's gossip, don't you understand? It's fools' rumour! It's put about by witches!'

'We've prayed,' said a squat, bull-necked fisherman, over the top of the priest's words. 'We've prayed, and still there's cows and sheep gone and places burned to ashes. And no fish. We needs a blessing to keep it off's. We needs more'n a blessing. We needs a holy man 'twixt us and it.'

'We needs tokens,' said a woman, investing the words with such menace that Alban reached out and put his hands on her shoulders – to restrain the fright in her.

'I won't listen to you!' cried Paul, laughing, as an after-thought, his laugh of wise good humour. 'You've all been listening to your grand-dams, you foolish, idiotic children!'

A stone hit him on the ear, and he stumbled sideways with a look of stunned surprise.

'We need better'n him for a holy man,' said the woman who had thrown it. 'We all know him for Judd's boy. All talk. Always was. We need more'n a talker now. We need a driver-out of spirits. He's not that sort. He never was. I've known'm since he was a babe.'

A child in the crowd picked up a handful of shells and threw them, cutting himself and missing his aim. But the adults came to his help, kicking up the dirt at their feet, peering and ducking like herons for the stones they unearthed.

Brother Paul crossed himself and turned to run. But a woman had caught hold of the rope round his waist and he had to tow her along with him three or four paces before she let go. Stones began to thud into the brown folds of his hood, making little explosions of dust and protest and leaving white circles on the cloth.

'*Stop!*' said Alban. 'Stop at once.'

He stepped up on to a tree-stump bollard from which a moored boat dangled on to the dry beach. He felt his habit fill with wind, so that he looked absurd, corpulent, pregnant. But the mob did not think he was absurd. They turned back to him, frightened of their own lust, hoping he would forbid it.

'The dragon . . .' said Alban, pausing as he had heard Paul pause, 'is not the Antichrist. Or if it is, 'tis a poor, miserable thing. The world's not fool enough to worship it.'

Mooing derision roared back at him.

'Ah, but I speak from knowing, you see,' said Alban. Behind the crowd, beyond Brother Paul who had turned his face to a wall and was panting or crying or both, Gwyne's horsemaster tumbled naked out of the fishing hut, hopping into his breeches. He had been caught unawares by Alban's unnecessary meddling. He had only been sent to rout the local priest; why words, too?

'How do you know?' yelled the crowd.

'I know!'

'How do you know?' The words were responsorial – a pagan catechism – *I know – How do you know?*

'The dragon is a beast of flesh and bone. It has only one head and that no bigger than a horse or a cow. It's sick – diseased – a poor, mangy specimen of a dragon and soon to be dead. I *know*, you see!'

'How do you know?'

Perhaps that was to be his special sin, then, now that he was an open jar in Satan's larder, ready for filling. To him was given the Lie. It came as naturally as speaking, as naturally as thinking.

'I *know*!'

'How do you know?'

'*Because I've seen it*,' he said.

When the rain stopped, Anselm got to his feet like a horse in a stable – all legs and clatter and things dislodged from the wall. 'I'll go, then,' he said. 'I'll go now, and fetch Elfleda tomorrow.'

'Ooh time enough, time enough,' said de Rochfoll, grinning. He tottered to his feet, and the boy came up under his arm like a church gargoyle. 'A week or two.'

'Please let me give the wedding feast . . . Father,' said Anselm (who had discovered one simple way at least of delighting the old man). 'At my house.'

'I'm not helpless yet, son.'

'No, no. But if you agree to the idea – a marriage service tomorrow and a feast later. It's Elfleda's whim, and I'm pleased to gratify her.'

'I wager you are, son!' De Rochfoll gave a coarse laugh and peered in the direction of his daughter. 'Silly girl. She'll marry when the arrangements are made. No reason to seem hasty in the eyes of others.'

Elfleda pulled her cloak round her and touched Anselm's sleeve. She pointed towards the door, indicating that she wanted to speak privately. Anselm pondered his chances. De Rochfoll was set to become surly, planning grander and grander festivities which would forestall the marriage weeks, maybe months. He was loath to renege on his word to Elfleda, but all in all, she looked the more open to persuasion.

He made an opportunity to visit the yard, and almost but not quite daring to rest his arm round Elfleda's shoulder, said softly, 'A hasty marriage might not do your honour such justice as befits it.'

'Don't say that.' She glared at him with fierce grey eyes bruised by lack of sleep. 'Take me with you now, and find a priest and marry me today. They were my grounds. If you delay, I shan't marry you later, Anselm.'

'Elfleda! Is there someone here frightens you? Is there something that chases you into my keeping? God forbid I should profit by your necessity, lady. I wouldn't have you think my help needs purchasing. I am your friend without debt. You know that.'

The whites of her eyes showed, and the muscles in her cheeks flinched. 'It won't do. I must be married. I must.'

Anselm felt his heart had been shrunk and aged by the day's hopes and disappointments. To lurch from exultation to despair so many times in so few hours left him nauseous and tired. He thought he understood. 'So.'

'So much said in such a little word,' said Elfleda. 'So.'

'There are other words,' he said bitterly, and stepped away.

'Say them, then. You cannot dishonour me, if I'm already dishonoured.'

He was grossly irritated with her. Bad enough to trick him,

exploit his gullibility, make a convenience of his dog-like love. But to make him talk about it took undreamed-of spite.

'Circumstance alone has dishonoured you, my dear. You should by rights have been married to the baby's father by now, I see that. It's Elshender's honour that's stained, to my mind.'

Her face expressed nothing, though her head trembled slightly on its long, hollowed neck. 'Come with me.'

She led him, by example and not by touching, to the outside steps of the house, and up them to the upper floor. Leaving him at the top of the steps, she went to her room.

The view from up there was all turbulence: barley and grass tumbling, and the sea in the distance.

She came back with a small vellum-bound book. It was a book of days. 'If you ask it,' she said, in a formal, reedy voice, 'I shall make this vow on a Bible – or on the relic at Saint Bede's, or on my mother's grave – anything you choose. I am a virgin intact, and I don't mean to foist on you any child but your own . . . Don't interrupt, Anselm. Since this is true, I ask that you take me with you now – today – and marry me.'

Anselm puffed out his cheeks and danced from foot to foot. 'So!'

'Again that little word. Do you think I'm lying, Anselm?'

'No! By God in Heaven! So, there's someone here that frightens you. Is it one of the servants? It is one of your father's boys? Tell me. How can I say it – if there's anyone that frightens you so sore that you'd pay your maidenhead to be away from here . . . I won't profit by 'em.'

'Anselm.'

'Yes?'

She thrust the book of days into his hands. 'Now swear that

you *won't* have me unless you know and like my reasons.'

'I . . .' Anselm blushed scarlet and dropped the book. It fell close to the edge of the landing, and they both reached down to stop it falling into the mud below. Their foreheads cracked together.

'Oh Jesu, I'm sorry. I'm an ox. I'm a dray-horse.'

She did not try to remove her head from his shoulder where he was holding it with both hands. But after a moment she said, 'I'm not dull to the fact that you have loved me since my fourteenth birthday, when you were recovering from lung fever at your brother's house during all the betrothal celebrations for Elshender and me. Do you have the book or do I?'

'I do.'

'Will you swear, then? That you don't want me unless . . .'

'*No!* No, I won't swear it! I won't! I bless the thing that drives you to me, whatso'er it be.'

So Anselm went back down the stairs and into the house where he told de Rochfoll, 'Time enough's been wasted. I think I'll take her with me now, Father, this evening. You can take my word, I'm sure, that everything will be done with your honour the first consideration.'

De Rochfoll puttered good-humouredly. 'No hurry! No hurry, lad!' He interlocked his fingers over his belly.

'Now or never. That's my thinking.' Anselm laughed, hoping the laugh would sound bluff and imperturbable. 'Strain enough getting wed without all this waiting. Look at me – haven't I waited too long already?'

De Rochfoll was shaken. His hands began to tremble as he saw the blurred movements of his daughter fetching down her belongings and handing bundles he could not identify to Anselm.

'Goodbye, Father,' she said, lifting his hand and putting it on her own head. 'I shall see you again shortly. Shall we try to make Leo pay for a wedding feast? Shall we? Wish me well, please. And remember your fastenings.'

Anselm was amused by the curt instructions. He had often imagined how bitter her life must be under de Rochfoll's crusty, domineering rule. But holding Elfleda tentatively against him as a carriage was rigged, he pitied achingly the old man's loss. He was taking, after all, the object he had always thought of as the hearth of de Rochfoll's house.

The wind coming off the sunset had a wicked edge to it. Inside the covered cart, Elfleda huddled down among her clothing, with a fleece rug under her. De Rochfoll stood at the gate, his hands cupped round his ears to shield them from the raw wind, and to pick up the sound of the cartwheels and horse's hoofs as they moved down towards the bay.

Where they first left the lee of the hollow in which the house sheltered, and the full force of the onshore wind buffeted them, Anselm's cloak lifted into the air – straight up into a column that towered over his head. He laughed out loud, and stopped his horse stock still, until Elfleda called to him, 'Can we hurry, please?'

If he rode directly to Bede Priory, the Prior could perhaps be persuaded to marry them in the morning. Beyond that point, his imagination ran away from him and could not be caught.

Everyone in the village was out on the shore. Was there an air of festival? Or was it the lamp of Anselm's eyes illuminating the ugly, wind-screwed faces? Certainly the eyes were feverishly bright which glanced up at the carriage and rider coming down the hill, but few took any notice. They were repeating to each other words they had heard, as if to memorise them.

'Heading north.'

'Old and sick.'

'Dead soon.'

In the heart of this extraordinary animation and noise (where Anselm had left behind inert silence just a few hours before) a young monk with overgrown tonsure and long, jug-handle ears was trying to extricate himself from the crowd. 'Yes, that's right. It's what I said,' he kept repeating, prising fingers off his arm only to find two more hands gripping his wrist. 'Yes, it's what I said. Please let go of me.'

Elfleda and Anselm spotted him at the selfsame moment, and looked at each other with the mutuality of an old married couple. 'Monk! Hey you, monk!' called Anselm. 'Over here!'

The crowd at last acknowledged the newcomers and made way for the monk, who almost ran to Anselm's stirrup.

'I have a service to beg of you . . . ah . . .'

'Alban, master.'

'Would you ride in my lady's coach, Brother Alban, as far as . . . well, a little way off?'

'Of course. Yes, master.'

'Is that Bruno from the castle with you?'

Bruno had shouldered his way through the crowd, dragging the horses behind, shouting and cursing at both animals and people impartially. Anselm did not like Gwyne's horsemaster. For some reason, his hackles rose like a dog's at the sight of that flat nose set in that perfectly perfect face. He could see that the monk was physically frightened of the man, backing away through the folds of his unbelted habit.

'Bruno, are both these beasts from my brother's stable?'

Bruno paused, as he did when asked any question – to look for catches, tricks, or an answer that would be to his best advantage. 'Yes. This is the Lady Gwyne's new chaplain. Sir.'

'Give one to Brother Alban, and tell the Lady Gwyne I will return both man and mount tomorrow.'

Bruno's eyes flickered from side to side, taking in the carriage, taking in the lady. He was gathering intelligence. Anselm surprised himself in wanting to ride down Bruno and trample him in the sand. He did not like himself for the feelings Bruno aroused in him. 'Why are you wearing the chaplain's belt?'

Bruno shrugged. 'He gave it me. Likes me, see. Don't you?' And he pinched Alban's cheek spitefully before running the horse up against him.

'Was that true?' asked Anselm.

Alban clutched his robe to him, trying to keep the wind from filling it. 'It doesn't matter, sir.'

'I'll speak to Leo tomorrow – get the man put off. He's a coxcomb.'

'Please! Pray let us go now!' called Elfleda from the coach.

A minute or two more they waited for Alban and his horse to circle each other. He apologised, said that he was unaccustomed to horses. Finally Anselm said, 'Tie it on behind the carriage and ride with the lady. But do hurry, friend.'

Alban got into the coach. He knew that he smelled of wet wool and sweat, and that he would fetch the crowd round the carriage with their horrible breath and their incessant 'Really, is it true?'

He and Elfleda stared down into different corners of the coach. 'I've just done a fearful thing,' he wanted to say, '– several fearful things today. Since I was excommunicated, I've done nothing but – tell lies.' This woman with washed hair and white hands would surely have the intelligence to grasp what he was saying and understand his confession. But if he opened his mouth, he feared some new blasphemy would spill out of it. He toyed with the idea that he was possessed by demons.

'Can you perform a marriage?' asked Elfleda suddenly. 'Tonight?'

'No,' thought Alban. 'I'm an unhousled, unshriven, blaspheming liar. Don't be absurd.' He said: 'I never have done.'

'The gentleman would thank you. So would I.' She rummaged among her baggage for her purse of money.

Alban tried to get up, to lean over the side and summon the rider's attention so that he would stop the carriage and let him out. 'No, no. It's impossible. It's Lent. Go to a church. There's a priory near here. They'll tell you. It's Lent. I can't marry you in Lent.'

Elfleda smiled, and the snout of eczema disappeared, altering her face astonishingly. 'A few hours. Will you marry us at midnight, then?'

Alban thought, 'Easter? Could anyone but the Devil's own man omit to notice Easter creeping up out of Lent? Where had he spent Good Friday? What had he been occupying himself with while Christ was harrowing hell all day today? Standing on a bollard drawing pictures of dragons in the air. Frightening frightened people. Lying.'

'Not after sunset,' he said. 'I can't marry you while the sun's down.'

'At first light, then.'

'Oh God!' he cried, so loud that she flinched, and clenched her cloak round her. 'I'm not in a state of Grace, lady! Do you know what I just did? Do you?'

At the noise, Anselm glanced back, but Alban had dropped his voice to a shameful whisper. 'Do you know what they were asking about when you arrived?'

'Yes,' she said, but he did not notice.

'Do you know what I told those poor people? I told them I'd seen a dragon! There!' He let his hands flop in his lap and, for the first time, the absurdity of the thing made him hinny with laughter.

'And have you?'

'Gracious God, madam, I said it to keep them from stoning the priest! They were going to stone the priest! They seemed to want me to say it. So I said it. I told them I'd seen a dragon – a mangy, sick old dragon in its death-throes. So they wouldn't be so frightened. If they have to be frightened, I thought, let them be less frightened, at least. Let them think the dragon's gone. You should have heard me. I was . . . I was . . . *ridiculous*. And no one noticed.'

After a considerable pause Elfleda said, 'But it isn't.'

Alban clenched his eyes and mouth and fists. 'Isn't ridiculous, lady?'

'Isn't mangy or sick or dying. Here. This is for you if you'll perform a marriage at sunrise tomorrow.' She put the money into his lap, and as she leaned forward he could see the grey of the hair at her temples and the unnatural arch of her eyebrows, fixed in permanent perplexity.

'She's a madwoman,' he thought as the purse rolled down his lap into his crotch, 'and with this money I can get away from her and the Lady Gwyne and Bruno.'

God's chiefest mistake, he concluded, was Free Will. The Devil would never have complicated the issue like that. The clarity of the Devil's directions brooked no disobedience.

'At dawn, then. Yes.'

Furnished with a religious, Anselm rode directly home. He was ashamed to take Elfleda to a place so unprepared for her. But he felt that while he alone had possession of her, no one could question or obstruct the marriage. He felt like an eloper, or an abductor, pursued by all the arguments against marrying: his age, her obvious fear, most of all his own disbelief in the possibility. He was a crocodile carrying an egg in his jaws. He must get out of sight and there, perhaps, instinct would tell him how to set it down without crushing it.

The house was bleak and undecorated. The only cover to the flags was a heap of sacks on which Anselm's two dogs slept. The walls had no hanging, no trophy, no crucifix, no carving, no colour, no decorous weapons, no birdcage, no mirror. The plaster simply bulged between the beams, like the white flesh of a fat old man slung in a net hammock. The leather of the chairs was slavered over by the dogs. The bed had no linen on it. The linen had had no airing for fifteen years.

Since the death of their parents, Leo had been obliged to keep up a certain grand style, but Anselm was free to slope in and out of his days as his dogs sloped in and out of the house, throwing himself down when and where he was weary, and rising when he was not.

Fortunately, it was dark when they arrived. Nothing but the smell of the dogs betrayed the barren squalor of the house. The indoor servants were slow to wake. His torch was slow to light. All the while, Anselm left Elfleda in the carriage for fear she catch cold. When at last he lifted her down, she was trembling as violently as a fawn in a trap. Her whole frame shook. And set down on the ground, she did not so much stand as crouch against the daub wall, hooped over from the knees. Even in the darkness, she was legible like a letter G sprawled on the house by gypsies.

Anselm took the young monk by the throat. 'Have you been talking to the lady? Have you been frightening her?'

But Alban only shook his head and said that he believed the lady was unwell. In the dark, something splashed on to Anselm's hand which he took to be the lad's tears, and behind him Elfleda said: 'Have you a roof?' She insisted on spending the remaining hours of darkness on a level with the pigeon loft.

Easter rose shortly before five o'clock. Witnessed by their own gangling shadows which sprawled at their feet across the neglected kitchen garden, Elfleda and Anselm took communion and were declared married by Brother Alban.

They ate a breakfast of kidneys and liver from the butchered paschal lamb.

6

Easter Sunday

For the woodgatherer the sky did not exist. There was no need to look up and risk a bramble across the cheek, a twig in the eye. No reason to balance on two legs after so long grubbing through the decaying vegetation, one hand down. No curb on speech or silence. No call to differentiate, in dress or act or thought, male from female. The gatherer was like a caddis dragging itself along where the green light percolated down, accumulating and festooning itself with ridiculously small fragments off the riverbed. Even as the gatherer worked, branches and twigs were rattling down from the canopy to replenish the litter which no gathering ever diminished.

Like a vulture on a battlefield, the gatherer went on and on and on, gleaning the scraps of dead wood, even though the tortured branches reached out and snatched and the unquiet brambles incessantly plucked. Every step was a trip; every trip brought the front foot down on some spiteful, nobbly detritus that bruised the arch, even through wrappings of leather. The woodgatherer cursed feet.

Rattling under the wet winter's leaves, birds and mice were indistinguishable. Under the dripping leaf canopy, the gatherer and the donkey, its shape scribbled through with twigs, were barely distinguishable.

Then the donkey began to bray and stumble about. One front leg was strapped up with a rope to keep it from straying, the hoof bent up to the belly. But all at once it began to lurch, three-legged, through the trees. The branches across its back baulked between two birch trees and splintered with an explosion of bark and dust. A volley of birds shot through the canopy. And then there was another noise – a succession of smaller explosions, like chestnuts on a hearth, and the furtive scattering of the creatures under the leaves.

The smell at first was a festive smell of bonfires and, because there was a deal of may blooming on the perimeter of the wood, cloyingly sweet. Then, as the lilac smoke turned black and the sodden leaves and trunks began to hiss deafeningly, the smell was of wet clothing left on a stove to char.

The fire did not spread of its own accord. The long white stems of dead grass fizzled and dropped, but did not ignite the wet mould. The ivy on the trees flared, then belched smoke and went out. The canopy, still black with rain from the day before, blanketed the fire and turned back down a denser and denser mix of smoke and steam.

As the wreaths rolled over the gatherer, some condensed into water-drops because the skin was still so early-morning cold. Heat was local to the flames. Only the donkey sweated, its mane already frizzled to the brittle consistency of stranded caramel. It broke its hobble, but though it put four feet to the ground, it had already used up its breath in screaming. It jumped twice against a tree, as if the trunk were an insuperable barrier, then dropped dead of heart failure.

The woodgatherer, unlike the donkey, kept silent. The bent old body could not be persuaded to run, and had to be stuffed into hiding under a log. Then the smoke made for coughing, and the log began to burn, and bark and grubs and a shroud of glowing convolvulus dropped down on the body beneath. The alternatives were to suffocate, to burn, or to roll out into the open and run.

When the dragon let fall fire from its long, flat jaw, the flames unrolled across the forest floor like carpeting. Crimson and orange, it fell in shreds on the ground, each shred a tuft of undergrowth that burned itself out. The dragon draped the dead donkey with fire until its colour, then its substance, changed.

It was a bad habitat for the beast, whose body stood shoulder-high to the squat trees. Its long neck had to be threaded between trees and low branches. The small eyes, set so far back to the sides of its head, made for poor co-ordination. And where the cheeks caught on twigs or rough bark, scales lifted. They were multi-coloured as they fell, and the light shone through them. The blood underneath the scratches was slow-welling, brown and glutinous.

It squatted to seize hold of the donkey, its nostrilled upper lip rolled back, and its far-sighted eyes unfocused; the jointed legs folded, and huge kneecaps showed bone-white through the ochre skin. The head shuddered from side to side in a reflex tearing, and the feline feet turned over on their sides to show stone-grey, stone-round pads, and claws that opened and withdrew, opened and withdrew. In a crouch, the rump made an awkward twist in the spine, a man's height higher than the shoulders. And the tail twitched incessantly, white and fleshy underneath like a whelk, and a drab, lustreless, speckled mustard colour where the scales flexed down the ridges of muscle. The creases of the body at the groin and withers were obscenely human – a glimpse of the scaleless cream underbelly bulging like that of an old man or a pregnant woman.

The workings of the gullet, as the dragon swallowed morsels of donkey, rippled the scales for half the length of the straining neck. The red palate flapped as the jaws turned and returned bones for the teeth to fracture so that the short tongue could prod for the marrow. The beast's hearing was sunk, like a fish's, in unshielded holes behind its eyes, and as it ate, it turned its head this way and that to catch the sounds familiar to it – of burning scrub and of scavenger crows mustering in the tree-tops. It was during this thrashing of the head that the vertical eyelids parted momentarily and glimpsed the wood-gatherer crawling out from under a burning log.

The gatherer looked back and stopped stock still, and the staring, whiteless eyeball rolled inside its vertical lids as the beast raised itself on its front legs. The back feet skidded in a mire of leaf-mould, the tail thrashing to and fro for balance, splintering a hawthorn bush. The woodgather's eyes rolled, too, in the ecstasy of terror.

Unable to see behind, the dragon barged backwards – once into an oak, once into clear space. Dragging what remained of the donkey between its lips, it staggered back, swaying, ungainly, feeling the way with its flanks, through the perimeter may bushes and out on to grass. For a moment, sitting back on its tail to make the turn, its head was of a height with the spruce trees. Then, reverting to a lizard-gait, legs moving in sequence, pausing now and then to readjust its grip on the carcase, it quickly passed out of sight among the interfolded dunes which ran down to the sea.

At the edge of the forest, the may petals lay scattered about like the aftermath of a wedding.

Elfleda ate the food like a harvest mouse, quivering. It marred

Anselm's appetite. Her head was held so far forward that her unplaited hair fell in two clumps down the sides of her face. It diminished her face. Her food looked hair-filled.

Anselm went and stoked the fire, but she went on shivering. Out of doors it was a perfect spring morning; no trace of yesterday's rain, the sun glaring on the dead, white grass and the river. It was Easter. The priory bell was ringing, and the servants, ready to go for their blessing, were sitting outside against the sunniest wall of the house.

'After mass, should we go to see Leo and Gwyne?' said Anselm.

'If you care to,' said Elfleda, pulling the chair-fleece forward over her shoulders.

'Or we can stay here. I only feel that this house is unprepared for you. I should like to make it more . . . pleasing. Before obliging you to live here. Gwyne would be quite happy to have you for a house guest.'

'So was my father. But I'm married now.'

'You mean you want to stay here?'

'Naturally.'

Anselm would have felt pleased but for the miserable little frown wedged between Elfleda's eyes, and the small smile-lessness of her mouth.

The monk was eating ravenously, cramming bread into his mouth between each bite of meat. Man and wife both watched him, rather than look at each other, and he quickly felt their eyes on him. Like a beast at a water-hole, he reared up his head. The bench under him rocked backwards. Wiping his mouth, he stood up, and the breadcrumbs fell like dandruff on to the table. 'Thank you. Thank you,' said Alban. 'Most welcome. I'll go now.'

'Don't be foolish. Sit down. Finish your breakfast. You can go to mass with us. Do you know the way back to the castle after?'

'No.'

'I'll take you over there and explain what kept you. Sit down.'

Alban was about to do so, when he caught sight of Elfleda glaring at him. It took smaller things to shake him. 'I'll wait outside then, sir,' he said and lumbered out, upsetting the bench with a clatter and reaching back for the bread left in his place.

'I'm sorry,' said Anselm examining his trencher. 'I thought you wanted the monk to stay.'

'We couldn't send him away without a meal,' she said.

'Strange boy.'

'Not really. Marriages must be unsettling for monks.'

He looked up directly into her smile, and blushed. His bowels ached with desire. He asked her to excuse him and went outside and walked up and down the stableyard. When he came back in, he started speaking before he had let go of the shirt collar gripped between his teeth. 'Let me show you the house,' he said, pulling her by the hand out of her seat.

It was a route march through the lower rooms, dirty and dog-smelling. Her dress caught on the wood of the open stair and had to be picked free of the splinters. The upper rooms were bitterly cold where she had left the trap open to the roof. There was nothing in the partitioned chambers to see, except the huge family bed Leo had not wanted. 'There's linen for this,' said Anselm brusquely. 'Somewhere. You have this for yours. I'll make shift somewhere.'

She responded with equal sharpness. 'Have I changed greatly, Anselm?'

'A little. Why? A little underfed, maybe. Or nervous. Chiefly nervous. I'd not have it if I knew how to ease your mind, but I . . .'

'You're regretting what's done.'

'No! By all the saints! On my honour! Why would I regret –? I'm sure in time . . .' His one hand gripped the opposite wrist and twisted and twisted until it seemed he would wear all the hair off his forearm. 'Time enough. Plenty of time.'

'You sound like my father.'

'Ah. Yes. A poor exchange, I dare say. One old man for another. If you want to go home . . .'

'How old are you, Anselm?'

'Ah. Ha ha. Well. Yes. Forty-six.'

'A long time not to marry.'

He shrugged and grimaced and plucked at his chest for the cloak edge that was not there to comfort him. Finding nothing to say, he shrugged again.

'They do say it makes a man sicken. To pent it up. They say an unpitied lover can die of the impostume. Elshender used to tell me so. I took it for wheedling. You seem quite well, Anselm.'

Helpless, Anselm opened and shut his mouth until at last she laughed at him, though the wretched little frown never once dislodged itself. 'He was wheedling,' said Anselm.

'Even so. I curse myself that I did not let him persuade me to it. It would have spared us both this indignity.'

'Lady! God quit me if I ever put you to any indignity!' The skin prickled across his shoulders. He wanted to rub himself against the doorpost like a pig. 'If only I knew how it served your purposes to marry me. I could maybe conduct myself more to your. . . . Let's go to mass. I'm not much accustomed to ladies, you know. I mean well enough, but . . .'

'*No!*' She stamped her foot and took hold of her hair as if she would drag it out. '*No, I won't go to mass!* I'm married and not married. I'm wife and no wife. If you won't do it, send one of your servants. Or send the monk. Send anyone you please, but I won't set foot outside this house a virgin! You hear me?' And she began unfastening her clothes with demented speed, throwing at him her sleeves and shoes and bodice.

He looked round in panic for servants who might at any moment come up from the far end of the house. He slammed shut the roof-trap as if the birds on the roof or the angels on the clouds might see in. He knew he must resist the temptation to step back, give ground, run away. He emptied his arms of the clothes accumulating there and stepped astride her feet and pressed her to the wall with his forearm.

Her cold nose touched the crease of his neck, and her hair was in his mouth. Beneath it he found her ear. 'Be silent! For God's sake, woman! Hear you? This world and half the next can hear you! Now you hear me. Get in. Get inside.'

Her head recoiled from the shout and hit the wall. He put both arms round her, body, breast and elbows all, and threw her, like a log on to the hearth, through the curtainless doorway and on to the big old bed. But her fists were knotted in the skirt of his jerkin and he was fetched off his feet on top of her, bruising his shins on the baseboard.

The weight of his body jerked the air out of her in a cry: he both heard and felt it against his cheek. He heard, too, the bell ringing way over at Saint Bede's. He heard his servant climb half-way up the far-end steps and presumably reach his head above the landing. He heard the man's foot miss a rung and slip down to the one below. He heard the withdrawal downstairs, an exchange with the other servant and a snort of dirty, good-natured laughter – laughter tinged with a cheer, such as you hear at a wedding.

Then all he could hear was his own breathing and the blood pushing its way through the flotsam of noise in his ears, like flood-water breaking a dam and cascading into the mainstream; and a drowning man's cry in the flood that dilapidates the boundary fences of Eden.

'Whatever are you doing?' said Gwyne.

Leo sat on the end of the bed, banging his feet on the floor. She had taken him unawares, and he stopped guiltily and pulled up his hose.

'Is it cramp again?' she demanded accusingly.

'Tingling, that's all it is.' He rubbed behind his knees furtively, trying to finish dressing with the other hand.

'You should be bled.'

But to his relief Gwyne did not pursue the subject. She was preoccupied with the news of Anselm and Elfleda's intended marriage. Her horsemaster had come back with word of it. The only emotion it stirred in Leo was a feeling of disappointment on behalf of his son.

He asked himself whether he envied Anselm his adolescent bride. But when he thought of his forty-eight-year-old feet, tingling as if they were stuck in a bucket of nettles, and of Gwyne, just ten years younger, her energy washing round him like Canute's inexorable tide . . . 'You'd think Elshender could have written,' he muttered. 'For Easter. Well, he's missed his chance of having Elfleda to his bed, and the blame's his own.'

They dressed in their best clothes. Leo said, 'So much linen. I feel swaddled.' But Gwyne fastened her skirt below the swell of her belly, admired the growing width of lacing below her armpits, and covered her hair with a lawn coif so thin that it floated horizontally with every downward step on the stair. Stumbling, because the shape of the stairs was not clear to his poor, prickling soles, Leo was wearied by the sight of her beauty.

The priory was live like a dovecote with monks in white surplices. The bright sun and the festive, unregimented speed of their movements hid the soup and sweat stains. Indoors and out, all gradations of people were camped about, sitting among their clothes, balancing their babies, squatting on their haunches, jumping from foot to foot. Old women had elbowed their way to the front and were already on their knees in a devout attempt to be first in the ranks of the blessed. Children playing nine-men's morris on the flagstones were kicked out of doors by a monk, and a mad vagrant woman had been tied to the church door by her wrist.

There were two stretchers on the floor of the church nave that were stepped on and stepped over by every newcomer. Bellies rumbled, nails scratched, and fleas as large as drops of holy water from an aspergillum arced through the cold gloom. Most eyes were glazed with waiting. De Rochfoll, propped into his two-armed niche, looked no blinder than the rest.

Leo stepped over the bedridden on the floor, gave them an encouraging smile, and propped himself in his own niche, nodding to the Prior that the service should begin. He chafed his feet alternately on the opposite calf, and winced as they finally came back to life. Beside him, Anselm's niche was empty. He considered possible explanations, and dismissed the foremost one; the melancholy bay of plainsong reproached him for having unclean thoughts. He also noticed, of a sudden, that his wife was missing. She had not followed him into the church.

Stepping over the bedridden again, he found Gwyne waiting irritably in the porch for his solicitude. 'I'm unwell,' she said. 'I shall have Bruno take me home.'

'I'm sorry. Am I to come? Should I come? Is it the baby?'

She flared her nostrils at him, murmured seethingly, 'Of course not,' and allowed herself to lean on the arm of the horsemaster who had driven them both to church.

'By next month the church will be finished!' he called after her apologetically. 'It won't be so far for you to come!' Then, since the service he had allowed to begin was proceeding without him, he ran back inside – and fell headlong over the bedridden.

Latecomers from outlying plots of land continued to arrive, with the noise of creaking axles and blowing horses, well into the service. But not until the Prior was fumbling the Host in the gloomy alcove, his back to the flea-storm, did Anselm arrive with Elfleda.

There was a stir by the door. One of the bedridden gave a shout to draw attention to himself in the dark, and Elfleda's hoot of laughter ricocheted round the dark walls, making heads everywhere duck and bob. Anselm nodded a greeting to his brother and adopted the uncomfortable, straddled stance needed to fit himself under the low perlin of the unvaulted roof. Leo was slow to acknowledge them. They seemed such an implausible pair. Elfleda, her hair plaited to the hem of her coif then left falling free to her waist, was back-lit by the paschal candle. She tugged on her husband's arm and drew attention to the fact that the roof above her own head was higher than above his. They changed places.

'Hello,' she said, beaming up into Leo's face like a child in expectation of a present.

He nodded and smiled. The Latin was enjoining him to rejoice, but that would have been both inappropriate and excessive. When he glanced sideways, he was deeply shocked to see Elfleda and his brother holding hands.

'So,' he thought. 'I am envious, after all.'

On the crazy canter from Anselm's house to the priory, Alban had let himself be swept along on their assumption that he would attend mass. Indeed, on the journey, he had suffered such physical mortification from bouncing about on horseback that he entertained brief hopes of being absolved. But then, when he saw the adulterers run ahead of him into the chapel, and thought how he had caused their unwitting sin, his despair was sealed, as a vault is sealed when there is no more room for corpses. He looked up, and a gargoyle over the door was gaping at him, vomiting congratulations over his head. He had given rise to the perfect sin – a mortal sin committed in ignorance so that it could never be repented.

He glimpsed Leo, propped like a mummified saint against the wall, and realised the likelihood of encountering the Lady Gwyne again. The overspill congregation eyed him from the porch. The Latin of communion jumbled in distant alcoves: he could not identify the separate words. An expatriate of God's earthly kingdom, he could not remember how to think in the language of the angels.

So he turned and ran, hoppingly, away from the church, leaving yet another horse displaced from its stable. There would be other horses in other towns and another harvest of innocence to reap. His belief in his demon was absolute. He felt no anxiety, saying, 'What shall I eat, what shall I put on?' He had money, and more money would be pressed on him as the sins arose for him to abet. Such a master – so attentive to detail – would not let harm befall his servant. Alban had only to put one foot in front of the other for the Devil to guide his footsteps.

He was pursuing this plan, walking across a hillock towards the Roman road, when he saw in the hollow below him a man lying on his face.

'No more,' said Alban to his demon. 'Not until I've slept.' He wondered whether to put up a resistance, but stood still, doing nothing either to leave or to become involved. The prone man was moving, so he was not dead. He had raised himself on his hands, and his spine was flexing. A fall from a horse, perhaps.

Able to see only the top half of the man, Alban walked a few steps forward and puzzled his brains about the bundle of cloth that lay in a pool under the man's nakedness. He took another step – and saw four legs.

It made his heart jibber so with fright that when he deduced the meaning of it he was almost glad. He looked for the woman's head, and saw it beneath the man's collar-bone. Having never seen the sexual act between humans, Alban watched for a long, long time. He made no attempt to hide.

Then the priory bell began to ring again. 'Chank. Chank, chank. Chank.' 'Am I responsible for this, too?' he wondered, and came to the conclusion: 'No, I am not responsible. This is sin independent of me.' And he was full of love and gratitude to these two little pagans, crushing the grass and flowers. It meant that he was not the sole sinner left on earth that Easter morning.

Where the stems of vetches were broken off, their strong-smelling milk spilled out luxuriantly. Alban was directly above the couple. As the man rolled aside, the monk looked down into the face of the lady. Seeing a face he knew, without immediately being able to place it, he gave a reflex smile and nod.

The Lady Gwyne did not return the smile.

One step back put him out of sight of the lovers below, but he heard Gwyne's voice say, '*Kill him*, Bruno.'

Alban gathered up his skirt in one fist and began to run. His heart contracted, his neck bulged, and his unaccustomed breakfast swelled in his crop. His ankle-bones slipped in their sockets, and his breath came and went unasked. His lungs spilled air like slopping wineskins. Bruno had a knife. He came up the slope of the knoll one hand down, and being squat and stocky, ran like an ape. *His* breathing made no noise, whereas Alban's was rabidly full of froth and made his lips flap and his teeth ache.

But, for all his physical superiority, Bruno did not stand a chance. A month before, Alban, with the promise of salvation, might have made himself obedient to death. But no sap-spent brute adulterer was going to muster the speed to catch Alban the Damned. This Gadarene swine, possessed by his demon, flung himself off the top of a high chalk bluff and fell, wheeling and squealing, through a bank of elder, into hogweed and docks.

7

ELFLEDA'S STORY

Anselm came down the steps in his shirt and bare legs, and discovered for the first time that his cook slept on top of the oven. He had never given a thought to where she slept, but she lurched up now on one elbow and surprised him at the bread crock. 'What's the matter, master? What is it?'

'Shush.' Anselm was flustered. 'We were hungry, that's all. I thought, a bite of bread . . .'

'Bless you, I'd've brought you that if you'd called.'

'Thank you. Thank you.'

She got up, almost entirely dressed, and fussed between the creaking wicker baskets and the rasp and ring of pottery jars, blessing Anselm repeatedly and being thanked by Anselm who felt thoroughly blessed. With plunder from the land of milk and honey, he climbed back to the draughty upper floor.

It was almost morning. Elfleda was sitting up, cross-legged on the bolster, her shoulders leaning against the bed-curtain and the wall behind it. Sunlight came into the room behind Anselm, overtook him, and fell rapaciously over her white shift. Her hair flowed down from her head as miraculously as water from the rock struck by Moses, and the skin of her face was as perfect as the petals of flock. Her eyebrows were the small accents over two rising notes of plainsong. When Anselm looked at her, his heart sang two semitones higher.

They sat with their feet intertwined, and ate stale loaf and honeycomb and drank milk, and Anselm thought how startled the room seemed by so much white. Its corners were still rounded with webs and heaps of dust, and the old linen spread on the bed was as yellow as cheese in the folds. But the dust was up and flying now, like the litter in a dovecote when a dove bursts into the darkness from sunlight outside.

'We shall draw rats up here,' said Elfleda, 'and ants.' But the honey strung in strands from her mouth as she said it.

Twice during the night Anselm had wakened wondering what he would find to speak of to his wife – had rooted about for stories or recollections that would entertain her sufficiently to excuse his being there, beside her. Then he would find his hand or his thigh drawn irresistibly to touch her, and she would stir and turn in towards him and he would protest that he had not meant to wake her, and she would protest that she had wakened of her own accord. After a while, his body would protest at the rent torn in it by ecstasy, and some short conversation would come of that that was neither planned nor necessary, before they both went back to sleep.

Now it was too light to sleep and too early to get up, though both of them had been accustomed always to rising at dawn. 'Leo was kind with his offer of a feast. But I'd prefer it here,' he said.

'I thought he looked in poor health,' she said. 'Perhaps his mind was running on Elshender . . . What does that face mean? Must I not mention Elshender? He's your nephew. I'm certain Leo will mention him often.'

'Yes. With regret. He regrets it. He wishes us well, but he does regret that you're not wed to Elshender instead.'

She set her head on one side and said dispassionately, 'I don't. You're a good, kind man. Better than I hoped.'

'And had you given much thought to me, by way of a husband?'

'I thought of it as I heard the drift of your words with Father. I fool myself if I suppose I had a choice: Father was set on it from the moment he understood you. But you must let me deceive myself a little: I like to feel I have some mastery over my life.'

'You had mastery over your father. It was for you to decide,' said Anselm.

'Not in that. The family was in ruins. Without an heir. You must get six sons on me, husband.'

'Ah! So!' Anselm had still not learned how to resist those flashes of insight. 'De Rochfoll's ill! You want him to see a grandchild before he dies! And this is your fertile time . . . and that's why there was a rush to be married!'

'No.' She brushed her hands free of crumbs with a large, conclusive gesture, then stretched herself like a cat and gathered her hair together between both hands. 'Not yet, Anselm. I'm not ready to tell you my reasons. What else have you to say to me before I get up and start to civilise this Barbary of yours?'

'That I love you.'

'Then I shall love you too, I think. It's all a matter of mutual need. I've finished eating now.' Picking up his hand, she placed it on her thigh, just as she had summoned her father's blessing on her head before leaving home.

'You'll let me pretend from time to time, won't you?' he said. 'That I have mastery.'

'I don't know what you mean,' she said, and moved his hand.

People would always judge them wrongly, thought

76

Anselm. They would look at his brutish size and temporal rank, and pity the fragile subjection of his little wife. They would never realise.

But the cook downstairs, listening to the sounds overhead, laughed out loud and said, 'Bless her, she has the bear up and dancing again!'

The day was spent in making the house fit for a celebration. It was chastening for Anselm, obliging him to admit what squalor had overtaken him. She had the long table taken out into the sunlight and scrubbed down. She had an inventory drawn up of the wine and slaughterable meat, and found that a whole tun had fomented where its seams had opened, and that there were boars all but adult still in with their sow. The pigeon loft was so underexploited that its birds stood shoulder to shoulder. Chicken droppings peppered almost every unoccupied room.

The servants quickly saw that an end had come to their era of autonomy when Anselm had pottered, preoccupied, through his frugal days, noticing nothing. Elfleda praised them for their honesty: they were opportunist only in liking to be idle. If they had thieved at all, it was too little to show. And her father's lack of judgement in choosing eye-boys had made her wise to most forms of embezzlement and pilfering. When Elfleda praised them, Anselm's servants thanked God for leading them clear of temptation, then resigned themselves to hard work.

But when Anselm saw his wife, her hair wrapped up in a kerchief, emptying a pan of rat droppings into the midden, his shame got the better of him. 'Let Leo give the feast. Or let your father give the feast. Yes, let's go over there and see him now.'

A shudder ran through Elfleda that was clearly visible from

across the yard. She recovered herself and laughed. 'By now that house will be worse than this one. Mine was a last-ditch battle against confusion.'

'Even so.' Goaded by his passion to understand, he was tempted to torment her. 'I think we should visit your father – tell him the arrangements – show him how well marriage suits you.'

'No, Anselm. I won't go there,' she said.

'Why?'

'And I won't tell you why. Now, if you'll say how many pigeons we're to have, I'll start plucking and dressing.'

'I have a cook, don't I?'

'And now you have two.'

Not until Mann's visit in the afternoon did Elfleda's self-possession falter again and Anselm see the rim of her eyes flash white with that strange excitability. Mann arrived in a cart, with a gift of three swans and the loan of six trestle tables from the Lord Leo. The old man seemed to hold some information Elfleda thirsted after. She wanted to help with the unloading. She would not leave Mann's side for long enough to take the swans indoors, but began plucking them at the cart-tail. And yet Mann was rambling on about nothing more sensible than dragons and sacrifices and dragon-hunts and fireproof armour and vagrant cattle-thieves.

'Ran clean mad,' said Mann.

And Elfleda said, 'Poor man.'

'Can't shirk it another day,' said Mann.

And Elfleda said, 'No wonder he looks unwell.'

'Off in the morning to find it and kill it,' said Mann.

And Elfleda said, 'He mustn't go alone.'

'Oh no, ma'am. He's taking me and two house-men. He'll maybe think of asking your husband, though it's a lot to ask of a man fresh married.'

The bird-like frown settled back between Elfleda's eyes. Anselm blamed Mann for it. 'Stop that, Elfleda. Do you think I can't afford women to do that?' He pulled the swan away from her angrily; its cold, dangling, broken neck wrapped itself round his arm. 'Do you think you're a kitchen woman? I don't want you smelling of rat shit and offal!' And he stalked away to the house, the swan's big feet swinging against his knees.

But she did not follow him, as she was meant to. Mann's ramblings kept her by the cart. Anselm watched her through a crack in the kitchen door.

She filled a bowl and washed. She freed her hair, picked feathers out of the weave of her skirt, and pinched the flesh over her cheekbones to give herself colour. Then she walked to the kitchen door – so fast that she all but caught him watching her.

She flung the grimy, balding swan off a stool and sat down. With a nod of her head, she signalled that Anselm too should sit, and he rested one thigh on the table. It groaned under his weight.

'I would prefer to keep silent,' she said, 'but it seems I can't. You must warn Leo, at least. He need not be in ignorance. I wouldn't forgive myself if I let him stay in ignorance. Don't interrupt. Do I seem to you at all . . . frantic . . . lunatic . . . unseated in my reason? I ask you not to recall yesterday, nor the day before. But now . . . do I seem to you distracted now?'

'No. No, of course . . .'

'No, it's an unreasonable hope. I'd thought to balance it out with a month's tranquillity before I asked you to believe me.'

'I'll believe you – truly!' The legs of the table grated across the flags. He hooked his foot round one of the trestles, angry that it should betray his excitement. He was about to find out who had harried Elfleda into a desperate marriage. Then he could disembowel the man with a blunt knife before living ever after in grateful indebtedness to the fellow.

'After Elshender had his Vision and went away,' she said, 'our house was . . . disturbed. It was not in my power to comfort Father. He was eaten up with anger. And I sometimes felt that my being there in the house was aggravating his disappointment. That's to say he flew into a rage whenever I was in the same room.

'I took to walking for hours along the cliffs and the beach. When I unpacked my press yesterday it was full of sand from my skirt-hems. I saw the tracks first at low tide.

'I was afraid. I knew just where they led. I could see them clear across the beach – leading to a cave. I was afraid then: I only realised later it's better to know. When I didn't know – when it was dark or just a noise in the bushes . . .' She stopped and collected herself, straightening her plaits and arranging her skirts with great deliberation.

'I told my father about the footsteps, but he thought I was distracted with misery over Elshender.'

'Were you?' His throat was dry. He had to cough and say it twice.

'What? Oh. I thought so. I remember thinking so. Huh! The weight I fixed on it! That little disappointment! Such things to be endured – and I thought that little disappointment was the world's end. Why did you interrupt me?

'I stayed away from the beach. I took to walking on the heath instead. One day I heard it. Do you remember the last time it

80

snowed? The cold was wicked. The wind was blowing the snow about so I didn't dare go out of sight of the house for fear I got lost. The sky was a dreadful colour. It plays such tricks with your eyes, that kind of light, and that sort of blowing snow. But I could hear the hissing when the snow turned to steam. Then a huge piece of the yellowness moved – like a piece of the sky falling out. It was rolling, you see? And its belly's so white that in the snow the shape was all broken up.

'I couldn't move. My feet wouldn't let me move. I couldn't pray. I thought, if there are such things in the world, maybe the Norsemen were right. This is Grendel. Ha ha! I even tried to remember the names of the Norse gods. Thor. I could only think of Thor. I remembered later: Odin the All-Knowing. But my brain was like a rock at the bottom of a river. I seemed to have drowned. In fright. On my hands and knees, my skirt snagged and snagged and snagged on the gorse. I might just as well have been nailed to the ground by it. I took it off. I remember feeling the snow through my shift. I was menstrual. My blood froze to my shift. The house was so far away. I could see it, but it was so far . . .

'When it saw me – the beast – I prayed to die before it could chew on me. It's foolish: I couldn't get it out of my head that my body couldn't rise on Judgement Day if it were scattered in pieces. I'd never thought of dying, except of a piece. I begged the beast to wait. I thought any moment my heart would melt and let me die. But it came on and came on and came on . . . The sound it made – oh Christ, it was like all the Damned in Hell. Maybe that's all it's ever heard. It touched me. It ran and put itself between me and the house. I ran the other way. Its leg was there. It touched me!'

She ran her palms up and down an invisible column too

large for her two hands to encompass. 'Its leg touched me! Then it raised itself up – not in a squat but right up on its back feet. Its belly was the colour of tripe. I could see its lights pumping and bulging through its skin . . .'

'Stop now, Elfleda. Stop it.'

'Stop? Why? It reared itself up over me. But one of its back feet slipped into a hollow. It overbalanced – clean on to its back. I ran and ran and I ran. I don't remember reaching the house. It looked like twigs and plaster – a thing you could push over with one hand. I thought, *It will batter down the house!* But it didn't follow. Not then.'

The trestle table crabbed across the floor. 'You didn't tell your father anything. Your father said not a word about dragons.'

'Of course I told him. I thought the gates would come in on us and the house would burn round us. I thought the beast would eat us out of the flames, one by one. But picture me. I came in off the heath mad to speechlessness. My skirt was gone. My shift was bloody. Oh yes, he knew in his own mind what had become of me. My wits had been gone since Elshender's Vision. Why not my maidenhead? If he listened close enough to hear me say 'dragon', it was no more than raving for him. He looked at me – I remember his looking with those stone eyes. White and red was all he could see, and blood was all he could feel. And I suppose shame was all he could think.

'He had the boys barricade me in my room to shout myself to a silence. And when he could bear the sight of me again, he took away the barricade and let me come and go around the house. I had no wish to come or go. After a while I felt safe up in the loft. And the gates didn't come in, and the house didn't burn. I thought the beast had gone.

'I kept watch all day. But when it got dark, I didn't think I'd be able to see it, even if it came. It was so cold – you remember how cold it came with that snow? Up until it rained? I got into bed mostly to keep warm, and then when I slept, I slept every watch of the night and day. I don't know why I woke up then. There was no noise – no roaring. But when I got up, the moon had set already. Its head butting up against the wall – that must've been what woke me . . . I got up and looked out of the slit.

'It was standing on the slope beyond the wall, back on its haunches with its jaws apart so that its head looked to be on fire inside. It was the fire that lit it up. It was putrid yellow – sour yellow – with its underbelly lifted up I could see every part. It held its head sideways – like that. That was all that moved. Its head. Sometimes its nose pointed east and sometimes it pointed west. Otherwise I would've thought it was dead. I've seen a badger dead like that once – rigid – sit-up-and-beg.

'But every so often it turned its head. I couldn't move. I was transfixed. Then I thought of the Scriptures. God, this time, not Odin, you see. I remembered about the dragon standing before the maiden, at the End of the World. There seemed no purpose in warning Father or the household or the village. How can you warn people against the End of the World? I thought of the sky disintegrating and the sea drying up. And I thought, yes, this is what Elshender called a vision – when your head's full of ideas and pictures that can't be said. But I couldn't remember whether the dragon ate the maiden or what. I couldn't remember, and it seemed sinful to be worrying about myself when the world was ending for everyone, but I couldn't help it.

83

'It was such a . . . *meaty* animal, 'Selm! I mean – what do I mean? – I suppose I thought the dragon of the Last Days would be vaster, or standing in the sky with stars for eyes, you know? It was the difference between the Golden Calf of the Israelites and an ordinary cow standing there in the garden. There it was, over the wall. I could smell its pats towards morning. It buried – like a cat. Then it walked away.

'I went to look for proof. The smell was terrible on the patch where it had stood. Its urine had burned off all the grass. But there was nothing my father would believe. Besides, I'd started thinking, wasn't I maybe mad? Or wasn't I having visions like Elshender? I didn't want to speak before I knew what I was supposed to do. Maybe none but me could see the beast. I thought I was so clever. I thought, *If it comes again, I'll wake Father's boy for a witness.*'

'But it didn't come,' said Anselm.

'Oh yes. It came. It stood where it had stood before. It rocked about more, though. It was . . . I don't know the word . . . excited. I fetched the boy and he was scared in that 'little' way children have of being scared. I told him it was all right – and he believed me! Then he was just . . . in awe – sort of in wonder at the adventure, you know?

'*Fetch the Master*, I told him. But he says, *No, no, not him. He won't see it and he won't credit it. Mam'll know what's best. Best I tell me Mam.* And off he ran, out of the house and home to his mother!' Elfleda was twisting her hair into stringy tails, her eyes focusing and unfocusing on the strands. She threw back her head and laughed. 'His mother's the Seer! What's her name? Mog? I never knew! Of all the lads to choose, but I never knew! Mog the Seer's son!

'He came swaggering back before dawn – all plumed up like

a jay. He tells me, *Mam knows. Mam knows what draws it hence.* I thought he'd burst with luxury. He stood by the window looking out at the thing, bare-faced as sin and sniggering and scratching himself. *There's only one thing for dragons, Mam says. Can't get it in the village and that's why it's come here. See how it's hot for you. See how it's up for you. Dragons want virgins, Mam says. Won't make do with less than a virgin.* And he grinned and sniggered and snickered.

'There's no keeping of maidenheads in the village. The men try for a child before they marry. Did you know that? Didn't you know? Yes, of course you'd know. They're not really sinful, you see. It's just that their blood is still paganish. *They have one foot in Eden.* I've heard the priest say that.

'The boy meant me to bribe him. He was cock-a-hoop. He said the village would come soon and be sure the dragon got its virgin. Unless there was no virgin to be had. He even meant me to pay him money. If he'd stopped short of the money I'd maybe not have pushed him as he stood by the slit. He's such a little fellow for his age. It's how I came to think he was younger . . .

'He slipped right through, and I held him by his belt with my foot in the small of his back. I wanted to drop him. God have mercy on me, but I did. I wanted the dragon to eat *him*.

'The beast stopped rocking on its haunches. It started reaching over the wall – as if I was feeding it something out of my hand, feeding it the boy. So I pulled him back in. Look. You can still see the mark his fingers made on my arm. When I looked out again, the dragon had gone.

'I kept to my room after that. And I waited for the rabble to come for me. I expected them every hour – as soon as the Seer persuaded them where they could find a fit sacrifice to keep the dragon off them.

'Then you arrived. My father must've thought God Himself had sent you . . . Maybe He did! What rubbish you both talked about honour and reputation. If you'd sat up that night and seen what I'd seen, and waited for the rabble . . . and thought of the end . . . and maybe the End of the World, too. If you'd sat up on your own roof, Anselm, waiting for it to follow the scent . . . Not to be a virgin sacrifice to a dragon. What would I *not*'ve done to keep from being that?'

Elfleda broke out from her obsession like a cormorant out of water, her gullet distended by straining on her story. Drops of salt water were rolling off her face. 'Do you believe in the dragon, 'Selm?' she said. 'If you do, you can't let Leo go after it in ignorance, thinking it's a fantasy. The old man who brought the tables – he said it's killing beasts and cattle every day now for food. But Leo still doesn't believe. It'll cut him down before he has time to repent. You have to convince him, Anselm. Help him to kill it – if it's not the Antichrist. Before the Seer of Worm Head finds another virgin.'

Anselm was playing absent-mindedly with the swan, tossing its limp head from one hand to the other and making its beak open and shut with a pinch of the jaw.

'Do you believe in the dragon, Anselm?'

'I'll speak to Leo when he comes here,' he said noncommittally. And then he added in a rush, as if in a hurry to get said something unpleasant, 'I have this to say, and I won't be gainsaid. I'll not ask your father to the wedding feast. And I won't have his person in my house.'

Elfleda seemed to shrink in stature. She shrugged her acquiescence. 'Because he sold you an unsound mare? Because he tricked you into marrying a madwoman?'

Anselm leaped off the table and sent it clattering to the floor.

'Certainly not! You foolish woman! Because of his boy! And his barricades! And his barbarous behaviour to a woman in her extremity. By God, Elfleda, he makes the beast itself sound human!' And he wrapped her in his arms in a gesture of apology for all men towards all women.

8

De Rochfoll's Siege

When Leo woke up with no feeling in his left hand, he was so petrified that he cared less than nothing about the wood-gatherer's donkey being eaten by a dragon.

He dimly guessed at some pagan, Saxon plot to test the Norman clergy and ruling powers. He wished his first wife was alive to explain it to him. He admired the woodgatherer's story-telling, but compared with the loss of feeling in his hand, it was a mime, an entertainment. He gave orders that the gatherer be put to the torture, to discover who had paid for such a ludicrous hoax. But nothing came of it.

He did not tell Gwyne about his hand. The fewer people who knew, he thought, the less importance it could have. And when she told him to put on a sword – 'At least make a *show* of hunting the beast' – it would have sounded wimpish to say that he had a bad hand. By closing his left-hand fingers round the buckle with his right hand, he could hold it still enough to thread the belt through. He did not think she had noticed anything.

He and his house-men rode up and down the heath from lunch-time until after dark and, having found no trace of dragon, came home spiteful with sarcasm.

But since Easter Sunday, Gwyne had been so pale and terse that Leo finished the day solicitously fetching her sunflower seeds and cordials. He had been married to Gwyne for long enough to realise that he was responsible for whatever ailed her.

Gwyne did not even want to go to the wedding feast. Leo concealed the fact that he did not want to go either, and said that it would offend de Rochfoll if they failed to attend.

But then, in the event, de Rochfoll was not there. Leo asked Anselm why, but got no straightforward answer, only 'I must speak to you privately.' It was not the stuff of weddings.

There seemed to be, against all likelihood, a love-match between his brother and the glorious Elfleda. But the guests would keep harping on Elshender. Had Leo had word from him? Had there been more visions? Could Elshender be consulted about the dragon? Did Leo suppose his son to be a saint? People seemed inhibited by this idea. They mooted it anxiously, almost distastefully. One woman even made excuses to Leo for not directing her prayers through Elshender. 'I can't forget how he kissed my daughter against her will – though they do say Holy Augustine was a whoreson lecherous lad as well.'

Plainly they did not relish the idea of a parochial saint. They tended to talk of Elshender as if he were dead and they must keep from wounding Leo with memories. But it did not stop them talking about him incessantly.

They congratulated Leo, too. What a sharp political move to salve de Rochfoll's honour by finding his daughter a bride-groom of equal status from inside the family. How fortunate that the girl felt so well compensated. How obliging of Anselm. They were watching, waiting for Leo to acknowledge how Anselm had helped him out of a delicate dilemma. No one there gave Anselm the credit for finding his own wife, nor for wooing her.

Strange kind of a favour. Leo wished there were someone for whom he could make the ultimate sacrifice of marrying Elfleda! Her eyes were the colour of morning glories, and she filled her dress as wine fills a cup. She also said, 'You look a little tired, brother Leo, and have you hurt your hand? It seems to be troubling you.'

'Well, you know, it's most odd. I seem to have lost the feeling . . .'

'May I chafe it for you?'

'No, no. Well, not when my wife's . . . I mean I haven't worried her with mentioning it.' Gauchely, he was stuck for words. She seemed so . . . unmatchable, what with her youth and her cheerfulness and her two hands. He said, "Selm's a pleasant enough fellow, isn't he?'

'Indeed. I trust we both think so.'

'Ah, yes.' There was a further pause. 'Your father's not well, then?'

'As far as I know he's well.'

'Ah . . . I mean, he . . . ah . . . doesn't appear to . . . ah . . . be here.'

'My husband didn't want him here. Have you spoken to Anselm yet?'

'Oh. No. What about?'

'Whatever he wishes to say to you, sir. If you won't let me rub your arm, we ought to take our places at table.'

The swan arrived – gilded and sewn back into its skin with all the finesse of darned hose. It was the shape of a pillow, and its head lolled drunken and bedraggled over a wicker support. The grease was starting to seep through and soil the colouring. It looked rather like a disreputable, shrunken dragon.

Leo should have sat to the right of Elfleda, with Anselm on

her left. He had looked forward to having her there. But he was given the chair to the left of Anselm, instead, and Gwyne sat on the bride's right hand. Leo heard her say, 'And what fowl are inside the swan, child?' and Elfleda reply, 'More swan, madam. Our cook lacks ambition.'

Leo asked his brother directly, 'What do you want to talk to me about?'

Anselm cleared his throat, plucked at his shirt-front and stared at his meat. Leo thought he was going to ask for money. 'Did you get back your horse?' said Anselm. 'That man of yours – Bruno – he's an oaf. By the way, did Brother Alban find his way back to you after the Easter service?'

'Who?'

'The monk we borrowed. Your wife's curate.'

'My wife doesn't have a curate. I don't know who you . . . or perhaps she has. I don't seem fully in control of things lately. I don't know, 'Selm. I haven't seen a curate. I'll ask her. Is it important? Do you need him again?'

'No, no. It was by the way. I had it in mind to join you tomorrow, if you go looking for the dragon.'

'Went yesterday,' Leo declared. 'Shan't go again.'

Anselm was startled. This risk to his brother, of which he had known nothing at the time, made him tremble now with its dreadful possibilities. When he could recover his non-chalance he said, 'Why won't you? The weather's pleasant enough. People seem to expect it.'

Leo was, as usual, rendered stupid by his brother's assorted conversation. But he determined to see this through and reach Anselm's meaning. The last time he had ignored the man, when he had called on the pretext of talking about dragons, he had gone away and married the glorious Elfleda inside the day. 'I know!' thought Leo, with blazing insight, 'He wants to be away from the house! The child won't consummate. He wants an excursion to take his mind off her body! By Jude, so do I! By Judas, I need to take my mind off my own body, let alone hers.'

'All right, 'Selm. Tomorrow, starting from my yard. Shall we take picks to brain it, or nets to bring it home in?'

'Oh, anything and everything. To make a good show.'

A cold shiver ran up Anselm's back as he clutched in his fist the little charcoal sketch Elfleda had made for him of the dragon. When he unwrapped it later, it was obliterated, and the palm of his hand looked charred. Charcoal had crept into every crease. He could leave a map of his life on the wall, simply by leaning against it. And the map could be brushed away just as easily.

Drunkenness set in by noon. By sunset the guests were frantically clinging to facts. They were shouting at each other the reasons for a wedding feast without a wedding. They were shouting the names and parentage of the bride and groom, the possible extent of their wealth, wild approximations of their ages. Elshender's Vision was bandied back and forth, gathering embellishments with every telling.

The older men, made bold by Anselm's example, were exploring liaisons with their nieces, their cousins and the daughters of their neighbours. Where they were rebuffed, they turned to the better trodden territory of serving-women and their tenants' womenfolk, while their wives complained shrilly to one another. One or two men even eyed Elfleda optimistically, stirred in their imaginings by the peculiar and immodest circumstances of her marriage.

The table where Anselm, Leo, Elfleda and Gwyne sat

remained like a raft in a trough of pitching sea. Leo did not drink for fear it numbed his remaining limbs. Gwyne did not drink, he supposed, so that she could remain competent to disdain the guests around her. Elfleda drank only for thirst, wetting her lips with the one cup of wine. And Anselm did not drink for fear his breath or his body failed him in bed where his imagination already lay.

Now and again they caught sight of Bruno, low-lying but constant like a buoy, at the other end of the flood. Mann washed up against him and, helped by a push, sank stonily out of sight. But apart from that one movement, Bruno simply stood and watched, and watched and stood. His eyes remained fixed on the top table.

Around it, the feast thrashed on, as heedless and needless of the host as an epileptic fit is of its victim. Finally it slowed to stupor and vomiting and the irritable flurries of women wanting to leave. It was Bruno who finally opened the house doors and spilled the festivities out on to the yard where they shivered and died. It was Bruno who came and announced that Mann was dead drunk on the kitchen oven, and wiped the table clear of food scraps. It was Bruno who leaned against the bride so furtively and suggestively that she sprang to her feet. Anselm stood up within the same second, having awaited her signal patiently for an hour. They backed, hand in hand, towards the staircase.

'You'll see the guests away, won't you Leo?' said Anselm.

'Oh. Yes. If you like. Where are you going?' Leo emerged ragged from a forest of thought and got to his feet.

Anselm plucked at his shirt-front and looked at Elfleda.

'Don't be foolish, brother Leo,' she said, curtsying to Gwyne before drawing Anselm away and up the stairs.

The few remaining guests threw lewd, excitable exclamations up the stairs as though they were shying stones at a fairground target, and the wedding broke up under the impression that it had paid the bride and groom all due honour.

'Damn,' said Leo peevishly. 'Gwyne! Rub my arm. I've no feeling in it. Here, woman, here.'

'Let me, sir,' said Bruno, stepping forward when Gwyne did not stir. He rubbed the arm as though he were drilling for fire with a twig. Leo's fingers kindled and burned. The rush of blood raged from wrist to shoulder and flashed hot and cold. 'Anything else, master? Anything else want rubbing? Lost its feeling?'

Leo pushed his servant away.

'You must be bled,' said Gwyne, leaving no room for argument. She waited for Bruno to hold her chair before she got to her feet.

Next morning, Elfleda changed her mind. She did not want to let Anselm go, and refused to dress in the hope that he would lose his resolve. But, heroically, he left before dawn for his brother's place, and surprised the manor-house in its early-morning indolence.

His two dogs rushed into every corner of the yard, disturbing the pigs and sending up frightened chickens on to the straw thatch between the buttresses. His horse was so big that the tip of his longbow, worn over his back, caught on the gate's keystone. Mann came out, praising God for Anselm. He, at least, believed that a handful of armed men could dispatch the dragon.

To his disgust, Anselm saw that Bruno was to be included in

the troop, as well as Leo's steward and ostler. They were none of them bowmen, and the steward wore sandals. An assortment of halberds, quarterstaffs and javelins were wrapped up in a blanket and carried between two horses. But a basket of hot coals had been abandoned, since the ostler valued his horses too highly.

Irritated past all reason by the superstitious chatter of dragons, Leo had assembled the only members of his staff who held (or said they held) the rumours to be nonsense. Anselm did not want to endanger the trip. He would maintain scrupulously his look of cynicism until they were far enough from the castle for Leo not to turn back.

'Why would you want to go dragon-hunting the day after your wedding feast?' said Leo, wheedling for an admission, a shared confidence.

'Oh, a little joke between Elfleda and me.'

'So shall we ride that way and show her the parade?'

'No. Out by the coast, I thought. If it's not finished, you can hear the blow-hole at high tide. Extraordinary. And the village below de Rochfoll's place is paralysed with fright. Ask your horsemaster.'

'And your father-in-law can stand us a meal,' said Leo, wheedling for information again.

Anselm ignored him. He rather hoped they would find some trace of the dragon, to deflect everyone's attention from him and Elfleda. He did not want to be questioned on his accidental bliss.

How strange that he could not bring himself to confide, even in his brother, the extent of his joy. It seemed illogical for one newly married man to tell a man long married the delights of marriage. Leo must already know them. But in that case, where was the spark in his eye? Had he really kept a similar rapture secret all these years? Why? Why such a universal conspiracy of silence among the world's married men?

Mann boasted about the agony of his rheumatism. The ostler boasted that he had helped hang a man once. The steward boasted that all his sons had died in the war. Why was it so unacceptable to boast happiness? Perhaps because it was not generally available. Or perhaps because it would sound like an unwillingness to die.

That morning Anselm was feeling a great unwillingness to die. Whenever they stopped, his horse began to walk backwards: he was yearning into his stirrups. He determined not to spend the night away from home. Not an unwillingness to die, so much as a novel longing to live – in Elfleda's company. Men of his station were accustomed to billeting marriage and desire in different quarters. A talented slut could relieve the marital misery of a man. That was the beerhouse myth. What the ale-oiled bawdy had not prepared him for was the impact of love and sex joining forces. It was enough to unseat a man.

His horse stopped and shook its ears irritably. Anselm tried to stop yearning into his stirrups. 'Even so,' he thought, 'I ought to say something to Leo.' It seemed a betrayal of Elfleda not to admit to *someone* that she was the loveliest of women since . . .

But when he glanced over at Leo, he saw that his brother was standing in his stirrups. He had stood up to let his horse relieve itself; but the lifting of his head had brought into view the copse ahead.

It was burned.

White branches and roots twisted among the ash. It resembled Ezekiel's Valley of Dry Bones. The fire had come and gone so fast that nothing but dead grass, leaves and twigs had burned. The fallen branches had been blanched clean, but only one or two had caught and smouldered and retained any heat.

'Lightning,' said Leo.

'No,' said Anselm. 'I think it's time to tell you.'

'There is no dragon!' Leo interrupted him shrilly.

'There is. Elf's seen it.'

'She's mad, then.'

'No.'

'You're mad, then. Why would you want to fool me?' Leo rubbed his biceps as if he were cold, but he was purely angry.

'Better to force your hand than wait for the beast to force it. She's seen it, I tell you. It exists.'

'No.'

'Yes,' said Bruno, relishing the impudence, and the attention it drew. 'I've seen it, too. It ate your monk, Anselm – the one who married you so helter-skelter.'

'Alban?' Anselm was unmanned. The sadness of it shrank him. 'He was with us on Easter Sunday. When? You saw it? You didn't speak up till now?' He wanted Leo to be right now: the dragon must be imaginary.

'How *dare* you,' Leo mouthed, riding his horse up against Bruno's. 'Is everyone trying to make a fool of me?'

'Came on the hunt, didn't I?' said the horsemaster, closing his mouth over a grin. 'Was looking for a fitting time to tell your lordship.'

In the centre of the copse they found the remains of two deer. Beside them, a clutter of footprints faced in every direction where the beast had turned and turned over its prey. They followed the tracks without any difficulty up to the remoter bounds of de Rochfoll's estate. They found a stone wall wilfully pushed down, a holm-oak burning in its core with its branches falling one by one. They found a cairn of droppings outside the stable wall, and two horses hanging in their headstalls with their throats cut. A wilderness had been made of the yard. De Rochfoll's cart had been plunged, shafts downwards, through the thatched roof of the stable. Every corner strut was broken; the planking swung like the skirt of a Roman legionnaire over the end wall. At the base of the wall they found a pool of blood. The smell of roasting pig from the corner sty was peculiarly delicious among the devastation.

The steward was scared out of all usefulness. He slumped over the neck of his horse or twisted about in the saddle, expecting every moment for the beast to leap out on them. He said he could feel its eyes watching him. He was a sycophant as a rule, and Leo liked him better for this honest, selfish terror, but it spread thin his resources if he had indeed to fight the dragon.

A dragon has been here. He found the words in his head and could not be rid of them. It was as though his brain had left a message by its door and gone out. Leo tried to summon up a plan, but nothing would answer but that one inane phrase: *A dragon has been here.*

Anselm too called on his brain for tactics, and all that he found was a precise, pedantic description of the yard – as if his memory were rehearsing a report for Elfleda. Each man's brain ceased to function.

The front door was barricaded from inside. Anselm called his father-in-law's name repeatedly and threw his shoulder against the door. But there was no reply. They circled the building and found an open doorway to a cellar.

Inside, it was completely dark. Anselm put out his hands and they met with a cold, damp flesh covered with sharp, cold hairs. It swung away from him with a groan of the rope by which it was suspended, swung back and nudged him in the dark. His back set another such slab of flesh swinging.

He shut his eyes and put his hands over them, pressing his eyeballs until the blackness was veiny with colours. When he opened them again, the darkness was less, and he could recognise the shape of a salted pork hung from the floor-beams overhead. With a whimpering laugh he fell up against the ladder, and pulled himself up it largely by the strength of his arms. He heard the ostler follow him in and meet the hung pig. 'It's salt meat,' he called, and his voice sounded like someone else's: a snickering, oafish voice.

As he pushed open the trapdoor and put out his head and called de Rochfoll's name, he felt a prick behind his ear that he took for a bee-sting. He brushed the thing away, and felt a prick in the back of his hand, and knocked the blade of a sword away from his jugular.

'You came back, then, did you?' squealed de Rochfoll. His voice was caked with phlegm as if he had not used it for days.

'Yes, sir,' said Anselm, holding the blade's end.

'How many of you? I'll have you one by one. Is my boy there? I'll have him gutted, so help me Mary.' The old man scowled down with his milky eyes, but his unshaven cheek was twitching, and his hand shook. He had not taken off his clothes since Anselm last saw him.

'It's I, Father. Anselm. Your son-in-law. Elfleda's husband.'

De Rochfoll's mouth dropped open, like a tragedian's mask, and he pattered one way and then the other, almost falling down the trap. 'They've all gone!' he bleated. 'Every last son of a whore!' And then he let Anselm up, and wept into his jerkin, his blotched hands clinging in the armholes.

The dragon had come in broad daylight. But to de Rochfoll it was just a noise of confusion and destruction. As his servants, bent on abandoning the house for ever, pillaged it for valuables, snatching up candlesticks, pewter, fire-irons and rugs, he raged at them. What was happening? What were the noises? What were they doing? But no one answered him. His blind eyes followed them about, but they paid as little heed to them as the stone eyes of a gargoyle. He grabbed at his boy, but the lad only jabbered hysterically that Elfleda ought to have burned – ought to have gone out to it or ought to have burned.

Then the outhouses were stove in – 'by some mighty instrument of war', in de Rochfoll's words – and there was no one to answer his calling. They had all gone, swearing their gutteral, heathen oaths, and de Rochfoll was alone with the noise and, subsequently, with the silence – which was worse, he said, much worse.

For three days he walked the house, trying to scrabble together, with his outstretched hands, a picture of his looted home. His authority flouted once, he could see no reason why the looters should not come back. Every villager in Worm Head would come, with carts and wagons, to complete the brazen task of stripping him bare. So, laboriously, he heaped furniture against the door, hid his personal valuables in the bread oven, armed himself and placed his chair over the trapway to the meat cellar. But nobody came and nobody came.

Anticipating starvation, he unbarricaded the door once and

made an attempt to reach a horse. But what horses had not been stolen by the servants, his blind hands found cold and wet with gore: he took it they had been slaughtered so as to cut him off from succour. He retreated to the house, blocked up the door again and waited. But nobody came and nobody came.

In a brain littered with memories of old military campaigns, the humiliation of a siege rankled. He lifted his chair off the hatch, wrote his will in Latin and, wearing it inside his shirt, continued to wait. He was besieged by silence, one generation away from the end of his Line.

Finally, Anselm and Leo had come. On top of hunger and starvation, the relief of it prostrated de Rochfoll. He slid on its slurry into that tract of old age, the valley between the bright plain and the bottomless sea.

When Anselm put him to bed, he was asleep before his hands let go their grip on his son-in-law's jerkin. Anselm sat by him, reading the sheet of writing de Rochfoll called his will. The sprawled words overlapped. Lines were overlaid, one on top of another. In among the briar and bramble of cursives, he could make out parts of his own name, his brother's name, his wife's name. When Babel fell, its library was more coherent than the handwriting of a blind man.

Leo disbanded the hunt and went home. Next morning, the old man rode to Anselm's house in tandem with his son-in-law, his spotted hands knotted in front of Anselm's waist. From Worm Head to within shouting distance of Elfleda, neither of them spoke a word.

9

THE DEVIL ON THE BEACH

His head, hands and heels hit the earth together, his back a moment later. All the breath went out of him. He waited for some bloody sachet of spleen or liver to burst inside him, but the only immediate pain was in the jarred bones of his feet. He stared upwards through the leaves, and concentric circles of darkness rippled outwards from the centre of his eyes.

Above him, Bruno started down the slope, absurd in his blood lust.

'Better be dead, Alban. If you be'n't dead when I get to you, Alban, you'll be sorry for the rest of your life! I see you, boy. I'm coming. Did you like what you saw, did you? What, and no confessing to your lechery before you die? No shriving? I . . .' His foot slipped and he cursed. The soil from under his boot spattered over the leaves and into Alban's face. 'No shriving, eh? Still, you won't want your body at the Resurrection – not when I'm finished –'

The noise of munching interrupted Bruno's itemising of the torments he had in store for Alban. All the birds flittered away.

It was only the loudness of the munching and the panic of the birds that made Bruno turn. And then it was only a hammock of shrubs that prevented him slipping down on top of the monk.

Like a lizard he went up the escarpment, knees and elbows out and his cheek pressed to the earth. Alban, looking upwards, could see the bias weave of his breeches stretch on one diagonal then the other. Another shower of earth came down in his face. The munching stopped.

Alban tried to lift his head, but the muscles in his back cramped and he dropped his head back and rolled on to his side. He would get up by rolling on to his knees, he thought. One of his sandals was missing. He must not leave the spot without finding it. He had some vague fear of the unseen cow eating it.

But the munching had stopped, and in its place was a sound of gagging and hawking. Alban looked up in time to see the dragon shaking its head and neck violently then extruding a firmly packed ball of yellow grass from its gaping mouth. It coughed, with hardly more noise than a horse, and strings of saliva hitched it by silver reins to a gorse bush.

Its head was sideways on to the monk. Its eye was fixed on him. An inner eyelid wiped mucus shreds off its stony eyeball. Placing its feet precisely, carefully, it came on, turning its head to right and left to look at him with each eye. The gait gave the beast an arrogant, mincing walk; its closed mouth gave it a smug, human expression and a bulbous nose. Every inward and outward breath registered in the nostrils, sweeping the long inner hairs like kelp turning over in the run of a wave. It picked out its path with fastidious care, placing one foot in front of another, wagging its head, blinking its eyes, and sifting the air through its nostrils. When it was within a stone's throw, Alban struggled to his knees. When it was within a body's length, he snatched the crucifix from round his neck, pulled the beltless habit over his head, and prostrated himself on the bracken. (It was difficult, down the slope, with his feet higher than his head.)

'Ave, belua! Vacuus coram domino viator sum.'

Though the beast uttered a dreadful whine that culminated in a bark which arced fire through its gullet, and though its head, overarching the monk, came gradually down on to his back, never for one moment did Alban expect the teeth to close on him.

How many signs can a man expect before he accepts a summons to serve in the lair of the Devil Incarnate?

If Scripture was precise, the Beast from the Sea (deputy and successor to the Antichrist) would hold authority on the Earth one hundred and fifty days. How many of those days were past, and where the seven-headed Antichrist was keeping himself, exercised Alban's thoughts often as he sat on a rock on Worm Beach and watched the sea reorganise the pebbles and shells.

He was confirmed in his choice of master by the spell of beautiful weather. In the lee of the headland it was even hot. Sandpipers were running maniacally up and down the shore, dodging the waves. Fat white gulls were sitting on the combers, rising and falling like minims on staves. The beast was stretched out on the sand, steaming in the sun. If it were not for the pestering flies breeding in the old seaweed and a certain smell of decay, the place would have been paradise.

The fine weather had allowed Alban not to enter the cave where the dragon slept at night. It looked unfortunately like the painted mouth of Hell on the set of a tawdry guild-play. He would avoid passing through it for as long as possible.

He had expected at first that the beast would speak to him – give him instructions. But though it had a tongue, it seemed incapable of articulate speech. Perhaps already its powers were declining. How could Alban know how far through its temporal span and rule he had become its servant? Certainly, the creature often whined and rattled its soft palate in a noise that approximated to misery or pain. Its body was covered with contusions, too, as if it had thrown itself repeatedly against a cliff, or been bombarded with rocks. When Alban, having walked alongside the dragon over the heath and along the beach, became steeled to the closeness of that huge flank, he fetched sea water and gingerly washed all the scrapes and gouges.

He never again saw the beast eat grass. And when he put up snares and caught a rabbit and offered it as a token gift to the dragon, it was snapped up and swallowed whole. Alban had to catch three more before he was able to cook and eat some meat himself.

When the sacrifices first appeared on the beach, they were no more than Alban expected. He was surprised that the dragon had not already gathered an entourage of worshippers. There was no one. Only himself. Perhaps fear had kept them away, the kind of fear to which he was not prey, being already damned. After his few hugger-mugger, overcrowded days in the service of Man, his first days in the service of the beast were pacific, empty, quiet. He slept for hours in the middle of the day, wrapped up in his knees, arms and habit among the grass of the sand dunes. The dragon slept too, or lay half-in, half-out of the cave, which it had blasted clean with fire.

Its fire was a source of stark terror, then of fear, for Alban. 'Fear' as in the Fear of God. 'Fear' as of the fire Abraham carried to the land of Moriah along with a knife, wood and his son. 'Fires' astonishment', such as made Saint Patrick in-vulnerable. The implications of it were far more dreadful than the flame itself. The faint glimmer which, at night, showed through the skull itself was no threat to Alban. It would not consume him as it had one day consumed a tree, for the sake of the birds in it. It would not scourge Alban as it had scourged clean the cave – not at least until the bonfire was set for the whole world to burn upon.

The villagers' propitiations on the beach were welcome. They appeared during the nights: a skewer of blackbirds, a bowl of sweet, immature wine, a brace of geese, and a live pig tethered by one leg.

At first, Alban went to fetch the gifts – in case of ambush: a volley of arrows, a covered pit or a petard. But the people of Worm Bay had clearly grasped their obligations towards this guest billeted on them by the Devil. Each day their sacrifices were surrounded by scrapings in the sand, paintings on slate, carvings in wood. And every symbol was the same: a fish.

'*Give us back the fish,*' said Alban to the dragon, by way of a translation. But though the Christian symbol lifted the hairs on the monk's neck, the dragon paid it no attention, often trampling the sand drawings and dislodging the slates with its clumsy attempts to eat the offerings from in amongst them.

And then one morning there was the girl.

They heard a commotion towards morning but, as usual, by the time beast and servant reached the place the anonymous acolytes had gone and there was the girl, screaming noise-lessly, or too high for any ears but a dog's. She was bound hand and foot and had been laid inside a boat – a sort of coracle with an outrigger, moored on an outhaul three waves off-shore.

She was about twelve, with a big head and thin white legs. In the madness of terror, she was no more or less than another child of the same age. The villagers had gambled that the dragon would not see that she was a thing spoiled in the making, an accident of birth. Perhaps her simplicity would pass unnoticed for the first time in her life.

As Alban approached the shore and gradually understood the situation, he quickened his walk. Distress revived in him like a dormant infection. Behind him the dragon too moved quicker. Alban broke into a run. The dragon plunged through the sandstorm it was forever raising with its big front feet. It ran too.

Alban looked from boat to beast and back again. He ran into the water – so cold that he might as well have been kicking his way through ice. The dragon came to a halt with its back feet out of the water and its front feet prancing over the broken waves. The sin of compassion broke down all telepathy between monk and beast. All at once he could not judge where the offset eyes were looking. He could not judge what the beast was thinking. He could not tell what pleasure the sacrifice gave it. Disobedience cut him off, as it had cut him off from his Order. He tried to put all scruples out of his mind. What – desert his only allegiance for a moment's squeamishness? In a hundred days or so the girl would be no more than fuel for the Final Fire. Along with the greater part of humanity she would be shovelled into the maw of Hell, and him with her. Why try to save her for a few meaningless weeks?

He waded out, floundering in the skirts of his habit, and slipped under as he tried to grab the outrigger. Then the girl saw the dragon. She thrashed herself so close to the rim of the boat that it tipped up, and she rolled into the sea. When Alban surfaced, she had disappeared from sight entirely.

The dragon pounced into the sea. Underwater, the girl's

hair washed into Alban's hand and he pulled her up and ashore by her head. The dragon backed out of the water. Its monk panted on his hands and knees on the sand. And between them lay the girl, torpid with cold and with her back to the beast. The dragon turned its head side-on and blinked. Alban stood up, stood back, and with a gesture of assignment, offered it the virgin sacrifice.

He fell back to his knees when the beast let out a bellow that echoed off three faces of the cliff. It flung its head about, first to one side and then the other, until its neck was snaking. The noises that came from its throat then were high, small and demented, like a gull's screams, and its movements so frenzied that it turned itself on to one shoulder and its cheek slapped the sand.

It ground its teeth on the rope of the outhaul until the coracle was swamped and sank, its rigger reaching out of the water like a drowning arm. Then the beast turned its excitement on the humans, thrusting its head into the priest's chest and throwing him across the sand. As for the girl, it skirted her, ploughing a half-circle of footprints that made her look even more of an occult object. Then the dragon broke away, and setting its front legs apart, began to sweep its snout through the sand. More signs, more signals, thought Alban. A candlestick? A right angle? A snake? Then its feet began to blur and deface its own work. It heaved its body up with a jerk of its head, and walked drunkenly to the mouth of the cave where it lay down, its head obscured, its rump in the sun. The heartbeat – visible where the skin was stretched rubbery white over the shorter ribs – slowed gradually to keep time with the breaking of the small waves. Every so often its tail lifted and snaked.

With his eyes on the beast, Alban untied the little girl. She was as rigid as a plank, and her limbs prickled with gooseflesh. He picked her up in his arms and wandered up and down the beach, tripping on his hem and accumulating sand.

He could not take her back to the village. There he could expect to be stoned like Brother Paul for misleading them as to the nature of the dragon – for telling them it was old, harmless and leaving. Their spies might even know him to be the dragon's chiefest acolyte.

He said to the girl, 'My master wishes for no human sacrifices. Do you understand? Can you give that message to your people at home?'

The girl shook her head. Her cold hair flicked in his face. Her prickly, stick-like arms were pincered round his neck like a yoke, but she took none of her own weight. 'What would happen to you if I sent you home?' The child looked at him with ill co-ordinated eyes. One of them wandered across his forehead as if looking for Cain's mark. She did not reply. 'Do you know where the Prior lives?'

'No.'

'Could you find your way there – to the Prior's house?'

'Yes.'

It was a waste of time talking to her. He was anxious to get back to his dragon. He felt his allegiance draining away from this clammy, helpless child and back towards his master. When he put her down, he had to prise his head out from between her elbows.

He dragged her by the arm to the top of the cliff-path and pointed in the direction of the priory. He did not know that he was right, but he sensed its position from some kind of old, devotional intuition and from clouded memories of passing it as he walked alongside the dragon to the beach. Since Easter Day, he had lost all sense of geography.

When he let go of the child, her legs buckled. She was like a fawn unlicked. She dripped. Her terror was already submerged in confusion. She wandered away in the direction he pointed, but he had to throw his hand out again and again to impel her to keep moving. It was like ordering a dog to its kennel. Long before she was out of sight, he turned his back and skidded, squatting, down the shaly cliff-path.

Mercy. It was incompatible with Satan. For a time it troubled Alban and made him think, when he had hoped that thinking was no longer a responsibility of his. In the end he explained away the dragon's hysteria as repugnance at being offered an imperfect gift. Such repellence left no room for charity. Revulsion was not mercy. So his dragon had been consistent. Revulsion is not mercy.

Alban pressed his back against the warm rock and not a louse moved in the weave of his habit. He had washed it and himself in the sea that morning, and he felt like a new man. The dragon stirred itself and lifted its head briefly to look back at Alban over its shoulder. It was troubled by flies. In the evening Alban would go and find a switch of leaves he could use to keep them off. In the mean time, he sat and looked up at the sky and watched a cloud form over Worm Head that was just the shape of a dragon. It swelled and rolled, lethargic, in the blue sky. He would have pointed it out to the beast but for the notion that his every thought sprang from and returned to his master. Their brains had melted together under the small warmth of May, and his waking and sleeping were all phased by the waking and sleeping dragon, as the sea is phased by the moon.

Never in all his strictured, structured, servile life had Alban felt so obedient to rule, and never had he felt so free. As the breeze brought downwind the rank, stale smell, like decaying whale, Alban simply turned his mind to the little girl – unconsumed – and he loved the dragon with a sharp, pitying love. Surely, in pitying the Devil Himself, Alban was only a little lower than the fallen angels. He was profoundly content.

Elshender derived more comfort from the man's grunts, snores and sighs than from any words he uttered. Where there was no language to point up the ludicrous disparity between man and beast, they could happily coexist – two beasts of a different kind, grunting and snoring, letting the small warmth of May melt their aching bones and solder their thoughts together, half waking, half sleeping. Lying on the sand, he heard the priest sigh and, lifting his head, he looked back at the rock where Alban sat. This happy imbecile in his shapeless wool could almost sway Elshender the Dragon in favour of life.

10

ELSHENDER'S VISION

Elshender's Vision was not written in the heavens. He preserved it carefully nevertheless, hanging it like a banner against the back of his brain, and trooped it out each morning and night. He had studied its fabric too closely and too often to forget each prick of the needle that had made it. His 'vision' was, of course, of Gwyne's making.

On the day after his father went away to attend the King's marriage, Elshender, who did not interest himself greatly in the domestic affairs of the castle, became dimly aware of excited activity. His sister, when he caught sight of her in a corridor, was white-faced and agitated. He was afraid she was about to confide in him something sorrowful about which he would not mind, or something banal by which he would be irritated. So he went out of doors for a day and a half.

She was a harmlessly pleasant girl, Frideswide, but her life was so confined by the castle walls that she rarely had anything to say worth saying. She had a tendency, too, to pry: an innocent, vicarious pleasure in the fleshed-and-bloody lives of men and peasants from which she was excluded. But she could not keep a secret. She lacked subjects for conversation, and he did not care to have his confidences reach the ears of waiting-women, servants and more especially his father and stepmother. Now and then he would let Bruno the horsemaster procure for him, but he would no more have confided in Frideswide than he would in Elfleda. He hoped his betrothed wife would have more spontaneous conversation.

In fact he had huge hopes of Elfleda, whom he loved heroically. His picture of her was against a setting of spreading family trees, under the streaming sunlight of history, with progeny at her feet and the tessellations of secure battlements at her back. Her beauty and grace would permeate his own body (which, as he watched it growing, rather disappointed him). Dignity eluded him in adolescence. Elfleda would give him the status and carriage of a man. He hungered after her in every way he could imagine.

When he discovered that his sister had been betrothed of a sudden to a Frenchman, his reaction was not to pity Frideswide (for he had no inkling of her feelings on the matter), but he was mordantly, peevishly aggrieved about the hasty arrangements. It was wrong of Gwyne to make such matches while his father was away. But what rankled most was the thought of his sister marrying before him. And of Elfleda unenjoyed. When a marriage could be arranged for Frideswide within the turn of a tide, why must he wait?

In his room, he fuelled his anger on barley ale, then he went and hammered belligerently on the beam over his step-mother's chamber door. He would demand a marriage of his own.

Bruno drew back the curtains.

While Elshender was still struggling to put a name to Bruno and to the sin he had interrupted, Bruno's punch laid him on his back. It was Gwyne, in her shift, who administered his undoing, while Bruno held him down, forced open his mouth.

Beyond the window, the moon nodded like the head of a poppy, and black seeds fell out of it into his eyes. His mouth filled with the taste of rank fish. He was awash in night air and encompassed in darkness. His blood ran cold and his skull kindled.

Geometric shapes floating in his head dwindled to the minuteness of gravel, and the gravel swelled to the hugeness of boulders, and the stars pelted on his back and the wind seemed to pass through the sieve of his skin and leave behind in it the salt of an ocean. When he licked himself, his tongue rasped and curled and ran with salt saliva. He had a thirst lake-deep.

All night long he suffered his metamorphosis. In the morning he suffered the sight of it – first only the front legs and the rim of his distorted cheek. At first his undersized brain could not impel movement in the distant tracts of his vast body. His flesh twitched, but his feet would not stir. Mice overran him. Beetles undermined him. Every defeat of his human body was magnified, from the impacted disc in his spine to the old pulled hamstring. It was a day before he could balance, swaying like the platform on which heathens prop their dead to be eaten by vultures.

His only and incessant thought was to put an end to himself. He settled on the means: a fall from the cliffs at Worm Head. But through his inadequate eyes, with which he snatched at light between uncoordinated lids, he could not recognise the place where Bruno had brought him. A day's labour took him mistakenly to the head of a tor which shelved away so gently into bracken that a baby would not have come to harm who fell down it. From the tor he could see on the one side his father's castle, on the other Elfleda's house and beyond it, three or four miles distant, a glimpse of the sea.

He thought, on that tor, that the ground had opened and

propelled a gout of lava into his belly. Yearnings, such as the lion feels for the lamb, swept up the slope from the castle. At the selfsame moment desire, when he saw Elfleda's house, shook his hindquarters. He realised that in his nostrils he could smell the smell of de Rochfoll's house: meat and dung and tar and leather and unenjoyed sweetness.

His brain was cracked open by massive lusts, his body was undermined by titanic instinct. Instinct strained at the out-stretches of his body like horses quartering a condemned man.

At the foot of the tor he lay down in the mire and determined to die of starvation. If he kept his head still, the fire inside it subsided from a white, searing pain to a dull dementia. In the act of thinking, he was Elshender. In the act of moving, he was a beast. He lay in the mire and lived in the confines of his mind, hoping to slip free of his green sarcophagus with the minimum of pain.

But hunger lay siege to his brain until he was forced to admit – by the stray intervention of a cow – that Elshender was not a mind inside a beast. Elshender was a dragon.

In time, mobility – even agility – grew along the tendons. He reached the sea, fed to fatness on cows and sheep and deer. He took shelter in a cave; he even walked for exercise along the cliff-top. His animal suffering was not (as he had often told himself when his hawk stooped on a rabbit or he wrung the neck of a duck) immediate, unrecallable. Even the possibility of self-destruction did not slip out of mind. But instinct bullied him along from day to day. Rage sufficed for motive.

He saw the dispatch of his sister to France. He was standing on the promontory on the day that a carriage brought her to the quayside below, with her trousseau and her marriage portion.

The tide was at its highest. The sea was bark-brown. The ship was wedged in it like an axehead. But the sails were so thin that the figures on the deck showed through in outline and colour. The anchor chain moved silently, like silk thread. And the bowsprit ran its length through the stones of the harbour wall without a sound. And though the stern faced out into the swell, there was no noise of waves breaking.

The gaudy pattern of shirt colours grouped and regrouped on the deck. They should have been sheep-coloured, wearing gabardine. If they were real. They should have been shapeless to the knee, not waisted and whippet-legged. If they were real. They should have been shouting over the hollow thuds of an unladen ship, not silent like a scene painted on a peeling church wall.

The bowsprit withdrew from the harbour wall like a needle out of flesh, and left no mark. The area of brown between ship and wall widened. The size of the genoa diminished. The hull did not leave a wake. It moved as far as the split rock beyond the promontory, then the sea received it like Excalibur, spun the mast three times and drew it under.

There was no flotsam. On the quayside there were no witnesses. Elshender searched, against the glare of the sunlight, for swimmers, rocking himself forward and back in distress. He had no doubt that his sister was under the sea. He opened his jaws to yell, and mouthed a shroud of flame over her. But the rocks themselves did howl. A fountain of water, forced through a cleft of wind-carved rock, let out a protracted, hollow complaint and fell flat along the sea. It was a thing so eerie that the beast on the promontory flinched away and cowered in a hollow as white spume fell on its back and head.

Elshender started at once in the direction of Gwyne. Had

she not been grossly stupid in her choice of magic? She might have silenced his witness to her adultery, but she had given him the bulk, fire, venom and strength to tear her in pieces. Elshender the boy had been thin and over-long in the back, his thighs hardly thicker than his calves, his eyes astigmatic and pale, his arms no stronger than he needed to throw dice or whirl the occasional jessy. He loved that inadequate body now: like Narcissus by his pool, he doted on its remembered image. He saw all its virtues, as if through the eyes of an enamoured woman. But even so, he was not so big a fool as to misremember. Elshender the boy had lacked the strength of a ploughman or a fisherman or a bowman. Only now was he dangerous. Elshender the Dragon.

'By Jude and Judas,' he thought, 'when I had my body, that woman could cow me with a look of her eye. Cow me – ah! but now the woman has dragoned me,' and his long tongue clacked against his palate, 'and I'll tear her and I'll tear that filthy ram of hers and I'll trample them in their blood . . .'

Then his flanks shook and his hindquarters swayed and his nostrils filled with the smell of tar and leather and dung and meat and the sweetness of Elfleda unenjoyed. He had wandered into the purlieu of de Rochfoll's house, and his dragony body would not let him pass by it.

His man's rational passion had hankered after Elfleda. Now his unmasterable, mountainous animal heat shackled him to her territory. He marked it, he patrolled it, he held it, and it held him, for a day and a half. When it snowed, the silent cold wiped out all smells and froze the sweat under his scales. The desire in his loins shrank. He thought to set himself on a path away from any place he knew: somewhere empty and open, where hunger would be the only instinct. He rolled wilfully in the snow, his body dissolving into a comfortable numbness and his mind made free to think again. To be a dragon was merely to be seen by human eyes and called a dragon. Away from eyes and away from impulses, Elshender could patrol some empty hinterland, no more loathsome to the things he killed than he had been when he hunted on horseback.

But when he stood up, *she* was standing just outside his shadow: Elfleda, kneeling in her small, fragile clothing of flesh while the snowflakes fell on his staring eyeballs and dissolved in trickles of darkness.

Surely, if he met her eyes and kept still, she could not fail to recognise him, to see Elshender in him.

His ears were sensitive to noise: Elfleda's noise hurt them. Her screaming knotted up his lights. When she ran away from him, he called after her with all the breath in his lungs: '*Elfleda!*' He could not associate the roar that came out of him with his shouting. He was Elshender, and, although she was ugly in her noise and her undignified terror, this was Elfleda, his betrothed, his beloved.

Still, he could not hold her. He even put himself between her and the house – another chance for her to recognise him – another opportunity for her to see that he was a man wrapped up in dragon, with no thought of hurting her. And she touched him! She accidentally touched his leg with her two hands! An intimacy he had never won in his days of flesh! It thrilled him into hoping. It made him tremble with the most delicate friendliness of love.

Then his dragonish liver stirred and his bowels rose up and his intellect recoiled. Even friendliness was submerged by the geyser of heat that her smell kindled. He reared himself up – not on to his haunches but on to his hind feet, and the dragon

118

displayed as it would to a she-dragon, before overbalancing on to its back.

She escaped him. But there was no leaving her afterwards. He knew what terror he must have caused her. He reasoned (when reason was in season) that he could only reassure her by giving her proof of his harmlessness. Time and rumour must teach her that Gwyne had 'done away' with Elshender. If he persisted doggedly outside the walls of her house, intuition must surely tell her, sooner or later, what had become of Elshender. Putting this plan to his body, it acquiesced with a sly eagerness and, as he stood behind the garden wall, watching her window, lust coiled like a worm inside him.

One night there was a movement at her window – a disturbance, a struggle. He moved closer, full of urgent, solicitous concern. Like grain to a budgerigar or salt to a horse, she held out to him a boy – a morsel of meat!

It so horrified him that he broke his vigil and ran and killed and ate cows, birds, rats, badgers, a horse – until the offence was replaced by revulsion at his own beastliness. Next day he was back again, as dogged and faithful as a hound. But he could smell only leather and meat and dung and the old, unrenewed smell of Elfleda, gone. There were other faces at her window. He pressed closer to the wall.

The house suddenly disgorged swarms of people, screaming and clanking like tinkers under festoons of tinware and furniture. It confused and incensed Elshender: he could make no sense of their pillage. He thought it might be an ambush for him, and squinted at the sky, fearing arrows. He damned his feeble intellect and he damned the looks on their faces when they turned and saw him. He damned the horses who strained in their halters, deafening him with their screeching, and he damned the boy who leaped about the yard, ferocious with terror, yelling, 'She's gone! Gone! Gone!' The barbarous dwarf suddenly freed all but two of the horses and slit the throats of the last. 'Eat! Eat! *Eat!*' he bawled, leaping this way and that with fists clenched and teeth bared. The air reeked of adrenalin and blood.

The mixture of such violence and terror so excited the beast that its jaws began to work and its claws to extend and retract and its saliva to run and its neck to thrash. The smell and movements of the boy drew down on him a reflex snatch of the head. And once the jowl touched, the jaws could not help but chew . . .

Once begun, Elshender's destruction of the outbuildings was mere flea-biting. At the finish, the walls of the house withstood more than his own grazable hide. But it was an hour before Elshender could repeal the impulse to lay waste to life, livestock and masonry.

Through his exhalations of sulphur and the rasping noise of his own breath, he could hear the 'chank, chank, chank' of the priory bell. It was Easter Day.

Remorse such as Satan must have felt when his belly touched ground and his mouth filled with ash drove Elshender through the countryside with his tail thrust up between his legs and his jaw trowelling through the under-growth. The ducts below his marbled eyes bulged like contusions, and he strained to swallow as if a boulder were wedged in his gullet. With the image of the boy leaping frog-like across his vision, he vowed never to kill another living creature. He would eat grass.

Cows and horses and all manner of large animals could sustain themselves on grass. So too could he – or would, in expiation for murdering a child. And snatching up clover and bents, fern, heather, rye, nettles, docks and cow parsnip, he stuffed his maw with an impacted pillow of stalks. His tongue could not crush them. His teeth could not shred them. He all but choked on the green ball.

The shock of seeing a human being in so wild a place, and on Easter Sunday, made Elshender slow and irresolute. If he had realised sooner that the man on the escarpment was Bruno, then he would have trampled the monk underfoot in his rush to chew on the adulterer. But Bruno was out of context and outside his comprehending. He saw the monk first, and Bruno after. The adrenal smell of fear in the air slackened as the frog-shaped figure topped the embankment and fled away across the heath. The monk, though he was a riot of smells, exuded only old terror and spent fright. When Alban stripped off his habit and prostrated himself at the dragon's feet, Elshender was filled with gratitude.

From the first scent to the first sunset, Elshender believed that at last he was known for a man shrouded in dragon. And when Alban washed his grazes, it felt like the unction of Mother Church. When they lay together on the beach, he dared to think that it even felt akin to friendship.

Until the virgin sacrifice, he believed that Alban knew. He believed, for all the silly gifts and tokens of the villagers, that the monk was a gentle divine sent by angels to sustain his spirit. Then the fishermen offered him a girl. And the monk bowed and stepped back, and offered her up to him as though she were meat on a platter.

Elshender was unmanned – undragoned, undone. He grieved like a child bereft, with empty, futile fury. He screamed his name: 'I AM ELSHENDER! ELSHENDER, SON OF LEO!' And he began to scrawl his name in the sand: E – L – S . . . But either his God's-man was illiterate or his dragon-body was clumsy. Misery had made a wordless beast of him.

When he reflected later on his mistake, lying on the beach with the madman (clearly as outcast as himself), Elshender thought he could see now the true value of the monk. Perhaps the angels had after all sent him this frightened imbecile for companionship. Elshender no longer trusted his remnants of human intuition, but sometimes he thought that the monk actually drew comfort from *him*. As far as a wordless dragon could deal in abstract concepts, he perceived that a kind of love had grown up between them.

11

High Ground

As panic rose, people looked around for high ground and ran to it. There were three areas of high ground, so to speak. The Manor, the Church and the Old Magic. Some thinking men compared the three and trekked towards (in their own judgement) the soundest. But for the most part geography determined where they turned: they chose the point of safety nearest home. And once a group had isolated itself, it scarcely knew or cared what had become of the rest of mankind.

The community at the priory was slowest of all to admit to the dragon's existence, whereby they partially lost their reputation for being first with the Truth. But they did present a strong, calm front. They were self-assured to the point of smugness. Besides, they were housed in a large, substantial building with water, animal houses, fish-ponds and orchards *inside* a perimeter wall. Serfs living within the sound of the bell gravitated towards the priory and demanded the protection of Mother Church.

With each new sighting of the beast they arrived, bringing their goods and animals. The gate had never been shut, but the Prior closed it now, turning away the common herd. Obstinately, the herd pressed back against the building, dismantling drystone walls without malice and rebuilding them when their livestock and chattels were inside. Then, as each particular panic subsided, they drifted out beyond the walls and took up their daily routines, one eye still on the horizon. The Prior comforted himself that this tidal flow would dry up in time, and ordered the gates to be left open again. He had also noted how, in penny pieces, his revenue had swelled thanks to the panic.

As an example to other susceptible souls, he excommunicated all the villagers of Worm Bay for stoning Brother Paul. Rumours of a disturbing nature were reaching him concerning the village, and the ban would also serve to quarantine any contagious sin. Witchcraft and magic were as virulent as the plague and, though he had never seen an outbreak, he feared the infection of his flock – that is to say, his Community.

For the Prior felt little concern for the laity. To him was given charge of a holy community. The chapel (which was used publicly only until Lord Leo completed a parish church) was one of the smallest rooms in the whole priory. It had not been built with the People in mind. And here were the People, with their cows and provender and wheatbaskets and pigs and lice and children. The Community was irked and unsettled. His own priests looked to him for a religious solution to the dragon, and he did not know what to say. Very well; death had no dominion over them, but that did not entirely instruct them as to whether they should fight this devil or die like Christian martyrs in its jaws.

In the short term, he instructed them that it was Lord Leo's job to destroy the beast, and that prayer alone should ensure his quick success.

One morning he looked out and a bolt of fear went through him. He saw what he took for two green heads hanging over the gateposts. Looking again, he saw them to be two felled yew trees propped up against the wall, outside; only the green crowns hung over. Someone had decided to augment prayer with something more . . . substantial, to fend off evil. How the trees had been felled and transported with so little noise or commotion he never understood: usually the peasants' behaviour was characterised by weeks of bovine inaction and bursts of noisy excitement.

Then the mill was evacuated. The dragon had come to drink at the river alongside it.

The mill was independently owned by a French yeoman who had done someone a judicious favour during the war. He accounted himself a modern man and, because of his humble origins, abrim with common sense. Latin had never sullied his lips. He could neither read nor write. When his little daughter came to him and said about the big animal in the garden, he had put his children under his arms, his money in a handcart, his wife's fingers in his belt, and he had run.

Partly out of fright but mostly to ensure that the Prior housed his family, the miller was now paying for a mass to be said every day for the Preservation of the People. And the miller's family was living in the Prior's solar, offering rewards to refugees and priests alike if they would venture up to his mill and assess the damage.

The Prior blamed the miller for what happened to the Pardoner.

A pardoner from far afield came riding along the ridge one evening, having evidently met with no danger or molestation in the world. He ran an eye over the yew trees and the children playing in the dirt, but made no comment on them to the Prior. He said he was simply seeking a bed for the night. Somehow the Prior could not bring himself to mention the matter of the dragon: he was a man of intellect and resented the possibility of being taken for a superstitious madman. He did not hide the situation from the Pardoner: he simply decided it was not worth mentioning.

Also he felt a nagging professional jealousy of the man who was carrying no less than three authenticated relics. The Prior had on his premises the earthly remains of the founding Prior, Ugo, and harboured hopes that one day Rome would elevate Ugo to the sainthood. But Ugo's sepulchre could not be called a shrine, and the Pardoner's tawdry reliquaries gave him a smug, superior status. He expected to sit in the solar after dinner to discuss the parish with the Prior.

But the miller was installed in the solar.

'A walk, perhaps,' suggested the Prior. The Pardoner looked dismayed but nodded, got up from the table and headed for the latrines. The passage from the refectory passed along the cavity thickness of the outside wall and opened on to the privy. It was at the end of this corridor that the Pardoner collided with the miller who shook his hand and declared his name and history before the Pardoner had even identified himself. The dragon arose early in the history and never really left it – or so it seemed to the Prior, hearing the echo boom down the passageway.

The Pardoner said nothing at all in response. He came back subdued, his face splattered with awe, and took the Prior by the elbows. 'I must set up my tabernacle here, holy father. This is the goal of my journeying. I never saw anything so plain.' His eyes meantime flickered and fleered, as if he were trying to see behind the Prior's disguise. *Does this one believe it?* wondered the eyes. They were cozening, greedy little eyes. The Prior coloured, and toyed with the idea of denying the dragon.

126

Instead he said, 'Take care. There is evidence of this dragon. It does exist.'

'*Populus vult decipi, ergo . . .*' breathed the pardoner, looking over one shoulder. *The People want to be deceived.*

'*Ovem lupo committo,*' said the Prior, shaking off his hands. And it was true: he did suddenly feel a paternal care for his lay flock menaced by this wolf.

The Pardoner set up his booth in the courtyard and began to offer up prayers of thanksgiving. The Prior guessed that a convenient change had overtaken the cherished relics: it seemed that the priory embraced in its walls the very sword-forearm with which Saint George had slain the dragon, plus the pelvis with which the saint had straddled the dying beast.

'These I will buy with every gold I own!' declared the miller. But the Pardoner would sell no more than a glimpse, a kiss, a blessing.

It was a miscalculation to set the fee so high. Many of the refugees from the dragon had no money and had come away without anything to sell. Cows and sheep were gifted over – something which filled the Prior with gloom, for it meant the Pardoner might become permanent.

'These I will buy with every blood in my body!' declared the miller. But the Pardoner said that God's mercy was not a commodity to be cornered by one man and withheld from others.

One man, rendered destitute by the dragon, realised that his only chance to buy a touch of the relics was by claiming the miller's reward. He volunteered to visit the mill and assess the damage. He went early one morning, before daybreak, and returned catatonic with fright. The miller intercepted him at the gate before he could spread his news: that the dragon had installed itself inside the mill, along with its servant, a profane monk. Already the seed-stores and meal house were untenable.

The miller swore the man to secrecy, paid him, then went to see the Pardoner.

'These relics I will buy with every wood and stones of my mill!' he declared.

The Pardoner took the man aside, spat on his palm, and said that in return for the mill, the miller's cows and the use of the miller's wife, he could just be persuaded to part with the forearm and pelvis of Saint George. Each man was too thrilled with his bargain to linger over the handshake.

The Pardoner decamped for the mill with the miller's wife to show him the way. The miller locked himself in the undercroft with the relics and foamed at the mouth. His belief in them was absolute. Their earning potential also made him dizzy. With his forehead pressed against the stone shoulder of Ugo's sarcophagus, he prayed fervently that the world should not come to an end before the King himself had paid tribute to kiss the forearm of Saint George! He prayed most fervently of all for the safety of the dragon, and that the loose shingle on the mill (he had been meaning to mend it) would not fall and injure the beast.

The miller's wife returned by nightfall, but without the Pardoner. In her coherent moments, she said that she had left him staring at the beast, profanely denying its existence, unable to move and blasphemous with chagrin. The cows had all been eaten by the dragon, hoof and horn.

The miller tried to leave the priory next day, to seek the patronage of wealthy men. He knew that he alone owned the only real money within the priory and that if he wanted to earn his fortune he must take his holy magic to Leo and other such people of substance.

He felt no fear. He carried his immortality in two boxes across his saddle. No dragon could harm him. He felt perfectly safe to leave with his wife and children and a horse bought for a kiss of the relics.

It was the purchase of the horse which alerted the refugees in the yard. He was leaving – taking the priceless bones and with them their protection. In the early morning, as he dismounted to open the gates, he was clubbed from behind with an adze and his body thrown into the arms of the dying yew tree outside.

The Prior placed the reliquaries in the top of the bellcote, and painted a red cross on the shingle. But his monks continued to sing mass twice daily for the Preservation of the People.

In Worm Bay, the blow-hole stopped roaring – blatant confirmation that the Old Practices were still potent. The fish did not return, but the ties with Christian feudalism were broken nevertheless. Paganism was restored and with it the right to hunt, rustle and poach. Blood which had run as thin as fish soup thickened with the juices of beef, lamb and venison. The children were sick on the richness of it, but the men put on muscle and ardour and daring.

They needed their strength for the erection of three monoliths to the north, south and west of the village. The seaward side they left to the protection of the waves. There was an ambivalence in the dragon-paintings on the sides of the monoliths. Did the inmates live under the siege or the protection of the dragon? But that was the joy of animal-worship. It had no need to be thought through.

Shortly after the sacrifice of the girl, the dragon left the beach, and their gifts lay untouched until the seagulls or children picked them over. They thought the beast had gone because it was content with the sacrifice. But its going left a vacuum, a hole at the centre of their obsession. They were regretful, like a child who plays a practical joke on a friend that sends the friend home crying. The dragons on the obelisks were no longer guards but look-outs waiting to sight the returning dragon with their flat, round, red eyes. The blight that had made Worm Bay exceptional left it to feel lonely, deserted.

Before the dragon, the Seer's following was on a par with the Church's. She was acknowledged, but with a certain kind of reserve. Her neighbours were almost prepared to believe Brother Paul when he said that Mog was a mad old harridan.

When they took her the mangled remains of her son from the wreck of de Rochfoll's house, they expected her to curse the beast with all the imprecations of Hell. She carried the boy away inside, and excluded them from her grief. And when she re-emerged, she appeared to have grown in stature. Rumours spread that she had eaten what remained of her child and ingested his energy (though time proved she had buried him under her earth floor). Her expanded size was partly due to a chemise she had quilted full of magic herbs and dried flowers – she reeked of aniseed. But primarily, it was to do with the restoration of her status. She put on flesh and arrogance because of the way they looked at her, and they looked at her with awesome expectation because of her stature and arrogance. She claimed that the boy's death conferred an honour on her – that if she had had other children she would deliver them into the very jaws of the dragon.

But then she did, after all, have no other children.

Her wealth increased tenfold in a week. The villagers were prepared to give generously to the beast, but always there was the thought, after all, that the beast could not discern between perfect and second-rate. There was no such possibility with Mog. Tributes to her must be of the best.

When the village exhausted its wealth, it turned to ritual. The old came out from behind their shrivelled, papery masks, their eyes gleaming with secrets, and shuffled ragged dances in their doorways. They recollected profoundly mysterious old rhymes. They gleefully arraigned their children with bringing down trouble on their heads by forgetting the Old Ways. They congregated in murmuring knots after dark, by the remains of a drystone byre they misremembered as a cairn.

What they lacked in recollection they made up for in imagination. Never did it occur to them that the Seer might be doing the same thing. Besides, they had no sooner invented an incantation or some spiteful abstinence for their children to endure than they believed in it as if it had been written on the backs of their eyelids at birth.

The Seer could outdo them in imaginings. Her magic was alluring. It had something for everyone.

For the old there were small, precise magics – binding little rules that could be kept with the mildest ascetecism – and a history of dragons who roamed the cliffs a day or so before the creation of memory, and whose spirits inhabited the hairy hawk-moth and vile slow-worm.

For the children there were black dragons rampant in the night sky, with maces of stars tied to their tails that smashed thunder out of the goatskin moon.

For the older women there was the intricate crafting of wood and wax into dragons and fetishes; the weaving of raffia browbands which would save the weaver from insanity brought on by fear.

For the young women and older men, there was imitation of the dragon's own lust: no prohibitions or inhibitions, no faces or names, but only the gross passions of a lascivious beast to be gratified under the illuminating moon. The dragon, it was supposed, watched the coupling unseen, from the outer darkness.

And for the young men there was the violence of the beast's cause – its need to be fed and defended. To them fell the honour of spilling the blood of the dragon's enemies. They fought each other for rank in the mystical militia. Mothers other than the Seer lost their sons to this ritual violence.

Mog, of course, had no more sons to lose.

With a steady, delicate hand, Mog orchestrated these separate strands of worship. They rarely overlapped. Only at measured intervals of a week or a fortnight did she unite the village in some gluttonous festive rite – a pig-roast, a horn-dance, a cock-fight, an orgy of drinking.

The dead deer was straddling a mound of burning peat, its head twisted over, and smoke belching out through its skull, when Brother Paul made his mistimed visit to the Bay.

He came, despite the Prior's advice, to tell his family and neighbours about their excommunication. The thing appalled him. His Life-Everlasting was suddenly empty of mother, father, relations and friends. He had pleaded with the Prior to think what terror and hungry desperation must have driven the villagers to their dark excesses. He offered to go and persuade them of the superior modern power of Christ. But on the same day, an incoherent girl-child arrived at the Priory and talked of being 'set out' for the dragon. The Prior set his face against Worm Bay and made it clear that if Paul were to return there, it would be at the peril of his soul as well as his body.

That was when Brother Paul surprised himself on the verge of mutiny. It was generally accepted by then that the dragon did exist. In such case, the villagers and the strange young monk had been right: he, Paul, had been wrong to preach disbelief. *He* was responsible, then, for their violence and for their flight into the arms of paganism. The more he reflected, the more yearning, paternal pity he felt for them. They took on the moist-eyed innocence of fawns. They must be rescued. The hysteria of self-sacrifice throbbed in Paul's sinuses and tightened his gorge. But excommunication? It stood across the road to Worm Head like a fiery dragon, and down its throat he could see straight into Hell.

So in the end he did not argue with the Prior, but left in secret for the Bay, hoping that he could reclaim his neighbours for Christ *before* his disobedience was noticed. Nobody knew he had gone there.

When they looked up at him, their eyeballs were distilled in liquor. They said not a word, as if each man was dreaming him and Paul was not there at all. He could not find his mother's face in the crowd. His gaze began to nettle each face it touched, making the lips curl back and the heads toss like horses'. The roasting deer looked fire at him through its scorched sockets. He did not want to stand too close to the fire, for fear of an ill-considered shove, a thoughtless murder. His paternal pity was beginning to bleed away through his feet. He searched about for something other than the deer to rest his eyes on. He found Mog's shovel-shaped face.

133

'So you've come here at last, Paul.' It was a friendly, fishwife's voice from inside a high priestess's garb. She was dressed in a red woollen cloak to which shiny sea shells had been sewn by the thousand. Even as she stood still, she rattled like a smashed crustacean. She scratched beneath a raffia headband. Her hair was plaited into a dozen muddied black spikes, and her face was daubed with chalk-dust.

All the children who played under the cliffs had at some time daubed their faces with chalk. Paul could almost taste it in his mouth as he looked at her. They were the same age.

Behind Mog the deer settled farther on to the fire, its rib-cage spreading with a sharp crack of the spine. Marrow hissed on to the embers. 'I came to see my mother,' said Paul.

'She's singing for the Worm tonight,' said Mog. 'Seen the Worm yet, Paul?'

He shook his head. He wished he had. He hated knowing less than they. Hoping it was news to them, he said, 'I hear it's up at the French mill.' That did cause a stir. Drunken eyes turned to Mog for confirmation. 'Oh, didn't you know? The Lord Leo is thinking to tackle it there – burn the place down over its head. It may all be over by Sunday.'

The aspic eyes struggled to focus on Mog. Her mouth opened up into a rectangular slit and laughed. 'Fire? Frighten it with fire, would he? Its vitals *are* fire, boy. It's Earth, Fire and Water. What's him? What's Leo? A bit of earth. 'Sides. If he downed one, the sea's full of worms would come up to fill its place.'

The drunken eyes all turned towards the sea, towards that purple accumulation of dragons hurling themselves in ranks on to the shore. Paul watched too, his nerves jangling at the irregular sea-sound.

'It fetched you back, then,' said Mog. 'The beast sent you back here. We's all obedient to its bidding. I've been wanting you. Your mother's been wanting you here, so I asked the Worm, and you came at its bidding.'

'I did not.'

'We conjured you here.'

'That's a lie.'

'As you please. Still, we're happy to have you back. We'd turn away none from the safety of here.'

He wagged his head at her and hitched at the belt round his hips as if he were Abraham girding himself to wrestle. The smoke from a three-legged brazier belched into his face. An attractive girl was fanning it towards him and giggling.

'And what makes this place safe, pray?' he jibed, in a shrill, womanish voice.

''Tis the Worm's place. Worm Head. Always been a worm place. Even before Time. The Great Worm of Mindowsely come down here. The first worm pair come down here off Noye's ark, after the Flood. 'Tis a worm's place, and we belong to the Worm. To be spared or eaten. But while there's unbelievers and rich folks and black monks to be eaten, we'll be spared to do homage. Unless we choose, of course. Unless we choose out of love to go to't.'

The spectators, who had squatted down leaving only Mog and Paul full height, shifted on their haunches, and their faces brooded on what Mog was saying. They seemed parched for the secret knowledge she served up to them in drips and drops.

'It's an abomination in the eyes of God,' moaned Paul. The smoke had begun to make him nauseous.

''Tis flesh and blood, lovely. You know it. No matter. You mistook, that's all. Easy done. We all mistake.'

'*Quem Deus vult perdere dementat prius.*'

She walked forward briskly and put a hand on his forehead. 'Look now. He's weary with fretting. Have a bite and a bit, my dear, and come and talk. The fish are gone from the sea, you know. They're away eating lice and fleas off the backs of worms. There's a place in the ocean – a trough full of worms, and every one as big as a boat from France, and each one coming for its fill of Christian flesh.'

He was suddenly convinced that the smoke off the brazier was a magic vapour, and lunged at it, meaning to knock the container to the ground. He misjudged the distance, pushed against the legs, and found they were the rigid remains of some waterfront winch. As he overbalanced, the girl saved his face from touching the hot container, catching him by the hair and holding his face in the column of smoke. His head filled with reeking vapours and ash. He felt terribly poorly, and dizzier than at the end of a penitential fast. The girl pressed his face into her side and stroked his hair. 'We do love the Worm,' she said, and kissed him on the mouth. He could hear a dog whimpering somewhere that was not a dog at all, but him. Someone pushed two fingers into his mouth and poured inside him a pint of juniper alcohol.

Then the sea sent in battalions of navy dragons which melted in their own sweat on the beach. And his mother, who had once been as old and brittle as wood-ash, danced across his horizontal vision, swooping and grinning and humming open-mouthed. Her tongue cleaved to the crimson roof of her mouth, like Zacharias dumbly proclaiming his unborn son. Or was it Elizabeth who rejoiced and Mary who sang the *Magnificat* and someone else again who scratched in the dust with a stick . . .? When Paul, in his struggle against mental disintegration, scrawled his name in the sand, it looked in every detail like a dragon, head up, looking back over its shoulder into a dragon-filled past.

They put him in his mother's hut. They put a woman in his bed. But when he woke up he hurled her out again. Didn't he? Impervious to their childish hysteria. Wasn't he? He could persist calmly in his faith. *Against the chants of false prophets, against sterile idolatry, against the spells of women* . . . Such a comfort. Even submerged under the bleary depths of alcohol, he felt smug: he knew that doubt, like gangrene, was in. Doubt must exist in the mind of Mog. The most terrible thing of all would be, would it not, to doubt when everyone else was certain? That was why Mog ranted so. That was why she cursed and vilified him, losing hold of rational argument in her rage. That was why she had had to use magic and demons against him. She was just an ignorant old woman struggling to convince herself, while he remained calm and dignified and coherent and brave. It was a sustaining comfort in his hour of trial. Wasn't it?

Immoveable as a shell-encrusted rock, Mog the Seer watched her childhood rival thrash and scream and writhe in the net of drunkenness, abasement and despair. She watched as he was laughed to a nothingness by the women who held him down. Mog, it was true, was ignorant of many facts concerning the Worm. But concerning people she was not ignorant. She knew how to make a man happy or, at worst, how to dispel his misery. It was a knowledge which gave her the calmness of mastery. It was a knowledge which equipped her to rule in Worm Bay. It was a knowledge which taught her what Brother Paul *really* wanted.

So it was not truly for the sake of the dragon, not truly for the sake of her acolytes, but chiefly as a kindness to the man himself that she had Paul bound hand and foot and thrown off Worm Head cliffs.

To succour the Worms of Deep Ocean, she said. That was why she had conjured him from the priory, or so she told the fishermen. They nodded their heads and passed on the news to their wives. Mog herself explained it all to Paul's mother, and invested her with the title 'Guardian of the Worm's Tears', and gave her two fine headbands decorated with the feathers of guillemots.

12

THE HUNT

The castle yard also accumulated refugees from the dragon, shifting in and out of shelter according to the ebb and flow of rumour. But, though some placed their trust in angels and others in magic, and some took shelter inside the castle wall, everyone held it in common that Leo must, ultimately, act.

Leo too supposed that he could not lie in bed and wait for the beast to die of old age. But as he gazed up into the invisible black eaves, and watched the moths fly through the candle-flames and their vulture shadows quarrel hugely over his head, he did wonder about its lifespan. He wondered about lifespans in general, and his own in particular, gouging at his flesh from time to time to see if it had any feeling in it. He felt like a sand-bar in a rising ocean. The cold was creeping up, and the tiny grains of his mortal dust were trickling away. The feeling came and went tidally in his feet and arms and knees and lips. But with each tide, a little more of the sand-bar washed away.

He had sent the leeches away. They reminded him too much of graveyard earthworms.

The hawk-moths were too much like dragons. It occurred to Leo that he did not know whether the beast could fly. Apart from a few singular clouds and a rash of starry dragons in the night sky, nobody had spoken of seeing it airborne. In fact, it was becoming domesticated: he heard that it had moved into the French mill.

And every time he put his nose outside the door, there were the refugees. At the sight of him they roused like beagles, all heads alert, all bodies turned in his direction. They asked each other loud questions: 'Is it today, then? Will he go after it today?' Now and then, a head turned its mouth away to conceal a heckling 'God save us, he won't.'

Then a brood of old women arrived, with voices like chickens, greeting him each day with raucous blessings. 'God keep you, Leo the Dragon-Slayer!' 'God preserve you in your day's strife, sir!'

Shrewd. So shrewd that this morning Leo awoke to a dawn chorus of voices under his window: *God bless Leo the Dragon-Slayer!*

Other voices joined in discordantly, then a rhythm picked up, and the flat, monotonous chant got louder and louder. Leo looked at his wife, expecting her to call for Bruno to put them out of the yard. But she tolerated the noise for several minutes while she cleaned her teeth with a hazel twig. At last she tossed her head, flared her nostrils and said, 'They're perfectly right, of course. How much longer?'

'I'll raise an army, shall I?' said Leo. He said it every morning, then snorted. 'They'll be sorry then, when they find they're fighting it themselves!'

The chanting droned on, jumbling and faltering from time to time, then picking up again. 'What bullies they are.'

'All children are bullies,' said Gwyne in her clipped, dismissive voice. 'You have responsibilities.'

'I have a pain.'

She breathed out through her teeth.

'Elfleda doesn't want Anselm to fight it,' he said whiningly.

'Oh yes, she's a selfish little whore, that one.'

140

'Quiet, woman! I won't have it!' (The chant went on under the window.) 'Don't ever let me hear you say such a thing! God, the pain's bad this morning.'

'Liar.'

He sat up and stared at her, but she was away to the window, arching her back and flouncing her hips. She lifted the window-flap, tipped out the basin of washing water and let the flap fall again, all in one movement. The chanting drowned.

'Gwyne, you should mind yourself. You and I, woman – you and I are going to . . .' But, Medusa-like in her morning hair, she turned on him such a look of contempt that his tongue turned to mossy stone in his mouth.

'Yes, Leo. You and I are women both. *In battle as in bed* – isn't that what they say?' And she left him to call after her down the corridor: 'I don't know! I can't remember so far back!'

Finding himself on his feet, he decided not to lie down again until he or the dragon was dead. It sounded valiant in the privacy of his head. He saved it up to tell the women in the yard as he passed them.

But as they gazed after him in open-mouthed disbelief, because he had empressed their menfolk to fight the dragon, he thought better of rhetoric. All he wanted to say, as he clattered off towards the mill, was '*Now* are you satisfied?'

He and Anselm could, in theory, empress some ninety men between them. In practical terms, they could raise only the male refugees in their own yards or at the priory. And many of the refugees absconded at the first whisper of a dragon-hunt.

A mile from the mill, twenty men straggled behind Leo and Anselm, including Bruno and the ostler. They all carried unlit torches and dragged them along the grass and fooled about

141

with them, so that streaks of tar marked the route they had taken. What horses there were grew irritable with the slow pace of those on foot and fidgeted with their bits and began to bite and kick. Such was the unwillingness of the pocket army that a mile from the mill it virtually ground to a halt.

Leo rode on ahead with his brother. He wanted to let him into the secret of his illness without disheartening the men further if they overheard. But somehow there did not seem to be a way in to the conversation. The subject was walled up inside him like a dog down a well, whimpering. He had got as far as to say, 'I have this pain just here,' and had pressed his fist in under his rib-cage . . .

So he felt the thud of his heart as the roof of the mill came into sight. It was as peaceful and pretty a scene as any sunny day could afford. Purple foxgloves and golden rod grew in drifts against the mill wall, and along the edge of the water beyond, yellow iris towered over their own reflections. The black shingle of the walls was striped white with the flour and husk dust that had settled there over the years. The bees from a neglected hive were wandering in a clearly visible procession over the flowery ground. Pollen hung so thickly in the air that it seemed the mill must be working. But the harnesses on the treadmills were *almost* empty of the mules that had once turned them. Instead, flies hung there in spectral clouds as big as the donkeys had been. Over the bones.

'It's not here, is it? It isn't, is it? It's not here,' said Anselm.

The day was beginning to be hot, and a peculiar smell fetched up from the ground, a smell like vinegar. But down by the mill, under its porches and lean-to and the open-fronted loading bay, there was no dragon.

'Could it be small enough to get inside?' said Leo.

The clatter of a latch made them both leap backwards in their saddles. Their horses whinnied and dropped their shoulders and pranced about. A dark figure, foreshortened by their high standpoint, came and crouched in amongst the foxgloves. He was tending a row of small, sickly beans.

Anselm shook one fist above his head and gave a great shout of jubilation. '*Alban! Hoi, Alban!* It's Alban! Don't you see him, man? Just there? That lying bastard Bruno. It's our monk!' And he stood up in his stirrups and waved at full stretch.

Leo could not think he had seen the fellow before. Untonsured, unshaven and unbelted, he looked more like John the Baptist than the itinerant monk who had annoyed him weeks before with news of Elshender going to the Holy Land. He did not believe he had ever laid eyes on this wild man before. 'You say that's Gwyne's curate? You're mistaken, I do assure . . .'

The monk looked up, shielded his eyes against the sun and squatted back on his haunches. He touched his fingers to his forehead and was partway through crossing himself before he pushed the offending hand between his knees and began rocking to and fro. For him, there was no recognising the two figures coming out of the blackening sun.

Anselm got off his horse to descend the mallow-covered slope down to the mill.

'Where are you going?' said Leo. 'The dragon may be hereabout.'

'Then Alban would hardly be gardening.' Anselm laughed.

'Maybe he has a charmed life,' said Leo wanting to laugh, too. 'Maybe the beast has scruples. It won't eat a religious.'

'Then it really is the Devil Himself, and being on horseback won't help,' Anselm called over his shoulder.

The monk cupped both hands over his eyes and looked up the long, shallow slope. Slowly he unbent his legs and stood up, bundling together his gown to look like a pregnant woman. His shoulders pulled up round his ears and his face crumpled against the light, he gaped past the two men then leaped clear off the ground, throwing his hands over his head and forwards. *'Go back! Danger! Go back!'* He leaped maniacally among the foxgloves and flapped his big-jointed arms and hands.

Leo struggled to turn both horses. Anselm hesitated, half turned. He peered down on to the mill, looking for the danger.

'Come on 'Selm! Believe him!' shouted his brother.

Anselm protested. 'We can't leave him!' But he was already labouring sideways up the slope. 'We'll fetch the others.'

The mallow was such that he had to pick his way. He did not lift his head until he was looking to take the reins of his horse from Leo. Then he looked beyond him and breathed, 'My God. He wasn't shouting at us.'

For Leo's silhouette was entirely lost against the silhouette of the dragon, which stood up behind him on its back legs. The horses got wind at that same moment, and bolted. Leo dropped his brother's reins, and Anselm made a grab at them. But he missed his footing and, as his horse plunged into a gallop, all he could catch hold of was the pommel. He was dragged along at a run, at every stride his horse towing him ten feet over the ground. Then the saddle slipped round and, in pitching under the horse's belly, he brought it down on top of him. He felt his sword bend under his hip and heard his longbow break. The horse rolled on to its feet again at once and ran on, but by then Anselm had a leg over its rump and his head on a level with its pumping front knees.

144

He did not fall off until the horse stopped, out of vexation, to bite him.

He was separated from his brother by a mile of undulating ground. He crouched on his hands and knees, panting, and several pairs of feet shuffled into his circle of vision. He was back among the pocket army.

They waited for him to get to his feet, but his legs had no more substance than his breeches. They caught his horse, but they would not lay a hand on him to help him up: the thought did not occur to them. He stayed on the ground.

He could not even catch his breath. He pulled out his sword and there was a nervous burst of laughter as they saw the bend in it. But, too winded to speak, he scratched on the ground with it – a picture of the dragon. It looked like a dove, with a fat tail and short neck. Crossing it through, he drew it again.

At once the men broke, like the head of a dandelion, and scattered, running in the opposite direction to the mill. Anselm needed to fetch them back and he had not the breath to do it. He needed help to fetch them back, and there was only Bruno left, standing over him.

Bruno said impassively (though he was breathing hard), 'Did it get him? Did it eat the Lord Leo?' And he pulled out his knife.

Anselm was deeply touched. To draw a knife ready to fight the beast if it had slaughtered his master – it was an almost poignant gesture. He said reassuringly, 'Leo was on his horse – I think he got away. And Alban – the monk – he's not dead. We saw him. The dragon's not eaten him.'

Astonishment registered clearly on Bruno's symmetrical features. He looked down at the knife, then pulled Anselm's jerkin as if he would pull him to his feet by it: he almost pulled himself over, Anselm was so much bigger than he. Letting go, he turned and ran after the other men, snatching at the backs of their jackets and thumping them in the shoulder-blades. 'Get back here, you turds! Get back. If the lord's not dead, he'll light you for torches. If he is, his brother'll do it. If he don't, I will. Get back and knacker that animal! You think it's got a brain? You think it won't gut like a cat? You think it won't burn with a torch down its gob? I'm warning you.' The men stopped running. They turned and gawped at him and at Anselm whose brother owned them: Anselm had perhaps already inherited them.

Anselm got to his feet and someone brought him his horse. Bruno was already mounted, and rode ahead, throwing abuse at the men on foot.

Nearer the mill, they did not shout or call out Leo's name for fear of attracting the dragon instead. But they reached the turmoil of hoofprints on the top of the slope without encountering either of them. And as they did so, the roaring began.

Men dropped to their knees and prayed. Men dropped on their faces and hoped that the long grass hid them. Two began to run, but were whipped in by Bruno in his frenzy to hold together the levy. When the roaring did not advance on them, they began to crawl forwards, in irresistible thrall to this beast which had dominated their lives for months.

It was standing beside the mill, facing the river so that they could see the bow-legged straddle of its hind legs, and its tail scraping up the dust. Trapped between it and the river was Leo, unhorsed and with his sword drawn. His horse had thrown itself into the river and tried to swim but was being swept downstream by the current, its head sticking up like the rudder of an up-ended boat.

The beast was leaning backwards on its haunches, its neck stretched out and its rib-cage heaving. It was bellowing at Leo – bellowing and bellowing as if to drive him mad or deaf, and pawing the ground with unsheathed claws.

Anselm took a longbow from Bruno and laid it flat across his horse's neck. Even then, knocking the arrow to the string was like trying to thread a needle. His intestines writhed; his fingers could hold still neither arrow nor string. His hand was sweating so much that he could not twist the bowstring as he pulled it back: the arrow flopped impotently off the whippings and rested on his wrist.

At the second attempt, his fingers were so clammy that the string escaped him half-drawn, and the arrow ploughed off under the grass: its fletches flew up like butterflies. He could hear the horsemaster beside him saying monotonously, ceaselessly, 'Where's the monk? Where's the monk? Where's the monk?' Anselm wiped his hand on the seat of his breeches and rattled and bounced the arrow over the whippings once more. He lifted the bow, drew it back. The borrowed arrow was much too short for his reach. The arrowhead drew back well inside the curve of the bow and he was lucky not to shoot it through his wrist. The next he drew up round-shouldered and with his elbows bent, like an adult with a child's toy, and loosed with an expression of futile disgust.

He did not shout out a warning to his brother. There was a strong possibility of hitting Leo, but he did not want him to look up and present his face to the arrowhead. Still, the men around Anselm gave a unanimous groan, as if their own backbones had been plucked and loosed in order to fire the arrow. Someone gave a shout of admiration, some other a grunt of contempt. Leo looked up. The dragon turned its head over one shoulder. The arrow, as slow as a tumbler-pigeon, fell out of the sky.

It entered the dragon at the top of its tail, and the back legs danced to one side. Leo, with clumsy movements and staccato shouts, sprinted towards the mill, climbed over the half-door at the back, and re-emerged at the front, dragging Alban by the wrist. The dragon stretched out its neck to narrow its shoulders, and pushed after him, into the building. Or perhaps it was taking cover.

Anselm's success thrilled the levy into a reckless aggression. They broke out the can of tar, dipped the arrows and lit them, cursing each other for the burns they inflicted. Their archery was over-hasty for the sake of not burning their left hand or setting light to their bows. Their shots were over-long for the sake of not lifting the dripping tar over their faces, or over-short because of the heavy-headed, tarry arrows.

Leo felt like Orpheus dragging Eurydice out of Hell, as he tried to drag the monk out of harm's way. When one arrow passed between him and Alban, who obstinately hung back, he was startled into letting go. He hurled abuse at the archers, but when he turned back, the monk had his habit clutched round his thighs and was dodging back towards the mill.

Two, three, four arrows hit the roof. The pale flames could hardly be seen in the sunlight. It seemed they must have extinguished themselves in the thatch. Then, like St Elmo's fire, they crowned the building in an ash-flecked halo. The clouds behind them warped with heat. The mill was melting into the sky. The ash washed away on the breeze.

The monk came to the entrance, darted out to look at the roof, and was showered with burning straw. He dodged inside again, glaring reproachfully at the men on the hill.

Bruno picked up the bow Anselm had dropped, and fitted an arrow to it.

Leo came up the slope grunting and panting, his face grey like a plaster bust with its rime of flour-dust. Behind him the burning roof migrated in flocks towards the sun. Then the rafters began to collapse, one by one, the corn-dust charred, and the water beyond took on colour. The monk's bent back pushed apart the leather door-flaps and he shuffled into the yard, pulling a heap of burning sacks into the open. Drawing up on his bow, Bruno took aim and fired. The arrow embedded itself in the leather door.

Anselm rode in front of Bruno. 'What d'you think you're about?'

Bruno pushed the horse in the shoulder, and levelled his bow again. 'He's the Devil's creature, isn't he? It's obvious, isn't it? He won't leave it. Well he can burn with it. I'll drive him back into the fire to burn with it!'

The levy agreed. A volley of arrows swarmed against the mill wall.

'Leave him be!' cried Anselm. 'Shoot the dragon! Keep the dragon inside! Leave the poor man be!'

But the dragon did not attempt to come out.

Bruno said, harbouring the words in the back of his mouth, 'He's burning now. Burning.'

Like a crusader burned in his chain-mail, Elshender felt the scales on his back glow hotter and hotter and begin to fall.

The interior of the mill was on two levels, split by the winding gear and by pillars of wood which held up the main roof-beams. The pillars absolutely prevented him from moving through the house and out at the front, as his father

149

had done. He had seen Leo leap the door and collide with Alban in the kitchen. They had spun in each other's arms, Leo trying to reach the front, Alban trying to reach his dragon. Leo had got a grip of the monk's wrist and dragged him through the house. At each post Alban wrapped an arm round the timber and clung to it, begging to be let go, but Leo was determined to save his life.

Elshender went on calling his father's name over and over again. He shouted his own name. He called Leo by every term of affection he had ever used as a child. But they all just made a roaring.

Before – at the riverbank – he had tried to scratch his father's name in the earth, but Leo would not look. He had looked past it; he had looked out across the river where his horse was foundering, he had looked up at the sky and called on God, but never at the beast. Then he had wielded his sword hilt for a cross and shouted, 'I abjure you, Satan, to get back to Hell!'

At that, a great sorrowing whimper choked Elshender and he had reached out his head (because he could not reach out his arms) to plead for understanding.

The arrow-wound was no more dangerous, no less painful than a wasp-sting at the root of his spine. It had made him momentarily nauseous, and his eyes watered. He reached round futilely with his head to try and pluck out the arrow with his lips. That was when his father fled into the mill. Elshender had to pursue him, had to hold on to him until he understood.

Once through the rear door, he could not retreat. In stretching forwards, his neck and flanks were contracted. But in backing, there were rolls of flesh above his pelvis and behind his withers which forbade retreat. The grinding gear splitting the house in two was, to him, the mechanism of a gigantic rat-trap.

And now he was burning, as he had seen hedgehogs cooked in clay by gypsies. His scales were shrivelling in their sockets and popping, incandescent, to the floor. He stopped calling to his father, who had long since deserted him, and howled for Alban to release his soul. Alban came through the fire carrying an axe. The membranes of Elshender's eyes would not stay open – the smoke was forcing them shut and sealing them with rheum. Through their opaque whiteness, Elshender saw the monk's outline as he swung the axe.

The roof broke its back. As the dais supporting the mill gear burned, the stones fractured in the heat and fell in pieces through the wooden floor. Thick, tangible smoke piled up in the yard. Smoke off the thatch hung over the exposed rafters in the shape of a dragon (or so one man in the levy said). When the half-doors at the rear fell off, the extra through-draught lifted the centre of the thatch clean off in a geyser of glowing stubble.

Between the empty jambs, Alban wielded his axe. He broke down the wattle and daub with the back of the axe and with kicks and shoves, but the jambs were heavy, seasoned wood and only splintered, even under the blade.

'Shoot the monk!' shouted Bruno, letting go another arrow. But his archery was sweat-soaked and risible. 'Kill the monk! It's the Devil's creature!' He repeated it until Anselm tried to lead him aside, soothingly, thinking he had the hysteria of killing on him.

But Bruno was apoplectic with arguments for killing the monk. He tore his arm away and fired all his arrows into the circling smoke. And when he had exhausted all his own, he ran from man to man demanding to use theirs. 'You see how hard the bastard is to kill? That's the Devil's protection. That's demon-magic!' They did not know whether to laugh at him or help him. They looked to Leo for a lead, but he was wrapped up in shock.

Then Alban, who had paid as little heed to the arrows as if he had not seen them, ran back into the building, and the tail of the dragon emerged – slowly, obscured by smoke – slowly, smoking itself – slowly, like a conger eel slipping out of a crevice. The monk had got in under its jaw and was leaning on its chest, pushing it backwards through the enlarged door. He pushed it like a cart, his sandals sliding and slipping as he tried to get a purchase, and his cheek pressed deep into the soft, loose skin of the gullet.

Then the levy dropped their bows. They saw what they believed to be a phoenix rising from the fire, something indestructible backing out of destruction.

Alban continued to push, and the dragon, its eyes shut, continued slowly to back until its tail slithered over the riverbank. The bank crumbled under the weight of its haunches, and it subsided backwards into the river, raising a horseshoe wave. The monk clung to its neck. It scratched at the bank with the claws of its front feet, but allowed the current to pull it away.

In mid-stream its feet must just have touched bottom, for unlike the horse it was not tumbled downstream, but ploughed a diagonal crossing to the far bank where trees overhung the water. And under the shadow of their branches, it waded downstream to the next cattle-drink before lumbering ashore. The cowl of the monk's habit was gripped in its teeth.

13

WORDS WITH AN ANIMAL

When his dragon came close to burning, and escaped so ineptly with its hide, Alban rejoiced with all the angels and archangels. For it meant that the beast was not an exhalation of Hell at all. It was just an animal, like a cow or a horse or a rat. The End of Time rolled away from him like a carpet down a bright corridor, and from its pile rose the dust of generations – future generations who would be born and die and crumble to dust and await salvation in hosts as numberless as all those who had gone before. The universe expanded abruptly. The circling spheres, which had seemed to bind the world like a steel garotte, cracked, and the world's brain expanded to comprehend infinity.

Infinity? Well, Alban had no great desire for an infinite universe. He would be satisfied with a few hundred years more before monsters erupted from the earth and dragons out of the sea. *His* dragon was not a servant of the Antichrist.

It was a dumb, vulnerable, inflammable beast who having walked forwards into a building could not walk backwards out of it. It was a gentle, defenceless beast who had not even blasted a man it trapped against the river and who threatened it with a sword. It was a beatific dragon!

He sat on the footpath inside a hollow hedge, with the dragon's head on his lap, and stroked its horrible cheek. An accident of birth, he decided: a collision of crocodile and whale that had somehow beached itself on a shore far from its exotic home. With the threat of Judgement Day lifted, there seemed no horror in nature's teeming variety.

'You're not a beast of Satan, are you?' he whispered into the dragon's ear. 'You're not the Beast from the Sea or the Servant of the Seven-Headed Beast, are you? No.'

The dragon flailed its clumsy legs in an effort to lift its head and stare at him out of one rheumy eye. It shook its head.

'What sense I credited you with! What powers! Ha! Nothing but a poor dumb animal, and I fell down and worshipped you. Ha ha! You're a poor sort of a golden calf. Look at you, you ugly, mangy old creature. Jesu! what blasphemies for an overgrown newt! No, no. Rest easy. I don't blame you. Blame a dumb animal? I must be mad, even so. I was a damned man before I met you, ghoulie. Poor benighted beast. Is there a heaven or a hell for you? Or were you in Hell from the moment your mother spawned you?'

The dragon shook its head again and, in touching its jaw against a switch of the hedge, triggered a reflex chewing that broke off several twigs.

'Yes. I'll throw sticks for you, and catch rabbits for you. There's nowt else to do. It's second childishness for me. Look at me, talking as if you could . . . Couldn't a man convince himself that you're understanding me? Even now?'

The dragon clacked its tongue against its soft palate, and wet saliva splashed Alban in the face. It was mildly acid and burned the skin. But the fire at the mill had, ironically, extinguished the head's inner fire. Burned scales were still dropping from time to time, like a handful of groats sprinkling from the pockets of drowned sailors as a wreck rolls in the current.

Alban stood up. 'Come on, then. Sea-salt for the burns. Come on, ghoulie. Come on.' And he walked ahead and slapped his thigh encouragingly at the dragon.

It rolled to its knees and groaned as it got up, hindquarters first. But then it moved so quickly that it was snuffling on Alban's heels. Its lips rolled back off its teeth and it gripped his hood and wrenched at it. Alban was flung about like a puppet. 'Stop! Let go!'

Meekly, the dragon set the monk down on his feet. But as he set off to walk, the same thing happened. 'Stop! You're throttling me!' The beast let go immediately. It thrust its face into the monk's back and knocked him down – then picked up a broken twig from the path and laid it on his chest.

Alban saw it as kindling, and threw it off. But with much twisting of its head to search the ground, the dragon fetched it back again and turned to find another.

'A game? Is it a game you want?' Alban tried to show good humour, despite being caked in dirt and intimidated by the pushing. He picked up the stick and walked with it to where the hedge opened up on to common. He was about to throw it, leaning backwards on one foot, when it was snatched out of his raised hand and the dragon laid it down on the ground again. It fixed Alban with one rolling eye, daring him to disturb it a third time.

The second twig it laid across the first, nudging it clumsily into place. Then it touched, alternately, the monk's chest and the twig-cross with its nose. It nipped Alban's cuff in its teeth, and threw his hand up against his forehead, against his body, and almost pulled it from its socket in wrapping it across his chest. Then it buckled its ungainly legs under it and lay down whining in an ear-splittingly high register.

155

Burned and torn and chewed, the monk's habit hung on him in rags. He plucked at its cuffs, his head on one side and hanging down. He had his eyes shut. 'My father had a dog,' he said wearily. 'I was little. It was big. It scared me. *Don't be frightened*, said my father. *It's as good as human. Understands every word. Waiting!* he'd say, and it laid itself down. *Devil!* and it would push its tail up between its legs and slink off. He loved that hound. *More brains than you*, he used to say. *More God-fearing, too.* Me, I was dog-fearing, that's all. *Understands every word.* One day it had me. It got me by the leg and it worried the flesh off me. He told it, *Get off. Let go. Devil.* But on it went, chewing and chewing. He had to kill it in the end. He never forgave me for that . . . Can you understand human speech?'

The dragon ducked its head emphatically.

'No, I'm sorry. That's not enough. If you understand speech get up and put your head in my right hand.' He spread his arms as the beast dragged itself to its feet.

Elshender hesitated, then turned his back on Alban and looked back over his shoulder in order to tell Alban's right from left. Then he placed his muzzle in the monk's right hand.

His name is John, wrote Zacharias, and the Lord restored his powers of speech. But Elshender had to be content with rattling his soft palate and exhaling the foul reek of decomposing rabbit over his comrade who was dancing and weeping on the path.

They returned to the beach and Alban constructed a circle of rocks. Each represented a letter, and in the centre were two – one white, one black – to signify 'Yes' and 'No'.

'I AM ELSHENDER, SON OF LEO,' said the dragon, and, in his haste to strike the rocks, sickened himself by running in circles. He swayed dizzily, and their converse soon degenerated into nouns, and questions to which Elshender could stamp Yes or No, on the white and black.

Names signified little to Alban. He had not been among people for weeks, and he was not of the district, after all. So when he asked Elshender who had laid the curse on him, he did not expect a name in reply, or did not expect to know it. GWYNE, BRUNO, wrote the dragon, and as the boulders rolled from under his feet, he kicked them with such spleen.

'Gwyne? The Lady Gwyne? You're the son of the lord. You're the Elshender who had a vision?'

So Elshender became acquainted with his 'vision' – long after it was common knowledge among the serfs – and found a shared grievance with the monk which bound them still more closely. And Alban became acquainted with Elshender's downfall and that of his sad sister sunk in the salt sea. He gasped and groaned at the horror of it; he laughed out loud at the wonder of it, capering backwards ahead of the beast and guessing its words before they were complete. '*Tell?* Yes? Who should I tell? *Your father?*' His face dropped childishly. 'Gwyne would kill me before I got near him! Bruno was there at the mill, trying to kill you. So was the man Anselm. He must be your . . . uncle.'

YES.

'Still, somehow I'll get word to him. I will. I promise.'

NO.

'*Tell dkekd* . . .' Alban realised that the code had slipped, but it took a long time to persuade Elshender to stop and go back, he was so intent on supplying Alban with a name: ELFLEDADEROCHFOLELFLEDAELFLEDADEROC –

'Yes! All right! Peace, Elshender!' said the monk soothingly, wandering away from the circle to the sea's edge to draw the dragon away from its obsession. 'I know the lady. I know the lady Elfleda. You must go in the water now. Save the burns cankering. Come away.'

But Elshender went on beating out the name, ELFLEDAELFLEDADEROCH . . . until it exhausted itself. The fluid in its ears drained into its temples, and it lurched about drunkenly, its scales falling suddenly in clusters, like dead flower petals a head at a time.

The pain of the burns was lashing Elshender into a frenzy. In the moment's realisation that he could speak to the monk, joy so possessed him that he had hardly felt the damage to his hide. Even on the way to the beach, pushing between the twigs of the hedge so that they prised off his scales and scratched the burns, he had thought only of the first words needed. What handful of words to choose for quickness?

Now he had said them – or Alban had said them for him. Elshender's thoughts were tenants of the monk's body. The depression of acute, unstopping pain suddenly brought home to him that together he and Alban amounted to less than a whole man. Then the sickness of shock overtook him and shook him like an ague. Poreless as a pig, he could not shed his fever in sweat. His intellect stumbled. He heard his own, loud, involuntary whine, and could not recognise it. He clung distressfully to the name of Elfleda, bleating it and beating it out on the rocks.

Alban led him into the sea. 'It's all right, Elshender. I know the lady. I know the lady Elfleda. Jesu! Didn't I marry her, myself? Ha ha, no. No. No. But I won't burden you with that . . . Elfleda? Yes, I married her to your uncle myself. After a fashion. Yes, I'll get word to her somehow.'

The mechanics of grief seemed to stave in Elshender's sternum.

Like a ship holed beneath the water-line, he foundered. Looking uncomprehendingly at the water round his chest, it might as well have been his own tears swilling in and out of his ragged body through his flaccid skin. Elshender dissolved and left only a dragon with a monstrous sense of loss.

A shoal of fish so big that it discoloured the bay swept in over the bar. It closed on the dragon. In the shallows the fish broke up the surface. The water seemed to boil with gouts of fish bursting through the shiny troughs. Alban's feet and legs were bombarded with fish.

He had seen it in the north, when a shoal of white gurnard was dragged ashore in a seine net by fifty villagers. But to see them come of their own accord, and close in so hungrily – it made him pick up his feet and blunder ashore, squeaking and beating the water with his hands. "Way! Get away! 'Way!'

The dragon began to swim. It flopped down into the water and began to swim, dog-paddle, out to sea. Its lips were rolled back off its top teeth, and its breath wheezed in its throat. All round its head the fish swarmed and rolled frenziedly. Elshender was infested with fish.

Reaching the shore, Alban began to pick up handfuls of sand and fling them into the water. But the fish would not take fright. In among the herring and flounders and horse-mackerel were bigger fish, deeper and more shadowy, but rolling through the surface from time to time like the fleshy curve of a thigh or a forearm.

They did not devour the dragon, though Elshender too took them for carnivores and snapped his jaws to defend himself. They simply jostled and bubbled against him then gradually dispersed. A female dogfish was the last to leave. She lay across his chest, beneath his jaw for a time, in a fold of flesh he

159

could not reach by snapping. He turned for the shore; the dogfish swam off.

But the salt stinging his burns, and then the motion of the water caressing his underbelly, and the unnatural stirring of the fish, touching and not touching, had stolen away the reasoning man and left behind nothing but beast.

The dragon's mate had been snatched from under his flanks, and covered by a wily opportunist. Only men are broken-hearted. Beasts are persistent, insistent, unstoppable. They have only to wait for the older beasts to pass their prime. It is the birthright of beasts sooner or later to oust their elders by violence. Elshender turned for the shore and for Anselm's estate.

When Alban's beast deserted him – left him standing on the shore with a circle of stones like a silent, open mouth – he was desolate. It had run up the beach like a diseased rabbit, its legs badly co-ordinated and its head sagging. But it had outrun the monk without once looking back. It had stamped out no parting word – just rushed out of the sea and the turmoil of fish and into the dunes, where its remarkable bulk was quickly lost among the amber ramps of sand.

Alban blamed the fish. He believed they had communed with his dragon in a language more subtle and fluent than he could achieve with rocks. He stood and looked broodingly out over the sudsy foreshore and wondered what secret they could have for Elshender that evicted him so utterly from the dragon's thoughts. He had been overlooked. Like a child's toy carved with outstretched arms, he remained behind, waiting to be remembered and rescued from the unsentimental rain.

He was, fleetingly, angry. Saved its life, hadn't he? But he could not put a name to the offence Elshender had done him. 'Ingratitude' was something suffered by God at the hands of His Creation, not by excommunicant monks. And, lacking the vocabulary, Alban lacked the ability to sustain his anger. He lapsed into despondent loneliness, and went and sat in the dragon's cave where the rocks were cold and unrelenting and damp.

Perhaps the place restored in him the passivity of those fifteen years spent in a similarly damp cell. Or perhaps the humidity and cold soothed his burns and, with them, the depression of physical shock. Although he was mindless of his own injuries, he had done himself no good while rescuing Elshender. No good at all.

Waking out of a sick, confused sleep, he could not understand what idle wickedness had kept him from his obligations. He had told Elshender he would get word to Elfleda, and here he was sleeping. He pelted himself with reproach. He sheared the wool off his brain. He careened all the slimy and impeding dross off his soul where it had accumulated while he rocked in idleness. He would go to Anselm's house and to the Lady Elfleda. As he stood up, he almost fell because the flat, wet rocks set into the floor were so slippery.

At the mouth of the cave a trickle of fresh water, oozing down through the cliff, dripped out of the roof and into an indentation of its own making. It was the interruption of this steady 'drip, drip' that first alerted Alban. Bruno stepped into the circle of sand-coloured, outer light and into the pool. The water dripped into his thick hair without any sound, and because of the silence Alban knew he was there.

Bruno could see less than he expected and retreated on to the beach, clearly deciding to wait for Alban to come out. But

161

Alban could see quite well the figure in profile peering into the dark with a knife in its fist. He crouched right down, against the cold sand, and found he couldn't remember how to breathe silently.

Wherever Alban touched the sand, the sea welled up out of it. He developed a moat: a halo of cold water round him. He could still see Bruno against the rock, beside the door, thinking he was hidden. He told himself that Bruno was unsure, guessing. Even when the man called out, 'Mussel! Sea slug! Is that what you are?' Alban did not move out of his puddle. 'So you found yourself a rock to hide under? Well. Shall I tell you how I get cockles off a rock? With the tip of a knife, that's what. A knife just under the tail, that soon shifts them. And then it's just a hammer to smash them and a pin to pull their insides out. What? Has your lap-dog wandered off? They haven't got the brains of humans, you know. You shouldn't trust them to stick close. 'Sides, it's not healthy, living so close. I know how you monks are – your tastes, so to say – your liking for animals . . . I'm weary of waiting, monk. Come out and get it over. Don't make me come in there and fetch you.'

Alban could hear his own breaths echoing round the cave. He was over-breathing. He began to be dizzy. In reminding himself that he was out of Grace, he realised with a shock that laymen fight in such circumstances. The undernourished little brother in his northerly cell would have let life drop, like excreta. But the excommunicant, nourished on rabbit-meat and sunlit exercise, had a different constitution. Life was quite wedged in his guts. It would take a substantial effort to part with it. He quailed at the effort it would take.

Bruno came on into the cave again, saying, 'I wonder why he didn't eat you. No taste for it, I suppose. Elshender always was picky with his food. Now me, that's different. I'll show you what Elshender should have done to you. I'll bite through your windpipe and let you whistle yourself to death. Shall I?'

He saw Alban when he was only two paces away. He raised his knife in both hands, jumped forwards – and landed on the wet rock shiny with algae. His feet went from under him, and he sat down in the wet. Alban leaped up and ran back down the cave until the roof sloped down like a hand to stop him. Then he picked up his skirts and ran directly at Bruno, howling and roaring and calling on God. He leaped two-footed straight into the man's lap, and kept running – one foot on his chest, one in his face, and on out of the cave door. As he broke out of the arch and looked back, those stage-prop jaws of Hell spewed up the damned Bruno clutching his head and roaring like torment. He had stood up under the low rock and hit his head on the roof. He ran three steps and crumpled up, one hand on his crown and one pointing after Alban '. . . eat you, monk! Chew on your . . .' The disjointed words came after Alban, but he was off and running, kicking up sand into the circular mouth of Elshender's alphabet and plunging in among the sand dunes like a sailor surrendering himself to mountainous seas.

So well did Alban run – so fast and so strongly – that he began to congratulate himself. He set himself targets: that tree within forty strides, this slope without slowing. He had called on God and God had not spat on him. He debated with himself whether Bruno's villainy had outranked his own in God's eyes. But he decided against flattering himself. Some throw of the dice had favoured him with one more move. He noted the flowers, the stippled cloud effect, the trees' leaves peeling like old copper off the sky, and stuffed the images into his heart like a defeated army looting its way out of a rout. He felt imminent destruction at his heels and he was going to take with him all he could carry: that silver grass, those azure cornflowers, that small, precious cross of a windhover hung up in the sky . . .

Then his legs disappeared. They sagged and staggered and filled up with lead, just as he reached the priory's outer wall. He stood slumped against the drystone walling, wondering if there was more to it than chance that he found himself by the shadow of the bellcote.

Just then, Bruno came out of the bracken at the edge of the Order's pasture-land. His legs were not lead-filled. His lungs were not withered and dry like peach-stones. Alban wanted to cry.

Instead, he rolled like a toddler to the front gates. They were locked shut and so he pulled himself up the branches of a yew tree leaned like a fortuitous ladder against the gatepost. The yew was dead. Its needles came loose by the million and filled him fuller than a hedgehog with prickles. His heels went over his head, and he landed on his feet at the base of the wall, yelling, 'Sanctuary! Sanctuary! Sanctuary!'

The groups of children squatting in the dust broke up and moved back a little. They squinted nervously at the monk, but he was not the first person to rush into the yard looking for protection. An hour or so earlier the dragon itself had lumbered by, and that was why the gate had been locked. They ran to the walls, and stood on one another's shoulders to look over. They did not see anything; they did not see Bruno, in looking for the dragon.

The monks came out, with the Prior himself at the back of

the group. The parents of the children stood behind the half-circle of clergy, calling their children to come and tell them what had happened.

'You're safe now, son,' said the Prior, who was not free with embraces and held himself at a distance. 'Come and tell your story to the manciple. He's keeping a chronicle of the times. What are you?'

'It's him.'

'Brother Alban, Father. Of the Order of Saint Front.'

The Prior was taken aback. There was nothing in Alban's appearance – bearded and long-haired, his habit burned and torn out of all recognition – to say that he was a religious. 'And where have you come from to be so dishevelled?'

'It's him,' a woman said, from behind the habited ranks. She was moving sideways through the crowd, towards the Prior.

Alban began to explain that he had been chased there by a man – a murderer, an adulterer in the service of –

'Not the dragon?' asked the Prior.

'It's him,' said the women. 'Harken to me. It's the beast's monk. It's the animal's man. Saw him that day at the mill.' It was the miller's wife, who had gone with the Pardoner to view his filthy bargain. The crowd gasped, shuffled, closed ranks. The older children ran back to their mothers, asking if it was true. The younger ones scowled with ignorance, then grudgingly followed the older ones.

Only one child remained on the middle ground. She had a large head and thin limbs and wore the gleam of unwonted understanding in her drooping eyes. She pointed at Alban and said, 'Yes, it's the dragon's man.' A monk came and snatched her arm and pulled her away to safety.

Weapons and bladed tools appeared.

165

'Fetch the net from the ponds,' said the Prior quietly. 'Look at his clothes. He has the very scorching of Hell on him.'

They threw the net over Alban as he tried to climb back over the gate. And they threw him, still entangled, into the undercroft, with the relics of Saint George and a huge wooden crucifix against the trapdoor to stop him breaking free.

All night the Prior swore that he could smell sulphur. He was doubtful whether common fire would destroy such a creature. But he pitched a straw bonfire in the yard in any case, and wrote a letter to the Lord Leo, offering to attempt it.

Because of the dragon's passage close by the walls earlier in the day, he could not find a volunteer to carry the letter until the following morning.

14

FAITHFUL BETRAYALS

Anselm folded himself into the folds of Elfleda's body, his knees in the backs of hers, his chin over the top of her hair. He contained her. He was a hand round a flame, to shield it from the wind. She scorched him, too, with an astonishment of fires. She cauterised all the wounds life had ever made in him. Only reasonable that the process should hurt a little.

If he could always lie still, holding her, he supposed that one day there would be no wounds left. But morning seemed forever to be interrupting, insisting he should get up and leave Elfleda. She was the purpose of life, and yet he seemed to spend most waking hours apart from her.

And he slept so well, too. At first, excitement and disbelief had kept him awake all night, wondering. But now sleep snatched him directly out of her arms and swallowed him whole. And in the morning, the delight in waking up alongside her lay on him more like a sunbeam than a sword. The pain came in realising that yet again, for the sake of convention, he must get up and pass the day pretending to be an independent being.

Elfleda took his hand between both hers, over her newly conceived child, and sighed without rousing. Outside the window the birds so vied with each other in volume and versatility of song that their exertions must surely fling them off the roofs and branches. 'We won't rise today while there's one bird still singing,' thought Anselm.

As he thought it, the rumble of a flat-cart obliterated all the birdsong. A pigeon escaping from under the horses' hoofs fluttered up to the window and hit the architrave with its wings. It almost came in on top of Anselm in his bed. Down in the yard, Leo's serving-man called out for someone to hold his horses' heads. Elfleda woke up, kissed Anselm's hands, and slid out from between his arms.

Mann had been entrusted with a secret. He was so eminently trustworthy that it was difficult to prise the message out of him at all, so tightly did he cling to it.

'The master says you've to come, if it please you.'

'Is it the dragon?' said Anselm.

'Well . . . no,' said the old man, pinching the end of his nose.

'Is it something else?'

'Maybe,' said Mann, a finger in one ear.

'Do you know why you've come?' said Elfleda.

'To fetch the Lord Anselm, lady.'

'Yes, but you do know why, don't you?'

'I know not to let the Lady Gwyne know that it's not about the dragon . . . although there is news about it. They've got its devil-monk at the Priory.'

'Oh, I am glad!' cried Elfleda.

'Fixing to burn'm,' said Mann, seeking to expand the good news and please her further.

She drew a sharp breath and covered her mouth with her fingertips. ''Selm! Do something!'

'I'll go there now. Leo can wait.'

'No sir. I think that won't be right, sir. Not with him bad the way he is.'

'Who is? Leo is?'

'Yessir.'

'Leo's ill?' said Elfleda. 'Is it a stroke?'

'Why should it be a stroke, for Jesu's sake?' called Anselm as he ran towards the stable.

'Is it his arm, Mann?'

'Arms, legs, corpse. It's the lot of'm, pretty much, milady Anselm. But he's keeping it from the Lady Gwyne, see. With the baby all but looking out on the world.'

'What? Is she in labour?' called Anselm from within the stable.

'God bless you too, sir,' called Mann who could not hear over a distance.

'If this is your something made out of nothing, Mann, I'll have you turned off. For Jesu's sake, woman, did you know there was something wrong with my brother? Shut the gates behind us. Don't leave them standing open for the dragon to wander in, you hear? Holy Mary! Why wouldn't you tell me such a thing about my own brother?'

"Selm . . . I didn't know –' But Anselm had gone, in a flurry of pique and anxiety. Laboriously, Mann turned the cart and trundled after him calling, 'He's not at the castle, sir! He's up at the new church, sir!'

Elfleda stood watching them out of sight, then pushed the gates to. Before she could throw the bolt, she was overwhelmed by waves of nausea. Taken unawares, after years of unimpaired health, she was panic-stricken. What if some dire plague had settled on the country to which both she and Leo had succumbed? The dragon should by rights fetch pestilence in its wake. The Scriptures promised pestilence poured from the seven bowls of God's wrath on to those with the mark of the Beast . . .Elfleda picked up her skirts and ran into the kitchen, colliding with the cook in the doorway.

'Bless you, madam, you're as green as watercress! Is it the morning sickness already? You poor lamb. How is it when the man falls sick of love, it's always the lady what turns green? Come and lie down, Lord spare you, and think of the joy to come. It'll be the baby puking soon enough, and you'll fret worse over that.' Elfleda climbed to her bedroom behind the cook in such a blush of self-scorn that she gave no more thought to nausea. Nor to the unfastened gate.

The new church was complete but for the interior embellishment of the fresco. There was a stonemason hanging in a creaking wicker basket up in the roof and a lurid green dragon was sprawling along the east wall in battle with Saint George, though the artist of that piece of decoration was not in evidence. The painting was covered in burr-like asterisks and hemmed in by scrolling clouds or wind.

The Lord Leo was in the gallery, which projected over the door and was intended to support a band of musicians. At present all it housed was the mason's tools. Leo was sitting on a block of stone with another, taller, under his elbow, and was tucked round with his cloak and the horrible slit blanket Mann was accustomed to wear. Anselm had never acknowledged before how much smaller his brother was than he.

'What's this about then?' he said, folding himself up into the small space between his brother and the gallery rail.

'It's a bit better. I can feel the stone. It's cold,' said Leo. He talked as if he had his teeth clenched.

'Are you in pain?'

'Grant that I were. Can't feel, you see. Part by part it's gone. Over the weeks. Gone altogether this morning. Like being dead.' He said this several times over. 'Like being dead. As if my body died ahead of my soul.'

Leo was cocooned in thought. Sitting up in the gallery, looking down at the church nave, waiting for Mann to fetch Anselm, he had had plenty of time for contemplation. He was distant and wistful in a way that Anselm knew would embarrass his brother later, if he outlived the illness. 'What is it, then?' he asked, intruding on the man's terror.

'Don't know.'

'Did you fall off a horse? Fall on your head?'

'No. Don't know what it is, 'Selm,' and a single tear crawled down into Leo's beard and disappeared. It was not self-pity, but a wealth of regret as the thought of things lost from his future filled him, day by day, drop by drop, to overbrimming.

'You fool. Why not say?' Anselm spoke snarlingly through the collar of his shirt which he was holding in his teeth. 'Told my Elfleda, didn't you? But not me.' He began pulling at the blankets as if he were unwrapping a bacon out of muslin.

'I didn't tell your wife. Why say a thing like that? She's just naturally sensible to a man's troubles. She knew. You didn't know. She knew. Gwyne didn't. Look, it's about Gwyne.'

'What is?'

'You know she's pregnant . . .'

'Jesu, Leo, where have I been not to know she's pregnant? It's that or she's been eating clover. My Elfleda's . . .'

'I don't want a regent manor, 'Selm. I don't want Gwyne to rule in place of me.'

'Regent? Leo, you're not the King, boy.'

'Also it may be a girl.'

'Yes, it may.'

'*And I don't want you, either.*' He blurted it out like a child admitting to a breakage.

Anselm squatted back on his haunches and picked fluff off

the knees of his breeches. A drop of sweat fell on the back of his hand. He could not understand what part of his brother had shed it, until he realised it was his own. It was clammy cold in the church as well. 'Of course not. Of course you don't want me. It's Elshender you want. I know that.' And his voice rose and fell in most unnatural, womanly cadences. He dreaded most of all that Leo would see through him to the witless and frightened younger brother. 'What's all this anyway? You're a young man.'

The muscles of Leo's cheeks tautened and flickered. 'Inside. Yes I am. Do you think I'll not die, then?'

'You said yourself – you're feeling better.'

'I lied.'

'I'll look for Elshender, of course I will. Tell him you're ill, of course I will.'

'Tell him there'll be time enough when the new child's grown if he wants to go off again.'

'Time enough.'

'Inside I'm still young,' said Leo and, as if to corroborate it, his voice broke. 'I feel the same as when I was twenty. Just as ignorant, anyway . . . You see that villain in the basket? I've sat here and I've watched him. He's on a level with me. You see? Our heads are on a level – to the inch. Equal heights. And I can't lift a chisel over my head, no more than fly. He can. So he's higher really. They call it the Leveller, don't they? He has two sons. I asked him . . . Oh please God send Elshender. Find him for me, 'Selm. Tell him I just want to see him. To the Devil with the manor. I just want to see him. Please. Please. Please.'

He cried silently, and then not so silently, the tears running down into his open mouth. The stonemason stopped tapping and crouched down in his basket like a dog: only the curve of his spine was visible. His head averted, he knew he could not get away until his boy came to work the winch, and his boy had been told to keep away by Mann. It was not his place to complain and, after the noise from the gallery subsided, he went back to his sculpting. The particular angel in hand was the most perfect, the most detailed on the whole ceiling. The stonemason simply hoped that if the Lord Leo died, he would not be entirely overlooked in the excitement, left to swing out the year in his basket. He was quite astonished when the Lord Anselm took the trouble of lowering him to the ground before he brought down his brother from the gallery.

Leo was a damp, awkward and insanitary burden to carry down the ladder. Anselm had to put him over his shoulder to negotiate it. He felt as if he had found the secret of eternal life only to suffer the penalty of watching the rest of the world grow old and sicken and die. He felt guilty for having no misfortune to compare with Leo's.

Mann arrived with the cart, having pushed the horses almost to a trot. 'To the priory,' said Anselm, laying his brother down on the flat-back.

'You think I need shriving, then?' Leo said accusingly as his brother's head passed the side of the cart, on his way to his horse.

'I don't know. How should I know?' Anselm retorted furiously. 'Jesu, man! There's no harm in being shriven, is there? Would you rather go home to Gwyne and explain to her why you don't want her babe to rule?'

'No.' Leo's fingers twitched a little as, inwardly, he made some huge restraining gesture against being taken home. 'I don't know why not. She ought to be the first . . .'

'Spare her the worry,' said Anselm briskly.

'I wasn't thinking of her. Maybe she's right: I never do. No, I was thinking how . . .'

'For the sweet Lord's sake, won't you ever stop talking? You never talked this much when you were upright.'

'She'd say it was nothing uncommon, and why all the vexation and commotion. Everyone dies, she'd say.' His voice grated like a ship touching bottom. 'Why should *you* be different? Quick, then. Quick. Get on and die. I'm busy. I have a lot to do today.'

'You're unjust, Leo. Don't.'

'No. Of course. It's the humour that's on me. Not the right time to be unjust . . . But you don't like her either, do you? You never did.'

'I didn't marry her. It's husbands and wives that go to the vexation of liking and loathing.'

'But not you and yours.'

Anselm pointed a finger in Leo's face. 'No more. Don't add envy to your charge, man.' He turned his back and mounted his horse. He had an irrational and superstitious fear of hearing Elfleda's name on the lips of a dying man.

But he rode close by the cart, looking down into his brother's face after Leo had closed his lids against the brightness of the sky. The large brown eyes were the face's reservoir of youth and animation: without them he was a lantern unlit, extinguished. He was padded with straw against the back-breaking jolts of the cart, and looked like a dead fledgling on a nest.

'Mann,' said Anselm quietly, so as not to wake his brother. 'Let's hope the dragon's not on the path from here to the priory.'

''S'over by the sea again, so I hear tell.'

174

'Good. What a trough of information you are, Mann. When did you hear about Brother Alban?'

'Who?'

'The monk held at the priory. The one for burning.'

'A messenger come over. He goes to the castle and they send him up to the new church. They want the master's say-so to burn the fiend.'

'And did Leo give his say-so?'

Mann grinned grotesquely, and the only remaining teeth at the back of his bottom jaw showed, as if he were shovelling the laugh out of his gullet. 'Never fear. We'll be in plenty of time to see it. The master sent to say "not till I come" . . . I've no fear for the master, sir. None in the world. You just see. While that bugger burns, the sickness'll rise off the Lord Leo with the smoke. I'm telling you. The sickness is its making.'

'Dear De'il! You'd burn the Pope himself for a good bonfire,' exclaimed Anselm in disgust. 'There's no harm in Alban, you pitchforker you.'

Alban, when they arrived at the priory, was sitting on a waist-high pile of straw with his arms round his bent legs, and his face on his knees. His hands and feet were bound. He was surrounded by more blades, picks, spikes and clubs than ever laid siege to Arras. And there were as many unlit torches as weapons. The crowd waved them like amputated limbs dipped in tar.

'Let him go. Now,' said Anselm to the Prior. He was profoundly embarrassed to find himself involved in such an adolescent, fairground atrocity. He was glad of his height. It separated him from their corporate stupidity. If he had been a man of common stature they might, he thought, have swept him to ruin like cows accidentally crushing a drover. It *looked* like a child's game, with Alban at the centre on his castle of grass. The people round about wore that crazed look of schoolboys corrupting a girl. On their own, each would have been ashamed of himself.

But the Prior was not ashamed.

'Let him go, or I'll do it myself,' said Anselm.

'I can't do that, sir. He's the dragon's groom. He's privy to its every thought.'

'What of it? It's just an animal. If a horse trod on you you wouldn't burn the rider.'

Anselm was rather proud of this. It fell trippingly off the tongue, as if he had just thought of it.

The Prior was unimpressed. 'Look at him, my friend. Look at him. His clothes are . . . That's hellfire. We can do little more than send him back to the fire he came from. He's not even asked for shriving! Think on that, sir!'

'I dare say he knows Leo won't stand for his murder. Now let him go. He's just a harmless clod who fell asleep under a wasps' nest and had the wasps steal his wits. You'd be better occupied shriving my brother.'

'I'm going at once,' said the Prior petulantly. 'And you, sir, might be better occupied in prayers for your brother, if you'll permit me to say it. I've had him laid on my own bed. I understand how . . . – . . . you must be.' Adjectives did not come easily to the Prior. He was mesmerised by Anselm's white knuckles emerging through the weave of his cloak where he held the two edges clenched to his chest. It was a hot day and the lord's brother looked cold to the marrow.

'I'll go to him,' said Anselm, unconciliating. 'In two minutes you can send Alban to do the shriving.' And he turned, scattering the eavesdroppers behind him.

'*To shrive your brother?*' The Prior ran after him and tried to see up into his face. 'The Devil's man? To shrive your brother? I forbid it! I beseech you! I won't allow it! It's my place. The everlasting soul of our own liege lord? I forbid you to jeopardise it! My spiritual powers permit me . . .'

'I'm Leo's heir.'

'Temporality! Pah!'

It was undignified. The Prior reduced them to little boys squabbling. Anselm fully expected him to say at any moment, '*My* heavenly Father's better than *your* temporal one!'

At the door to the Prior's quarters Anselm turned and put his hand on the cleric's chest to hold him out while shutting the door in his face. 'Send the lad,' he insisted. 'Send Alban.'

Just in time he saw the deceitful flicker in the eyes and snatched open the door again. They raced each other across the yard: two grown men racing – last one home's in peril of damnation.

'*Burn him!*' shouted the Prior, and Anselm stretched his stride and took the Prior's feet from under him. '*Burn him!*' The Prior fell on to his hands but regained his feet, like a horse pecking over a jump.

Alban rose up like a swan on his huge straw nest and gave a scream that froze all movement in the yard. But only for a moment.

Anselm singled out one man running from the chapel, his torch lit at the paschal candle. 'Don't think of it,' he warned, colliding with the man and picking him up by the armpits. 'I'm Leo's heir and he's dying, and I'll turn off any man who throws a torch!'

The air between Anselm and Alban began to waver and to fill with gouts of smoke: the torches loosed it like squid loosing

177

ink. It coloured the air and it smelled of fear. Anselm reached the bonfire and half demolished it in the collision.

Alban let himself fall forward over the big man's shoulder and felt the spittle spatter the back of his head as it hung down.

'If you'd heard what he said of the lord!' said a voice.

'That a's a cuckold,' said another.

'God's a cuckold, is He?' said Anselm. He had no difficulty in pushing through the crowd: they shrank away from any physical contact with the monk he was carrying.

'No! The *lord*! The Lord Leo! The *master*! 'A says such things about the Lady Gwyne!' A pox-scarred face in the crook of Anselm's arm breathed awe and garlic up at him.

'And you believed it? If a fool believes a madman, who's the bigger fool?'

No one attempted to stop him this time from annexing the Prior's cell. He set down the monk, slapping both his shoulders in the most masculine gesture of sympathy he could think of. The monk crumpled between his hands as if he had burst, and sank down into exactly the position he had kept in the yard, his knees pressed into his eye-sockets.

'Anselm,' said Leo, who was sitting on the Prior's cot with his back to the wall. 'Come here, will you?'

'You seem better.' Anselm sat down beside him with one hand on his knee. They sat like this, backs to the wall, their eyes resting all the while on the huddled creature in the centre of the room as they exchanged comments under their breath for fear of disturbing him.

'You take a lot upon yourself, don't you?' whispered Leo. 'A nice act of gentility, but I don't want to be shriven by a lunatic. I want the Prior. Go and speak civilly to him. And while you're about it, tell him you're not my heir. There's gentle.'

'You heard that, then? We needed the monk, to tell us about the dragon.'

'Yes. I appreciate that was your thinking. But the fact is, I don't want shriving by Legion here. Look at him, anyway. He's past speech.'

'He's a good lad, I'm telling you; at least he's a common, ordinary lad. He married Elf to me. He's your wife's chaplain!'

'And I'm telling you I've never seen him before. And when I was down there, at the mill, with that beast reaching out for me, that madman was shouting at the *beast* to take shelter. He didn't shout to warn us. Don't think it. He was shouting to the dragon to keep hence.'

'So it's vulnerable. Flesh and blood.'

'It's poxy big, 'Selm. And that one there's a lover to it.'

'You waved your hand.'

'What? Yes. It's coming back, thank God.'

'Thank God. How is the rest of you faring?'

'It comes and it goes. I told you. A cramp or two. They'll be gone presently. Then I'll be . . . fair for a time.'

'So I was right to take time to save the priest, was I? For the information. Wasn't I? I'll take him somewhere and ask him about the beast. And I'll send the Prior to shrive you.'

'I don't need him. I'm recovered now. I don't need shriving. I'm not going to die.'

'No. Of course. But there's no harm,' said Anselm as diplomatically as he could. 'We all die one day.'

'Except your swyving monk. And his dragon. The Devil keeps them in health somehow every time. You be careful of him, 'Selm. You just . . .'

'And you receive the holy oils, lad. I've known you in better health.'

179

'Of course.'

'All right, then. You know . . . You know I only said I was your heir so as to make 'em pay heed?'

'Of course.'

'Of course.'

They continued to sit, until the Prior came and knocked at the door. He shouldered his way into the room without waiting for a summons, though his bumptiousness was curbed by his terror of Alban. Seeing the improvement in Leo's health, he praised God for it, indicated the monk and said, 'Don't you agree, my lord, that it would be better to dispose of this?'

Leo shot his brother a look borrowed from Gethsemane. 'Yes,' he said. 'Burn him.'

Alban's hands crept round the back of his head and he began rocking to and fro.

'Hold it in mind,' said Anselm, removing his hand from his brother's treacherous knee, 'that the monk is under my protection, and should my excellent brother die within the next few months, I shall lay siege to the title and take it from Elshender who is not only mad but absent.'

The monk on the floor looked up at the two on the bed, the pattern of hessian imprinted on his face so that his skin looked like cheese-rind. The name of Elshender had sparked a sly, covert excitement in him.

The Prior was alarmed, aggrieved. He took it for a personal test, this tug of war between the lord and his brother, with him as the rope. He wondered if a bet had not been made on his reaction, before he came into the room. 'This is serious, my lords. You are answerable to God for your . . . Master Elshender is eminently suited to inherit, my Lord Leo, but where is he? Didn't you say yourself he'd gone to the Holy Land?'

'*I* told him that,' said the monk, as though he recognised an old acquaintance in the fact. 'It was a lie.'

All three stared at him. Then the Prior said, 'You see what a Devil's snare he is?'

'Did he *not* go?' Leo demanded, sitting forward from the wall.

Alban puckered up his lips belligerently. 'You tried to kill him. I won't tell you spit.'

'Damn your scrawny dragon! What do you know about Elshender? 'Selm, make him say what he knows about my boy. God damn my legs! If I had my legs I'd kick it out of him. 'Selm, make him tell you!'

'I'll take him aside, then.'

'All right . . . No, damn you. You'll lie after!'

Anselm shoved the collar of his shirt into his mouth and stood up. He recinched his belt. He washed his neck at the Prior's washbowl. He tucked in his shirt, then said to Alban, 'Come on. Get up. Out.'

'Are you going to get him to tell you?' Leo demanded, griping at the back of his insensate knees. But his brother said nothing, helped the monk to his feet and pushed him urgently into the narrow cavity passage within the wall and through to the general dorter.

The voice of the Prior followed them down the passageway. 'Now gentlemen. Don't we have hardship enough? Have a care, sir! He has the smell of sulphur on him, that one!'

Each time Alban hesitated, Anselm pushed him on. They came out of the dorter and into the chapel, which was dark all but for a crack of daylight where the door hung ajar, and the paschal candle standing in drunken readiness to serve as a spill-lighter.

When Anselm began to speak, his noise vaulted into the roof and came booming back down on to them. 'I own you.' He dropped his voice and began again. 'So tell me what the dragon is and where it is now. And what do you know about Elshender?'

In the dark, Alban fell up the altar dais. 'I don't know where he is.'

'But you said yourself – You're a liar. So where?'

Alban shrugged like a delinquent, and shambled off to the far side of the altar where Anselm lost sight of his outline. 'I'm cold,' he said. 'I'm fearful cold.'

'Should I weep for it? My brother's dying and you can help him towards seeing his son one more time.'

This idea seemed to capture Alban's interest, because out of the dark came a highly animated voice. '*I've* been dying. Did you know? I've been dying all morning. Over and over. You know when you sleep, and dream that you've got up for matins and keep finding that you've only dreamed the getting-up? Well I've been dying – imagining it, through and through, and still holding my balance on my haunches because I weren't dead yet. It's a mad thing. It pushes everything away to a distance. Can't hold a thought together. Faces shouting down a well at you, and there's no substance to 'em. Even you. It's there. It's waiting. We've all swallowed the poison before we were born. It's just the waiting now for the pain to begin – that's all there is to it . . . Have I really met that man in the other room? Is that Leo? Is that Elshender's father?'

'Don't you know?'

'I recall I told a man a lie about his son. The son was called

182

Elshender. I can't recall what lie. It was some lie. I've lied a lot since I came down south. Hardly another thing.'

'Why lie to a stranger?'

'Oh. The Lady Gwyne told me to, of course. Why else would I . . . You don't walk into a strange house and straight off say . . . I would never have done it out of . . . Why would I? I didn't have the call to. I'll tell you the fact of it, but you'll only take it for mischief and kill me for it, so it goes on, you see. Still dying by the minute. Well, I'm in sanctuary now! *There!* never thought of that, did you?' He had set himself down in the middle of the dais, legs crossed, hands cradled in his lap, petulant.

'You simple bastard. It's me who just broke with my brother to keep you alive. What's it to me where you sit? This is the man that wouldn't be shrived, is it? And now you want sanctuary? Christ, you're a mooncalf, Alban!'

There was a slight snuffling in the dark, and Alban got up.

'True. You have it. It's no good to me. I'll tell you what, sir. I'm still deadly cold.'

They went back into the light of the dorter, and Alban wrapped himself in one of the blankets on the cots. He began to move about with the largeness of movement and gesture that bond-men never achieve in the presence of a feudal superior and which servile monks never achieve at all. He sat down on a crib and waved at another saying, 'Sit down, Anselm. Rest yourself. Save your strength for killing me. You see? I'm quite recovered. I've got back my Acceptance. I'll keep it on my lips always from now . . . Acceptance. It's a great watchword at Saint Front's. Acceptance. Acceptance.'

'I know the word,' said Anselm sourly.

'Ah yes. But then of course you can put it in your pocket and use it if you choose. It's different for me. I should teach you its merits. If you knew them, I'd be a safer man. Acceptance. It means feigning not to mind death – so as not to spread panic and cause a stampede. That's what it means.'

'They say madmen sound plausible,' said Anselm. 'What I need to know is who drove you out of your wits: the mob or the dragon?'

Alban showed his palms, like a conjuror denying subterfuge. 'You're wrong. I'm quite recovered now. I have accepted it. My beast's forgotten me. There's only a thing or two left to be done. I need to see the Lady Elfleda. Your . . . Is she well?'

Anselm was shaken to the core. 'My wife? What do you want with her?'

'I should only speak to her. I have a message for her.'

'From God I suppose.'

'God? No, of course not. From Elshender. Do sit down, Anselm. I'm fit to tell you now.'

Anselm, too, picked up a blanket and sat with it in his lap and unravelled its weave. Having exhausted his powers of intuition, reasoning and guesswork, he still did not know whether or not he was talking to a madman. But he sensed a terrible impending misery. And all the while half his mind was on the brother he had betrayed in the next room. In an effort to stop up bad news, one last little attempt to discern if he was listening to lies or nonsense, he interrupted: 'Why would you not be shriven?'

'Not that I won't. I can't be. Excommunicant. I was excommunicant when Gwyne made me her creature. I was excommunicant when I married you to the Lady Elfleda. I haven't been a Brother now for . . . I don't know . . . time's lost its measure . . . since before I came south. I hadn't the power to marry you. I didn't marry you. You aren't married. Well. When I say it, it doesn't seem past remedy, as sins go . . . Yours, I mean! I mean yours, sir, not mine! Easy to remedy yours.'

'Yes,' said Anselm, and for a moment he could see no harm in the world. Then something dimly suggested itself. 'Is Elshender still a Brother? He did take Holy Orders after his vision, didn't he?'

'Oh, but there was no "vision", sir. That was just a story put about by his stepmother. She cuckolded her husband – that's to say him in there. I dare swear his sickness is her doing, too . . . Don't sir. Keep away. It's better to know than to guess. She was the ruin of Elshender. His sister's drowned in the sea. Frideswide? Is that the name? Drowned. Yes.'

Anselm stood over him with his hands round the monk's throat. But Alban had stopped, thoughtful or vacant, with his eyes full of the middle distance.

'And Elshender?'

'Oh Anselm, sir,' said the monk wearily, almost pityingly. 'You haven't understood. I thought I was speaking plain. Elshender's a dragon, of course. The dragon's your nephew. He asked me to tell the Lady Elfleda. I shouldn't have betrayed him to you. I don't suppose I can trust you to tell her.' The monk could not have gone on, because of Anselm's hands round his neck. But he had finished in any event. Acceptance was written all over his long, unshaven, elongated head. Anselm relaxed his fingers.

'*You*? Trust *me*? You scabby lie-monger. Where have you been to fetch up lies that big? The Devil sent you to spread alarm. It's a beast. I've seen it! If it speaks, why didn't it speak to us, eh?'

Alban rubbed his neck. 'It's all one to me, sir. Believe me –
don't believe me. I suppose the woman means him to be killed
by his own kin. Otherwise she could have strangled him – or
poisoned – but she was more fond of giving pain. Or maybe
she hoped to stay free of a damnable sin. Or maybe she wanted
everybody to suffer everlastingly – the kind of regret that can't
be outlived. Everlastingly wishing you'd done different –
anything different. You'll shun it, if you love yourself, sir.'
Anselm showed no alteration of expression. Alban sighed
deeply. 'You'll kill him, then. It's to your charge. The old man
in there – he's too sick to kill his son. But you'll kill him, won't
you? I can see it in you. You'll kill my dragon, won't you, and
suffer for it ever after – just like the woman intended. Clever.
God give you joy of your intellect, and send you hot wire to
rest your weary soul on!'

The malediction emptied Alban's lungs, and in breathing in
again he choked. He began coughing, and coughed and
coughed and went on coughing until his face was as blue as the
broken veins in his cheeks and tears oozed out between his
eyelashes. When the coughing ended, the tears continued,
rolling in and out of the contours of his face like flies on a
corpse. He plucked forward his hood in a gesture acquired in
the cloister, and rocked from the hips.

When, after a time, Anselm pulled back the hood by its
crown, Alban was crying open-mouthed like a child and he
took hold of Anselm's wrist and held it against his sodden
cheek in supplication.

'Please don't kill my beast! Please don't kill him! I'll show
you how to talk to him if you promise not to kill him. I've
betrayed him. I told him I'd tell Elfleda, and I told you. It's
true. It's true. Everything I told you is true!'

186

'I know,' said Anselm expressionlessly. 'I have corroboration of it from my wi . . . from what Elfleda told me. Where is Elshender now?'

'You won't harm him? Please – you won't harm my dragon!'

'He's my own nephew. Why would I harm him?'

'Well then, I don't know where he is, but I'm glad he left me when he did. Bruno's out there looking to finish me because I saw him enjoying the woman.'

'*Bruno?* Did you say *Bruno* whored Gwyne?'

'I saw them.'

Disgust made Anselm splenetic again. 'What are you, the eye of God? Seeing and knowing what no one else does? How came you to lose your beloved dragon?'

'I don't know!' Alban clutched his knees to his chest and howled it. '*I don't know!* Maybe he didn't trust me to take his message. He was so set on her name. Elfleda, Elfleda . . . over and over and over he told it me. I said: I'll tell her, I'll tell her. But then the fish came and he seemed to forget all about me. Maybe the fish told him something. Maybe he went to find Elfleda. I can't keep up to him, you see, not when he runs. I can't keep up. I should've, shouldn't I? I should've followed him. Then Bruno wouldn't have chased me here. Then they wouldn't have burned me over and over and over on that fire. Look at the burns on me. Just look!' He fingered the burns on his scalp where his hair had burned, and on his thin, big-jointed arms. '. . . But that was somewhere else, wasn't it, Father?'

'Yes, son. That was somewhere else. Lie down and sleep.'

Alban obeyed at once. Anselm crouched down at the head of the bed and put his face close to the closed eyes. 'One thing, Alban. Does the dragon . . . can he *comprehend*?'

'Oh yes, Father. As much as you and I. And he feels, too – and likes and hates. So I never told him about me.' The eyes flashed open, wide and round, but the pupils were only pinpricks. Tears continued to roll freely out of the ducts. 'I should've told him about me, shouldn't I?'

'No matter. Go to sleep.'

'Will you tell the old man, sir? About Elshender and the woman and Bruno?'

'My brother? He's not old, Alban. He's only a twoyear older than me. I don't know. What would you do? Would you tell him his son's a dragon and his wife's a whore?'

'Me, sir?' Alban's eyes focused all of a sudden, and the burned stubble of his cheeks creased up. His peculiar face reorganised itself into a smile which confused its features. 'Me, Father? How would I know such things? You shouldn't be asking the like of me. I'm out of the way of people. Me? I don't know. Why don't you ask Elshender? He'd know. He knows everything.' He went to sleep before he could muster another sentence.

Anselm lay down on the next bed and looked up at the ceiling. He could see the dragon in his mind's eye as clearly as he could see Elfleda's face. The two images vied for the foreground.

If someone came to you and said that your son was a gross beast and Elfleda was . . . what would you do?

Run mad, like that poor fellow there (replied the ceiling, dead pan).

So would I, too.

Better than killing him and finding out after.

Better than rejoicing in a bastard heir.

Better than bequeathing the estate to a dragon.

And Gwyne may have a remedy. Or it may not be lasting. Elshender may be restored.

Imagine – finding that your wife's been covered by an ostler.

'Imagine finding that your betrothed has been covered by your uncle,' said Anselm out loud, and Alban stirred in his sleep. 'Still. Remediable. A recoverable sin, as the lad says.' If Elshender were restored, he might accept what amends could be made. He might be magnanimous. He might be prepared still to take Elfleda, according to contract. He might be prepared to take Elfleda . . .

He turned his head and looked at Alban sleeping. 'I wish I had let you burn. I ought to have built the fire myself. Taste this one, son. What am I supposed to tell *her*?' His arm flew out and he shook Alban by the hair. '*Wake up and tell me!*'

Alban's eyes rolled down out of sleep.

'Tell me . . . If the dragon goes seeking Elfleda, does he know where to find her? Did you tell him that?'

'Oh yes, Father. I told him about the marriage. I told him about you and her. But I didn't tell about me. I should have, shouldn't I?'

'No son. No matter. But get up. I need you.'

Anselm threw himself at the opening out of the dorter. His bulk all but filled the passageway. He had to move down it sideways into the cell where he had left Leo. The only person there was the Prior, kneeling at his prayers. He flinched violently as Anselm burst in on him.

'Where's my brother? Is he fit to ride?'

'Yes, Lord Anselm. He made shift. Word came from the castle that a son's born to him. When the good lady's pangs began the Lord Leo couldn't be found. But the Lord sent her an . . . easy time. God give you humility, Lord Anselm. He has

189

barred you from the sin of vaunting ambition. His son will follow him, God be praised.'

'Little Lord Bruno, eh?' said Anselm, and spat – as was not his custom – on the unrelenting stone floor.

15

SILENCE AND THE SCENT OF WOMEN

'If you won't give me a horse at least send a rider to fetch him back. He mustn't go home!'

'I'm afraid I won't do that, Lord Anselm. What kind of man would I be to keep a father from his new-born son? I'm afraid your hour is past, sir. I shall do everything in my power to prevent you overturning the . . . rightful order.'

'I pray you, save your soul from the sin of meddling, Father.'

The Prior narrowed his eyes and mouth at Anselm: he made it immediately plain that he saw it as his duty to obstruct this usurping younger brother. Alban hung back in the passageway, too nervous to come out. Anselm took him by the arm and thrust him at the Prior. 'Father! Absolve me for my stiff-necked obduracy! My brother and I – we commonly rub up against one another. It's a game. It's a sport – well, a vice we never threw off from being boys together. It's no sooner blown up than blown over. There's no harm meant. And this simpleton here – ' he dismissed Alban's sanity with a wave of his hand, 'he's newly mad from being with the dragon. He's lucid then he's raving. But I think I've got to the root of the truth, and I think Leo may be riding hard on to the dragon. He must be stopped.'

'Ah.' The Prior's dilemma was painful to see.

'Look. This one's brains are cracked. But he says that the beast's no more'n a cow – a big cow. And I believe him. What's more he has a way with cows. I need him if I'm to destroy the beast. That's why I need two horses.'

Alban said nothing, but looked at the swollen veins in the back of his hand where Anselm's grip was cutting off the blood.

'Ah,' said the Prior. He wanted earnestly to believe that brother loved brother. If Anselm had been threatening, the Prior would have held his ground, at the cost of life itself. If only he would detach himself from the diabolical ragamuffin, it would be easy to like him again. In fact it was hard to dislike the man.

'Leave the devilish monk behind,' wheedled the Prior.

Anselm made a show of sitting Alban down on the cot, then took the Prior aside to whisper in his ear. 'I've told you. This is the only man who can track it. If you like, I'll slit his throat when the dragon's dead. If you rule it in holy law, I mean.'

'Merciful God! That's not the way! No, man! Fetch him back here. It must all be done according to law – and be seen in the doing. If it's as you say, and the beast's not . . . from Hell . . .'

'By no means! A cow! A big ox! Now quickly – a horse for both of us!'

The Prior said, 'But there aren't any horses, sir. Your brother took yours. There's only the cart from the castle. We can unhitch the cart, I suppose, but that only makes one.'

Anselm gave a shout of exasperation and set off for the yard. He had to recollect, and go back for Alban who had rested his head on the crib and shut his eyes.

Only by good fortune had Mann delayed driving off in order to discuss the bonfire with the squatter-refugees. Anselm put Alban in the back, took the reins from Mann and shouted at the fat, ponderous old horse. They were gone before the crowd in the yard could rekindle the excitement of the morning.

But the cart rolled so slowly that its progress through the countryside felt like the casual drift of a sunken hulk shifting in a slow tide.

'So the master has his son, God be praised,' said Mann, who believed he was being driven post-haste by a man urgent to see his newly born nephew. He was uneasy, even so, about the monk on the flat behind him. The refugees had told him just what *he* was. The old servant rode side-on, so that he could watch the man feigning sleep on the boards of the cart. Foolhardy for Anselm to take the Devil's groom anywhere near the new-born baby.

'Sir? Are we not going to the hall direct?'

Anselm resented having Mann in the cart. It made him responsible for the old man's safety. He more than resented having Alban in the cart – Alban who, if he could just have died in his Northumbrian cell, would have left both Anselm and the dragon in innocent ignorance – Alban who might well have set the dragon on to Elfleda like a ferret set to a burrow. The monk seemed entirely ignorant of what he had done to Elshender. He seemed not even to guess at the relationship between his beloved dragon and the woman at Anselm's hall. It took a monk to overlook jealousy.

Most of all, Anselm resented sharing the cart with himself, whom he despised. There was no fault in Mann or in Alban – no more than the floating logs that wash about in the ocean for ships to founder on. He, Anselm, was different. He had the choice of chasing after his poor unfortunate brother or running home to save Elfleda.

Leo's failing life surely no longer served the uses of his appalling wife. He might be riding towards a sudden death on the point of Bruno's knife; or to toast the birth in a draught of poison. At best he was riding to pour out admiration on a bastard, and to thank its mother for her efforts. There he would stand, treating his household to bounty. And there, on either side, would be Bruno and Gwyne, their allied contempt hanging like buckets on a yoke. What brother would allow it?

Only a younger brother, surely, who harboured his own usurping ambitions. Such brothers did exist. They climbed like beans or peas, by subtle, spiral courses, and clung with such vigour that death itself found their tendrils enmeshed in the canopy of power. How strange, then – what an interesting phenomenon for the chroniclers – that a younger brother devoid of ambition should still betray his brother.

Anselm pictured himself climbing down the ladder from the church gallery, his brother small and trembling in his arms while his own huge shadow filled the porch floor. He pictured himself leading Bruno aside from the levy to pacify him. And that moment, too, when Bruno stood over him with a drawn knife: and Anselm too ignorant to be afraid. He drew these pictures like the border of a page. For written central was Elfleda's name. She stood like the maiden in the Revelation, great with child, and in front of her stood the dragon.

'Sir?' said Mann. 'Are we not going to the hall direct?'

'No,' said Anselm. 'We're going to my place. My wife's in danger from the dragon. Do you quibble? Eh? God quit you for having the slowest horses in England!'

A hand reached between them and took hold of Anselm's shoulder. Alban was pulling himself up on to his knees. He opened his mouth to speak.

'And you hold your peace!' bawled Anselm. 'Haven't you done harm enough?'

'But I was only going to say . . . you mustn't fear for the lady. If she's dear to him he won't do her injury,' he said quietly.

'Except fear enough to stop up her heart,' and Anselm gave the monk a push in the face. But as he lost hold, and the cart went over a rabbit-hole and threatened to pitch Alban out altogether, Anselm caught hold of his wrist and held on to him. He nursed the kind of hatred for Alban that a parent feels for a child who hurls itself on to fire, water or sharp edges. He hated the man's innocence.

After a mile in which the ribby cart kept up its unceasing, hysterical, grating clatter, Anselm said, 'Mann. Tell this foreigner what Elfleda was to the young master.'

'To Elshender, sir?' said Mann. 'What, before's Vision and Calling, sir? She were Elshender's betrothed wife before the Vision, sir. The sun itself he thought her . . . and so she is, you Devil-man, so I pray you won't hold so much as 'er name in your filthy mouth.'

'I see,' said Alban. And when Anselm next looked into his face, there was pity enough there, to prove it. Alban did see.

'You seem recovered,' he said.

'Much,' said Alban. 'I'm sorry for your wounds, sir. But you'll forgive me if I grieve for my dragon too.'

Mann made an attempt to strike him, but Alban caught the fist between his own and placed it back on the rail. 'You'd best hold on, old man. The ground's right bumpy.'

If Elshender had not gone to drink at the river just after sunrise, he could have seized on his uncle as he set off with

Mann for the church. All night long he had kept watch outside Anselm's home, as he had done once, long ago, outside de Rochfoll's cliff-top house. All night long the gates had been closed, and though his anger was hot, his fire was not. He knew, without resort to logic, that he could not burn or claw his way through the gate to chew on Anselm or to steal Elfleda. So he waited. And in waiting he thirsted. And in being a beast, he could not but go looking for water.

Mann came for Anselm. The cart and horseback rider disappeared over the hill in the direction of the new church, and Elshender came back to find the gates open. He held up his nose and sniffed the air. He could smell the flesh and blood that had escaped him. But he could smell too the sweetness of Elfleda.

The rage that had sustained him all night was swamped by the immediacy of desire. Surprised like a jackal finding an abandoned kill, his movements became covert and furtive. Dropping his shoulders and neck and hesitating at each step, he allowed his slow eyes to travel from end to end of their vertical slits. There was none of the uproar that commonly greeted his approach to a house. There were no wild arrows, no sheep tethered outside the gate to placate him. There was only silence and the scent of women.

His outstretched head touched the gate, and it swung in a little, then swung back. He pushed his head through the gap and turned it awkwardly, examining whichever section of the yard came into focus – the astigmatic oval of the well, the warped trough, the confused straggle of washing on a post, the plank doors of the stable whose lines converged, for him, like the segments of an orange.

There was a noise from the kitchens. Someone was singing.

The sound reached Elshender like the adult sounds of evening reach a child already in bed. He was excluded from them. At the sight of him such sounds invariably dissolved into shrieking and prayers. For a moment he stood and listened, disorientated by a small gentleness. Then the scent reasserted itself.

The name 'Elfleda' was still in his head. It rolled about there like loose cargo in a ship. This time the house was quiet while the shrieking was inside his head. He mistook it for triumphing. After all, he effectively held the gate to a box corral in which Elfleda was his captive.

Hunger began to chew on him. It was fairly akin to desire, except that it made him feel weaker whereas desire gave him the illusion of energy. There was a pigeon loft in the end gable. He dismantled the thatch stook by stook, until the birds began to flutter against his nostrils. It was difficult to snatch them off the wing. Their clattering feathers and noisy panic mesmerised him. He found himself jerking his head into the air like a cat pouncing at butterflies, his front feet lifted off the ground.

A dog came round the house and tumbled into a fit of barking that spent itself in a whine. It shuddered, back arched, shanks shrunk down, then bolted into the kitchen. A protest greeted it. 'Get out, animal! What's the matter with you?' Then the cook came to the door.

She shut it.

She placed a stool against the inside of it and sat down.

She got up and pushed the table against the door, then sat down again. She heard scales scrape along the wall and the timber. The latch rattled. But the beast exerted no force to push in the door.

The cook picked up a cake of cheese and put it in her pocket before going to the foot of the stairs and calling up quietly, 'Madam.' She repeated it as she climbed. 'Madam. Madam. How are you now, madam?' She met with Elfleda in the doorway of her room, took her by both hands, like a child, and said, 'Now I want you to be a good brave girl.'

'I'm mending now, Mary. Truly I am.'

'Of course you are, darling. Now just you get your cloak and come up with me.'

'Has something happened? I didn't hear anyone come.'

'Of course you didn't. It's just some animal's got into the yard. Now get your cloak like a good girl.'

'I see.' Elfleda turned her wrists, so that her hands were on the outside of Mary's. When they still did not stop trembling, she put an arm round the cook's shoulders and led her along the corridor to the roof-hatch.

Mary said, 'Your lord Anselm will be back soon, lovest, so you mustn't fret. 'Sides, I dare say it'll go off as it came. And you've got me with you.'

'Yes. That's good, Mary,' said Elfleda and helped the other woman on to the vertical ladder, freeing her open-weave skirt from the splinters and loose joints of the rungs.

'We'll be all right up here, for as long as need be. Now I told you to bring your cloak and you didn't, you bad girl.'

'No, Mary. I'm sorry,' said Elfleda and shut the hatch behind her as she pulled herself on to the roof.

'I dare say it just wants chickens and doves. I dare say. So you mustn't fret. It won't do the babe no good to fret.'

'You're in the right,' said Elfleda. 'It's good to have you with me.' And she sat the cook down against the roof pitch.

'It's like with dogs, you see. The great thing is not to show you're afraid. They won't tear you, then. I hear tell you only have to say "Bo!" to a lion and it's off and running.'

'I think I heard that too,' said Elfleda. 'Why don't we just sit here where we can see the road. Then we'll be able to see Anselm coming.'

The cook squatted with her legs to either side of her body and held her skirt over her face as if she were washing with it. It was a posture Elfleda had seen widows strike in the villages, the tendons of their feet tightening and loosing as they rocked to and fro. Elfleda stroked the woman's hair and wondered if their plight was in any way helped by being on the roof. There was still the dragon's fire to be considered.

She held herself to blame. She had left open the gate. Fear hardly had time to breathe inside her. Come what may, she would prevent Anselm returning, unwarned, to a yardful of dragon. Also, keeping to the far side of the roof, watching for him to come, she could not see the yard: the idea of catching sight of the beast again was not even to be contemplated, though she could imagine every scale of its head, every tooth in its jaws, every string of saliva. Behind her, in the yard, the dragon crunched on a dove.

The chewing stopped. The beast began to sniff.

Not finding Elfleda at once, Elshender was easily distracted by food and the quick movements of dog and pig and horse. Only smell rekindled his purpose. Though once or twice Elshender snatched at a rational thought, it eluded him like the doves – and the source of the smell of Elfleda.

The shape and nature of the house did not elude him. It remained familiar in his memory, and he was aware of its weaknesses. It was part thatched, part slated, and beneath both coverings the roof slats and rafters were all that separated outside from in. On the single-storey sections he had only to nudge the slates off their batons to see into the rooms below.

Up on the roof, Elfleda heard the slates tinkling and cracking on the cobbles of the yard, in twos and threes.

Where there was thatch, Elshender had only to fire it to fetch out what livestock was sheltering there, human or animal. But he could not find the kindling in his gullet, and he felt somehow an unreasoning distaste for fire of late. So he began to pluck up the thatch, bale by bale, wherever it bulged within his reach.

Up on the roof, Elfleda heard the hiss and rustle of straw and the twang of the wicker staples as they were pulled out and flew across the yard. One came over the roof ridge and rattled down the slates to land beside her. She picked it up and held it this way and that, for use as a possible weapon against the beast's eyes. Its eyes, she thought, were its only weakness.

Elshender exhausted what areas of the roof he could dismantle, and circled the house itself, looking in through the holes he had made, and through the windows.

Up on the roof, Elfleda heard the flaccid sniffs move round the building, and the woman beside her began to moan on a rising scale. 'Quiet now. Let's keep silent,' said Elfleda, but the cook began to howl: in the intervals she took for breath, the sound of the dragon's breathing became excited and moved up and down in shorter and shorter passes below where they sat.

Elfleda crawled to the base of the pitched roof and began unlatching slates herself. And when the breathing became a stationary panting directly below her, she threw a pile of slates over the parapet and heard them smash futilely on the ground. She flung them singly then – broadcast like seeds –

and heard the beast grunt and prance. The slates crunched under its feet.

The sound of the cook and the rain of slates pin-pointed precisely for Elshender the target for his efforts. The shaped slates had no cutting edge: only the shards under his feet punished his soft soles as he pranced and reared up against the wall. The wattle dented under his feet, and his leaps brought his nostrils on a level with the parapet.

Up on the roof, Elfleda cradled a half-dozen slates and waited for the dragon to rear up a second time. When it came, the head was turned side-on, blinking its vertical lids. The first slate she threw wheeled over its skull. The second hit it below its lugless ear. The third hit the cook as she leaped to her feet and fled along the roof, yelping and keeling over away from the precipitous drop. Half-way along, she seemed to be stricken with guilt at leaving the mistress, and stopped, overbalancing so that she had to make a grab at the stonework to keep from falling. She pulled the slab of cheese out of her pocket and hurled it at the dragon. She saw it squat back on its tail which twitched on the broken slates, then spring forward irritably against the wall, driving its forepaws into the wattle, and barking over the parapet.

Up on the roof, Elfleda's self-possession deserted her and she spread-eagled herself against the roof pitch she had stripped bare of its tiles, reaching up for the remaining ones. She missed her handhold and almost slipped between the batons. Then, seeing the canopy of her own bed directly below the rafters, she lowered herself through, slowly, slowly, clutching at the splintery timber until her feet came to rest on the canopy.

Elshender turned full circle, sweeping the yard's litter into a heap in the crook of his tail. It had occurred to him that by retreating a little way and rearing up at full stretch he could gain a clear view of the roof. He saw the cook cowering in a corner. He saw the bare hole in the gaping roof, like the flesh flayed off the rib-cage of a man. But of Elfleda there was no sign at all.

When Anselm was still three furlongs away, he could see the amber head of the dragon bobbing up above the wall of his house. Alban could see it too, and stood up on the flat, calling out delightedly. Mann could not see well enough to make it out, but deduced from the other men what they were seeing. He leaned across and hauled on the nearest rein, so that the horse reached round its head and snatched at the bit: 'Woah! Woah back!'

Anselm pushed him away roughly, but the cart had already lunged off the path and was rolling through a bog. The horse came to a halt, the steam rising off it in clouds.

It took an hour, a month, a year to unfasten the shafts and free the horse and cut short the reins. There was a clamour of noise around Anselm while he did it, but he was entirely deaf to the serving-man and the monk. They were no more than horse-flies or wasps. He was brass. He was barricaded with terror.

Clambering on to the horse, he felt it sag and empty its belly – an old saddle-horse that had thought to have escaped the brutality of the gallop and heels in its groin. Anselm, splayed over-wide on its balding back, thought how he was too old for riding bareback. He was too old for griefs like this. He was too old for the kind of love that cleared a channel through his clay as wide as the Severn. He was of an age only for losing friends and relations in increasingly frequent bouts of death. But he would never reach an age fit for losing Elfleda.

There was only one pocket of energy trapped in him, like a parcel of air trapped in an overturned boat. It sustained life and panic without sustaining hope at all. He was too young and would always be too young to lose Elfleda.

'*Elshender!* Elshender, son of Leo! Elshender, you dragon! *Come out!*'

He rode directly to the wall and round its boundary until he saw white garments flapping on the roof like a surrender. He rose up in his stirrups: '*Elfleda!*'

But it was only his cook, the wind and sun catching on her petticoats as she waved her arms over her head. 'Master! Poor Master! Filthy murdering beast! It ate her! It's ate her! She's gone! It reared up over and she's gone! Kill it, master! That poor, lovely girl! Kill it! Kill it! Blast it to hell, master! Sweet Christ! *Don't let it take me the same!*'

Suddenly the amber head with its flaccid white jowl reared up between Anselm and the flapping figure on the roof. It parted its white lids, and the yellow eye inside contracted as it focused on Anselm. Saliva as white as seminal lust ran from between its teeth.

16

CONFLICTS

It was extremely dark in Hell, with red asterisks and a heat-shimmer off the coals, and the throbbing of blood and the shared ache of Sisyphus in the perpetual bursting of his heart, and the communal agony of Prometheus in the first perpetual slash of beaks at his bowels. The place was full of silent screaming.

And all of Hell fitted inside the kernel of Anselm's brain. And one blow from the dragon's claw would crack the shell of his skull and spill Hell over the surface of the world. Let it.

The still, ruthless trees made smug spectators. The knots in the wood of his gate boggled after him. The grass infested the earth in a green swarm. Anselm pulled a plank rail off the cart to use for a quarterstaff and he tied clogs of wood – the cart-chocks – to either end of the broken rein to use for a mace.

All the while, he was fly-blown with monk. Alban picked and tugged at his clothing, repeating, 'You promised! You said you'd not hurt him! You lied! You lied! You lied!' Anselm had no time or care to swat him. He supposed the damned should expect to be fly-blown in Hell.

He mounted the horse off the tail-board, and the clogs swung and clacked beneath its belly, startling it so that it yerked and pitched. The gates swung out. The dragon pushed its way out with its chest distended and its head back. Its lips were rolled off its teeth. It dragged a flotsam of yard rubbish and dung in the angle of its tail, and its head sawed to and fro, to and fro.

Only flogging moved the horse forwards – in diagonal leaps, its ears back and its eyes rolling in time with the 'whaa, whaa' of the mace whirling.

Anselm let fly, and the chocks missed by a chain. The dragon scuttered, lizard-like, dropping its head and stretching out its neck. Anselm rode clear round its reaching jaws and into its neck, beating at it with the quarterstaff.

At the sight of Anselm, bestial envy and resentment flared up in Elshender. To be challenged after gaining possession would have completed his achievement. But to be challenged while still unsatisfied, ungratified, and by the animal that had covered his mate, galled and baited him. His organs ached. He felt like a beast buried in quarried earth full of sharp stones. He loathed his body for its lethargy. He loathed it for its meagre smallness. He needed to be a beast tor-high, made of granite.

But when Anselm made his puny assault on his neck, Elshender recouped energy. He had only to snap at the horse's flanks to send it bolting under his neck and leave Anselm unhorsed, sprawled beneath his front feet. Elshender trampled. He dropped his head and snapped. A tooth caught in Anselm's tunic, but he slipped out of it, leaving the leather to flap and gag in Elshender's mouth.

Anselm pulled out his sword. Elshender trod it out of his hand, breaking the blade off short. The claws slit the suede of his uncle's split-skin summer boots.

But there was no self-protection in Anselm, no retreat, no respite, no strategy. He was simply flinging the big weight of his body into Elshender's throat, battering at the loose pectoral flesh where it sagged within reach. Both hands on the haft and the sword over his head, he thumped it in, over and over and over again, and the little broken blade crunched through the skin like teeth on gristle. He was strong to bring destruction down on his head – as strong as Samson in the temple.

The force of the blows on Elshender's neck jarred the breath out of his windpipe. He arched his neck like a swan – and then Anselm had him by the nostrils, by the fronds of knotted hair in his nostrils, by the spindly cartilage that kept his nostrils apart.

Elshender's jaw closed. His eyes closed. In flinching, the blistered burns on his hide scribbled 'pain' along his flanks: P – A – I – N. A word which could by rights be confided without shame to a boy's uncle . . . Elshender gave a whimpering cry and fell on his knees.

Anselm picked up the broken blade of his sword and wedged it into the serried scales over the beast's clavicle. He turned round to pick up the wooden stave and drive home the metal.

Alban was holding it high over his head. He meant to bring it down on Anselm's head, but missed entirely and only broke his arm. The second blow, to the back of the neck, knocked him unconscious.

Elshender waited before opening his eyes. He was suspicious of the shadows he could see beyond his opaque lids. And he was soothed by the caresses of a hand over his skull. His nose throbbed. The familiar smell of Alban was a comfort. He set free a shuddering sigh and blinked his eyes.

His uncle was lying, bound hand and foot with leather reins, in the angle between his dragon-legs and body.

'This is your uncle,' said Alban condescendingly. 'Your kin. And he knows who you are.'

'Mmmm,' said the dragon – his only approximation at a human expression. His uncle did not stir. Other recollections dribbled into his mind.

The monk put a tentative hand on the man's shoulder. It flinched. 'Sir. This is your nephew whose life you are bound to defend.' But Anselm did not respond. Elshender was puzzled. He struggled, too, with an explanation of the pain in his nose.

Alban bit his lip and stroked his dragon. The old serving-man had disappeared and was running cross-country to raise hell, to raise Bruno. 'You must stir yourselves,' he said without conviction. 'You both have worse enemies than each other.'

At last Anselm began to speak, breaking off in paroxysms of mirthless laughter: 'He ate . . .' The fact was death by inches, but the words were too absurd to speak – too ludicrously comical, like the anecdotal tragedies that reduce a table to raucous hilarity: 'They amputated the wrong leg . . . slipped in the slurry and the pigs ate him . . . his heart gave out on the wedding night . . . and he ate my wife . . . he ate my wife . . . he ate my unborn child.'

There were no rocks for an alphabet. Alban installed a log, a clump of fungus and the cart-chocks to signify 'Yes', 'No' and 'I don't know'. Then he invited Anselm to question his nephew.

' "Why" is the only question I have for him,' said Anselm. 'Why?'

'Don't be difficult, sir,' said Alban. 'Whatever he's done was done out of nature. His nature's to blame.'

Elshender was angry. He wanted to express his grievance at being robbed of Elfleda; he yearned to trample Anselm where he lay. But nothing could be said with 'Yes', 'No' and 'I don't know'.

The monk was bent on putting him through his paces. 'Are you Elshender, son of Leo and nephew to this man?'

Laboriously Elshender got to his feet.

YES.

'Did Gwyne do this to you?'

YES.

'Is the man Bruno her associate?'

YES.

'Is your sister similarly cast down?'

Despite himself, Anselm had to watch the dragon go through its tricks.

'Is she drowned in the sea?'

Elshender went to the same marker, then paused and turned to register his uncertainty.

'You don't know if she's drowned?'

I DON'T KNOW.

Anselm began: 'Did you know Elfleda was with . . .'

Elshender drew back his head and snarled.

'Please! I beg you, sir! Think how to mend the harm!' cried Alban, his hand over his face. 'In God's name! I can't stand all this warring!'

'He ate . . .' Anselm shook his head and was silent. He began to brood on his broken arm. If it came to fighting Bruno, the dragon made a sorry ally, with its shiny patches of burned skin and curled scales and treacly blood, standing there resting on the sides of its paw-like feet. Its neck was sunk between its shoulders and its eyes were rheumy and dull. 'You lump of anthrax,' he said. 'Gwyne's men will cut you in pieces.'

The eye-slits flickered, and Elshender pounced forward on the clump of fungus as if to cry 'NO!', and tore it and tore it between his teeth and scattered the orange-spotted caps all around in the grass.

In the new church, the stonemason and the painter were working, with each other for company, despite the dwindling evening light. Whereas the one had first-hand knowledge of the Lord Leo's sickness, the other, a monk from the priory, had witnessed first-hand Leo's recovery and the dispute over the dragon's monk.

'Well, I always took the gentleman Anselm for honest. Passing honest. I'd hold his part in most quarrels.'

'Not if you'd seen the way he treated with the Prior. Jesu! I thought a thunderbolt would strike him down when he took the feet from under the Prior. Mind, I don't hold with burning men for being mad. The wind was in a few tails, if you have my meaning.'

'So where are they now?' said the stonemason, beginning to chip at the ceiling again.

'Who?'

'Lord and brother, course.'

'Gone to the castle's my guess, but I'd sit down with the Devil to dine before I'd take that dragon's monk near the child. He might be powered to swallow it – or sprinkle plague on it – or turn it into a pig!'

'And I'm telling you, if Anselm values him there's good in'm someplace. Two brothers are bound to fall out now and again. There's another reason I'd lean to Anselm if it came to't. I mean, you don't know where you are with a man what's whipped in with his wife's tongue. If you're going to judge a man on his wife, I mean Anselm would have an army and a half. I never saw a woman the like of that de Rochfoll girl since she married.'

'But he ain't lord, is he? Nor ever showed a wish to be till now. I've no down on Anselm, but you can't talk about choosing between. He's never wanted the castle. And now he's got a woman like that . . . faith, what's to get him out of bed? At least Gwyne keeps Leo jumping. He gets things done.'

'Won't be much doing from now on. You didn't see him like me. Like a pod with no peas in. Dead as a brick.'

'And I'm telling you he was fit to ride home and see his heir. 'Sides – there'll be his son now, if he dies.'

'And fifteen years of Gwyne in between.'

'Maybe. If God wills it.'

'Oh yes. That too. And if the dragon don't eat us all and it ain't the End of the World,' said the stonemason.

'Do you ever think it? All this work, and then the world up and ends next week?'

'God spare us.'

'God spare us . . . Someone's out there.'

'Let me down, will you? Who is it?'

Before going to the hoist, the painter went to the door and opened it into the face of Anselm. The low sun dazzled round him, and the painter stepped back in deference to his size. 'Praise God, it's the gentleman Anselm, sir,' he said loudly, for the benefit of the man strung up in the basket.

The stonemason peered over and wondered if, in good time, this whole pleat of history would unfold below his basket. 'Is your dear brother well?' he called down to Anselm.

'Father to a boy, master. There'll be a thanksgiving here shortly. Is the church ready?' It was Anselm and not quite Anselm.

'Not what you'd call ready, sir. But it's fit after a fashion.'

'Well, now I think me,' said Anselm, 'the place isn't sacred yet and I have a thing to stow here. So let's say the castle. Tomorrow early. Can you make it known? Generally? Abroad? It's the mother's wish for everyone to join in celebrating. It'll go amiss if there's only a handful there. Can I trust you, masters?'

'Yes, sir!'

'Oh yes, sir! If the paths are safe, sir, we'll tell everyone there is!'

'In the mean time, I've a thing to stow here. So if you'd clear the floor . . .'

'A thing, sir. Excellent, sir.'

The mason and monk looked round at the few chisels and shards and pans of paint lying about the floor. 'What manner of a thing, sir?'

'A harmless creature that's dying of its injuries. A big cow. A lizard of a thing. To my shame I did it a mortal injury.'

The mason grabbed up his tool-bag and stared round for the nearest way to leave. 'De'il and damnation, he's brought the dragon here!'

'To my church?' said the monk, and for a moment there was no morsel of fealty left. Only Anselm's size and quarterstaff made them glad to have him there – between them and the beast.

'And have you killed it, master's-brother? Is it out there now? Why can't it die out there?'

'Dead on its feet,' said Anselm, though speech itself seemed to be a hardship.

They scampered this way and that, sweeping the floor clean with their feet, scattering chips of stone into the corners, while Anselm heaved open the double doors. The men bolted out through a nave window, one helping the other through; and

211

he let them go, knowing that ghoulish fascination would fetch them back to spy.

The dragon stretched out its neck, lowered its shoulders and minced in under the keystone. It was a dragon-shaped door – a door that might have been built for a dragon. The beast turned and turned like a cat, following its tail into a cringe, and whiffled through the hairs of its swollen nostrils.

The monk and mason ran away leaden-legged, in the direction of the priory. Night ran up from the horizon to meet them, and the sparse rain from a ripple of high cloud.

On the dark, solitary walk between the new church and the castle, Anselm reflected on the day, on the past days. He tried to envisage the shape and brightness of Elfleda. Like a dream of rare and pleasurable clarity, she might be reclaimed from fragmentation if he clung tight to the image in his mind's eye. The shape and scent of her within the bow of his body, holding his hand over her child, and a pigeon ricocheting off the window-arch. In the pitch darkness the rain struck him front and back through his clothing, as if he were a substance that the rain passed through. But he had her image perfect. A book was open at a page: it could not have been more clearly legible: the book that she had fetched from her room and made him swear upon, the book he had dropped and which fell on the landing and which lay open where an angel illuminated an English sky – an angel with hair like spun sugar and brows like the risers over two notes of plainsong . . .

A dirty night wind full of the smells of the castle midden blew in Anselm's face. It turned and muddled the face of the angel, the page of the book, the face of the owner, the scent of her body in the bow of his, the fluttering pigeon. And all of the sky behind it, as far as infinity.

'I am stillborn,' said Anselm. Having quickened so late and so soon died, he resented the need to haul himself out of the vacant darkness into some bloody, tangled knot of intrigue at the castle. It would benefit none but his kin.

But being dead, he had no volition, of course. All he could do was to refrain from crying. He scorned to cry while events dragged him out into the light. Only silently, in the dark.

17

Mouths

Bruno was not sitting on the bed when Anselm entered, but there was a crescent-shaped crease in the cover to show where he had been. He was dressed according to his new position – steward, at a quick estimate – in a knee-length coat inappropriate to his age. It was like seeing a young woman in matron's headcloths. He was also wearing red leather shoes.

They exchanged wholly vacant looks. Behind Anselm, Mann was on his knees in the passageway. He had brought incomplete news to the castle of the fight with the dragon; incorrect news, but now here was Anselm happily to contradict him. 'Praise the Lord! Praise God and all his spirits! What a day in a week in a year!'

'Be quiet, Mann,' said Gwyne loudly. 'So, 'Selm, you've truly delivered us all from our peril?'

'And you, madam, have delivered us promise for the future. The baby's well?'

'Perfectly, I thank you. But you are not. What am I thinking of to keep you standing untended? Sit here by me, on the bed, and tell me again. You've killed it?'

Anselm did not sit down. 'I have, madam. Outside the walls of my house. I'll need to borrow drays tomorrow to drag the stench farther off. Where's my brother?'

Gwyne distorted her nostrils in an expression which had often been called charming when she was younger. 'Where would he be while you are conquering our dragons? Paralytic with drink. Sleeping in his cups.'

'He has great cause to celebrate, sister. You mustn't be harsh with him,' said Anselm smilingly. He guessed that Leo was, for the time being, still alive somewhere in the castle. 'No man could have been more mindful of the birth. I was there. He made arrangements then and there with the Prior for a thanksgiving tomorrow –'

'A thanksgiving?'

'. . . at dawn, yes. And he put such terror into the carls and serfs up there that they'd crawl through the teeth of the dragon itself to get here, as he told them to. He was up with the angels in his rejoicing.'

'And now he's down there with the pigs,' said Bruno, pointing his thumb at the floor and smiling. Anselm considered which way to split him.

'Steward! Off with you,' said Gwyne, as if to a toddler, and Bruno, having given this some thought, settled his coat on his shoulders and left, pushing Mann along the corridor ahead of him. Sodden with tearful rejoicing, Mann could be heard all the way down the stairs by Gwyne and Anselm: 'I *saw*'m go down! I *saw* the Devil's monk hit him – wop! – like that, yes, just like that, sir – and I never thought to see'm again! So I ran. Went at it like a dog at a bear, he did, sir, but I thought he was done for when the Devil-man grounded him. If I'd 'a stayed on – God blight me for running – I'd 'a had a thing to tell . . .'

The bundle of linen on the bed beside Gwyne started up a little yelping cry. It startled Anselm, who had not thought the child was even in the room. He could not help suddenly wondering in what part of Elshender's labyrinthine gut his own child lay decomposing.

215

'Thanksgiving? What simpleness!' Gwyne was saying. 'Only your brother would think to rattle me over every rut in the countryside for the maggotty villeins to gawp at. I wouldn't stand at the window to be gaped at by my own chattels.'

'Oh *here*, madam. *Here*. He'd not make you travel so soon. Here at the castle. Everyone of any credit or birth will be here who can travel in the time! The way things are, I think he was wise. Sister, you must know how sick a man he is – I don't want to cast gloom over such a joyful day, but you must surely know it in your heart, lady. He's sick to the edge of death, as I'm a Christian. If he wants clearly to disinherit Elshender in favour of this new son of his – I know that's his intent – he spilled it to me at the priory. And if that's his intent, he'd best do it clearly and publicly and soon.'

Gwyne's scowl was a thing to see: it contracted her features into the centre of her face as if the sides of an altar-cloth had been lifted and all the church silver jumbled together. She ran her eyes over Anselm and decided all this was too fortunate by half. When she pounced, Anselm felt like a leaf in the jaws of a locust.

'Leo was expressly preparing the new church in time for the birth! Why would he say *here*? I don't believe he sent word to anyone. Besides – they won't brave the dragon.' Her voice was rising in such a way as to fetch soft red leather shoes up the stairs again to a place of concealment beyond the door-hanging.

'Madam, madam, calm yourself!' said Anselm solicitously. 'I'd not realised you were still in the fever of childbirth, or I'd not have taxed your peace and quiet with politics. The dragon's dead, madam. I killed it. Send your horsemaster –

216

forgive me, your steward – to see. I'm fair sorry about the church, but the masons up there found spoors of the beast inside the nave and they think it made its den there after the burning of the mill. In time it can be hallowed, cleaned, finished, sanctified and so forth. But you see, time's the thing we lack! Time's the thing my brother lacks if he's to lay his mantle on your child, sister. I'm fair sorry about the church. It may be rumour, of course. The beast maybe never went inside it. But that monk Alban – the one they call the dragon's monk?'

'I know it, I know it. Well?' said Gwyne smoothing out her features with her fingertips, reassembling her handsome face.

'After I killed the beast, the lad did this,' he nodded down at the one arm he was cradling with the other. 'And though I hurt him in recompense, and went after him a mile or more, I had nothing left in me for the taking of him. It's my belief the boy ran to earth like a dogfox – to the last earth. To the new church. He went in that direction. He's surely there now, and maybe he'll die there, seeing how I cut him.'

Gwyne reached out her arms towards Anselm. 'Brother! I'm the folly of the world. Come here and let me see your arm. You poor creature. You great lion of a man! I hope your sweet wife didn't see you struggle with the dragon. She would be dead of fright, poor lamb.'

The red shoes lipping under the door-hanging withdrew, and the sound, or rather the breathing silence, of Bruno spiralled down the end staircase and unfastened the bolt on an outside door.

'Oh my dear sister, did you not know? Did Mann not tell you? The beast destroyed my wife before I could kill it. You're a realistic judge of men, Gwyne, you know when it's time for a horsemaster to be a steward. I dare say in your shrewdness

217

you know I lack ambition entirely. Once I've seen the estate settled and my brother's wishes served, I'm content to lay my head down on the earth and let the rain rain me back to dust. Now she's gone.'

Gwyne was scowling again, unwilling to believe in her own good luck. But when she looked into his face, all her powers of intuition, divination and common sense combined to say that Anselm had just told her the truth.

There was no real risk that Bruno would go in search of the dead dragon. Alban's survival obsessed him, the need for him to be silenced. He must be cut off for owning the one lascivious secret that could set the whole countryside against Gwyne. But Bruno had his own reasons for being dedicated to the enterprise. Alban had made him run and sweat and shout, had demeaned his physical dignity. The giant Anselm he had had at his bidding, had had within reach of his knife-point. At least twice he had let him live. And Anselm had been made a cat's-paw, too, in slaughtering the dragon. Alban was a different matter.

He had with him, for light, a tallow wick-cord round his waist. He paused to light it only when his horse was in the lee of the church building. He struck for a spark against the flint wall. Rain was running off the roof on to his shoulders in a sparse curtain, and it took some time.

Inside the church, Elshender lay listening to the flint smash against the wall over and over again. He heard Bruno graze his fingers. He heard the grunt of satisfaction as the shred of sheep's-fluff kindling caught and the tallow lit. He was back in the mill, listening to the quiet, breathing sound of the thatch catching, the gradual crescendo. His gullet swelled with fear.

His lower jaw began to judder. His claws scratched horribly on the stone flags. His nostrils dilated.

Bruno opened the door and hesitated for a moment, catching his breath against the smell. But having worked with horses and murder, he was inured to the smell of dung and decay. He came on, whirling the wick-cord so that the glowing end made a wide halo round his beautiful head. The angels' heads up in the roof were not half so perfectly finished and were set on poor, miniature, disproportionate bodies – not like this scarless head planted on its classical torso. Bruno breasted the darkness, with his hornet-light whirling and his body swelling with conquest.

'Monk! I can *smell* you!' he called, as with deliberate movements he shut the door and barred any escape.

'Please don't kill me,' said Alban's voice from the altar end.

Bruno let the wick hang, so that its glow increased to a flame. The radiance grew round his feet. He was as beautiful as Lucifer landscaping Hell. 'I'm coming for you, monk. Soon you'll be as dead as that dragon of yours.'

The glow spread to encompass a paw-like foot, a scaly flank, a pale area veiny like tripe. And then, swinging into the aurora, came a lip and a lobeless ear and a white eye crossed through with a vertical line. The vertical lids parted and an amber eye as dull as soapstone stared at Bruno.

From a standing start he jumped half-way up the ladder to the gallery. But Elshender, though he allowed the man to finish his climb, simply reached over the gallery rail and took him as he stepped off the top of the ladder.

The width of the narrow lower jaw was scarcely the length of Bruno's back. But the top jaw was wider. Its soft lips creased across his chest and thighs. Only his head and shins hung

219

down, and one arm could feel the saliva ducts trickle hot and viscous on to the tongue, heaped up beneath him.

'Think on, Elshender,' said the monk's restraining voice from the altar end. Bruno stopped screaming.

'I've brought you your mull,' said Gwyne, swooping into Leo's arc of vision. In his confusion, he put one arm up over his face, thinking she was a scavenger bird.

'Not carrion yet,' he said.

'So. You can speak still, can you?' she said, lifting his head by the nape of his neck to push another bolster under it. Huge with milk, one-handed as she clutched the baby, she seemed more than ever to outclass him in weight and strength. He supposed she must, in fact, be weak – enfeebled – but he had no way of putting her resources to the test.

'The boy?'

'As lusty as his father,' she said, and wrapped his numb fingers round the goblet.

When he looked down into it, he could not recognise the reflection he saw. 'This is poison,' he said.

'That's right. Will you drink it, or go thirsty? Only a day or two either way. I've said I'll let no one tend you but me. Well? Aren't you thirsty? It's palatable enough, isn't it? You've drunk it for months and relished it.'

'And the boy?' said Leo. His eyes filled with tears.

'Bruno's. You know Bruno – the one who used to exercise your horses. All of them. He's very fond of "riding", Bruno. He's my steward now. He'll be back soon from killing a creature. Then he'll come and help you drink down your mull – or maybe cut out your tongue. Can't have you speaking against your own little heir at the thanksgiving. One sip now,

220

and there'll be no need. That's it. Just a sad presence clinging on to the hope of seeing his heir established. They'll love you for it. The rabble will talk of nothing else for months.'

'Still need me. Need me to . . .' Words were like snails in his mouth.

'To speak for the babe? Not at all! Your wet bladder of a brother has smoothed every obstacle. He can't wait to speak up for your little son. He saw you dancing like David at the news. He'll swear you mean the little fellow to inherit. And the whole county will hang on his words: he's the hero of the hour, didn't I tell you? If your sickness abates tomorrow I'll simply lock you in here and say you're too unwell. Anselm will speak for you. Ah, but I must give you an incentive, my dear! I know! I swear by your cuckolder, by my own dear Bruno, that if you give a nod of assent or a cheerful grunt when you're asked to invest the child, I'll let Anselm live. At least this year. Maybe next year, too. I'll have to persuade Bruno. He's right fond of slitting throats. But then I can persuade Bruno to near anything. And you know what? If you frown or mouth or look askance, I'll treat that brother of yours to a tun of this same Rhenish. Agreed?'

'Do it. Let him go. Elshender. 'Shender's my heir. Won't.' Leo wept, and the tears crawled into his ears. He could not speak again.

'Oh, but Elshender's dead.'

Having waited so long to say it, Gwyne inevitably mistimed the thrust. Cherishing it too profoundly to let go, she repeated it:

'Elshender's dead. I can't forgive you for thwarting me, mind. You sank down too fast under the philtres. I should've known how tardy you'd be – what a coward you'd be in

221

fighting the dragon. I lived for the day you'd come home with its head in a bag and strut and crow and have the monks bless you and have guests licking wine off the cellar floor. Like at our marriage.

'And I'd have let you stand up on the table and make your oration and say how you stabbed it here and gouged it there, and what torments you put it to in the killing. And then I'd have drawn you aside and said to you, "I made that dragon."

'*I made it*. And I'd ask you, "D'you know what matter I made it of? Not a dog nor a cow nor a lizard, nor a villein nor a foreigner. Not even a string of monks. No, only the best. I made it from Elshender. By magic. I made Elshender into that dragon and made your daughter into a fish of the sea. And the sea's too big ever to find your finny Frideswide – unless we ate her last night at dinner. And isn't death too good for the man who slaughtered that poor boy while he was wrapped up in dragon?

' ". . . Not *me. I* didn't kill him. Not though he stood in the way of my own child, I didn't kill him. *You* killed him, with your own hands and sword." Wouldn't you have searched the world over to find yourself a worse death in penance? You got off lightly.

'Burn till Doomsday and I'll never forgive you for robbing me of that joy. Your brother had to do the thing for you. He had to cut off his nephew. Oh and look now – what a sin and a sorrow! – not before Elshender had eaten his own sweetheart. Just think of that! They do talk of devouring lust, but I dare swear Elfleda didn't take much delight in *that* consummation!

'So. No straggling branches on this family tree. There's been a hard pruning this year. Only the new stock from a healthy graft. What, Frog? What does that gawp mean? Should I get back to my cauldron and brew up a magic to spirit you into the next world? Should I use my precious fluid to change you into a rat before you go? Don't think I've not thought of it. But there's too little to waste on a dead thing. I'll save the distillation year by year – to give wings to my Bruno. Should I do that? Should I transform my Bruno into an angel – a demigod for men to fall down and worship? No, he's that already. And I'll need my honey to stick his affections to me, him being younger. Think. When you're dust, and my bastard boy is full-grown, I'll still be young; I'll still be Queen-of-the-May. Even the boy will love me. Yes. Yes, I'll see to it. Even the boy will pant for me. Like you did. And Bruno.'

She wandered, sweating, through this imagined era as she held the cup against Leo's mouth. She tipped his head forward, so that the hot wine covered his lip and nostrils. Even in such a small cup, she could have drowned him.

But the sound of several horses in the yard below hurried her away to her bed. Guests arriving for the thanksgiving were told that the Lady Gwyne was still too weak after the birth to conduct any audience. They were, however, welcome to every comfort until such time as the Thanksgiving and Declaration of Heir could be arranged.

Palely adorable – both statuesque and fragile – Gwyne appeared wearing loose white linen, cradling her sleeping son. Four waiting-women held the posts of a canopy over her, to keep off the rain. A ripple of applause circled the yard, followed by a murmur of devout pity as a stretcher bearing the Lord Leo was brought down the outside stairs. Women wrung their hands in lament. Men bit their lips at the alarming slant of the stretcher and the way Leo rolled almost to the edge. One strengthless arm flopped down and had to be folded back across his chest by his brother, who was there in deferential attendance. A similar canopy was erected over Leo. It put the Prior in mind of the Transfiguration on the mountain and Peter's suggestion of booths to shelter Moses and Elijah. The Prior was tearful with mixed emotions.

Leo was an earthworks, a barrow, a mound of earth. And somewhere under the crushing weight of clay, buried alive in some small, dark recess of trapped air, his mind was a grave-robber clinging to one small hope. Snatched up before the barrow caved in, the hope seemed somehow to have the shape of his brother: Anselm the traitor, Anselm the ambitious usurper. Up at the priory, Anselm had wanted the title for himself.

Now Leo lay and waited. All his hopes were vested in Anselm's treachery. He longed for the sounds of the crowd to fetch him the news – that Anselm had knocked out the baby's brains on the ground. Leo closed his eyes and listened. But the noises were a jumble of nonsense.

Then the Prior was touching him on the shoulder, asking him to signify that the new-born child was his intended heir.

He turned his head a hair's breadth. He opened his mouth a sliver. He moved his tongue a morsel. And the grave-robber buried in the heart of the barrow bawled, 'NEVER!'

'I do believe I saw a nod!' said the Prior, beaming round at the assembly. 'Yes, I do believe the Lord Leo spoke his assent! Praise be to God our Father.' And he blessed Leo with expansive, theatrical gestures.

He wasn't to blame. He had made a perfectly genuine mistake.

18

Bartered Magic

The Lady Gwyne had not wanted to begin the ceremony until Bruno returned. His failure to appear unnerved her. She remembered how irritably he had taken the abstinence forced on them by the last weeks of her confinement. Besides, she hungered to know that the troublesome monk was at long last dead. At each pagan festival there should be a sacrifice, and what better than the blood of Brother Alban at the investiture of Bruno's son?

Still, Anselm forced her hand finally. Wretched Anselm, with his melancholy eagerness to settle his affairs. Confounded Anselm, with his damnable recent discovery of etiquette: the minor nobility should not be kept standing; the Prior should not be kept waiting; the horses should not be left in one paddock for too long. The man would hardly sit still long enough for his arm to be splinted. And he kept on asking to see Leo.

That was the final obstinacy to which Gwyne gave way. She declared suddenly that the ceremony should begin, and sent word that Leo's litter should be carried down by the swiftest route – the outside staircase (rather than through the castle where it risked a collision with Anselm). She conveyed to the Prior her gratitude for his prompt ceremonial, but said she was feeling rather weary and could not be kept on her feet past half an hour.

The babble of peasants was hard to subdue. There was a raucous exchange of news: Anselm had finished the dragon! Lord Anselm, the master's brother himself, had single-handedly finished it. It was dying, probably even dead.

Dying?

Gwyne heard the word repeatedly. She tried to believe that rumour was slow to get its facts right. But where was Bruno to put the lie to it? In one whole night he had had plenty of time to ride on beyond the new church, to Anselm's house, and to see the carcase. Where was he with confirmation of its death?

Screwing up her eyes against the low morning light and the occasional sharp drop of rain, she watched the rumour wash round the courtyard and lap nearer, to where it was audible. The dragon was dying. The mason and church-painter had seen it. The Prior had to ask Gwyne twice to consign the grimbling baby to his arms.

'. . . up at the church. They saw it. Did'n look as dead as they'd 'a liked. Stretched out to die, it did. Or was about to. 'Swat the Lord's brother said it was about.'

Her eyes came to rest on Anselm. He was standing so still against the doorpost, watching her; so still that he made the lumpen statue beside him look fidgety. He never once looked at the Prior as the cleric leaned over Leo and asked him to confirm the child as heir. He never even wasted a glance on his brother when the crowd greeted his heir with a cheer. He just went on looking at Gwyne until she crossed her hands over her breasts, feeling naked.

He was barbarous. Without his cloak in his mouth or his shoulders drooping, he was huge, as a bull is huge beside a cow. As he went on staring she began to tremble. He was not a ludicrous dancing bear at all. He was something dangerous and hungry, lured down to these festivities by a smell he savoured. He went on and on staring.

He was barbarous. She felt her bowels melt a little, and concluded then and there that she held Anselm in a thrall of desire. She merely wondered at what time it had begun.

'And you, Lord Anselm,' said the Prior as the cheering died down. 'Will you lend the strength of your arm to defend the rights of this little child and the wishes of your brother who was born lord over you and all of us?' The Prior was anxious – still nervous of usurpation. Hence the rhetoric, the grandiloquent gestures, the stirring-up of the crowd to bay for Anselm's 'yea'.

Anselm blinked slowly, then pushed himself off the doorpost and went to the foot of the outside stairs. He climbed a few then turned to speak to the assembly, stopped, looked across their heads, and climbed a few more steps. From there he could see both the courtyard and over the castle wall.

'Yesterday I fought with a dragon.' A unanimous cheer buckled the courtyard. The baby began to cry in panic. The Prior looked dismayed, wanting to give it back to Lady Gwyne, but Anselm was making his speech. 'I should not have fought with that beast, knowing it to be an innocent and blighted creature. But it had just given me a grief which left me . . . which cut out of me that part that makes a man human. I was brute beast for a time. Just like a priest without a god is a piece of blanket wrapped round a stone.

'And what when fear cut the nature out of those pagans up at Worm Head? What did they become, eh? A great ravening beast with a hundred legs, ripping its way through my father-in-law's house without shame or fealty, till the place was carrion-stripped.

'And what was that mob I saw up at the priory if it weren't a beast? It murdered the miller with one of its claws while all of its fifty pairs of eyes watched out of the darkness. I saw it coil itself round a poor mad lad, breathing fire and sulphur and bristling with spikes and clubs. There was no reasoning with it. It was a beast, see – without humanity, you see – though it looked uncommonly like fifty men and women I thought I knew for better.

'Wait! Don't stir! The man next to you might be a beast! Not breathing fire or eating cattle, no, but what if he crept one night on all fours into your house, into your room, into your mother's bed and made the two-backed beast with her? What would it make him? What would it make your mother if, in place of sinking down under the shame, she rose up and poured a potion down your open mouth that robbed you of speech and form – a potion that wrapped you in gristle and filled you up with fire? Afterwards your face is so bent that your neighbour screams to see it. But in all your toils of scale and stench – are you a worse thing than her? Do you deserve a burning? More than her?

'Look now! Here's a wonder. There's no blemish on this child. Nothing to show it comes of such a coupling. Nothing to look at but you'd take it for the child of Leo. My brother Leo, poor creature – though he has no more speech or movement left to him than a plant – he's still a Christian man inside that carcase of his and merits justice more than's been done here. Is his place to be filled by the child of Bruno the Horsemaster – Bruno the Mucker-Out – Bruno the Cuckolder, who stole that part of the good lady here that made her upright and set her rolling on her back like any farmyard beast . . .'

The courtyard began to heave, like a drying pond under a

228

hot sun when the fish break surface and gape for air. Gawping faces mouthed at Anselm, but the only actual noise came from the dogs which were hurling themselves at the gate and barking themselves off their feet. Gwyne's face was empty of all expression.

'Ah, but Gwyne is no common animal!' continued Anselm, and the blue veins grew like convolvulus up from the base of his throat. 'She's a civet-cat with pouches of poison in her private places. One poison slow and undetectable, to empty her bed of a husband and make way for a whore-master. The other for her stepson – that slighted husband's despised son, Elshender – who made this one, this only mistake: he found out Gwyne and Bruno when silks and velvets weren't hiding her dark fur or his ramshorn. He saw them for the beasts they were. And for that the civet-cat wrung out her drops into his mouth and made him just one more beast among the rest.

'There was no Vision. There was no Calling. There was no Saint Elshender. There was only a dragon lying alone in the open. And you and I baying with fright, hounding him through fire and water. I swear an oath that Gwyne is a sorceress and the downfall of my brother Leo, my nephew Elshender and, by her works, the source of every mischief to beset this Hundred. Open the gates and be quick to make amends, before God in His disgust blots out all of us in blotting out her!'

More than one looked up at the sky. They were pushed and trampled as the others shouted, 'It's out there now! The dragon's out there! Don't let'm open to it!'

The waiting-women with the canopy had already begun to back away from Gwyne, and now big raindrops twitched at her face. But only at the realisation that Elshender was alive

229

did she register any kind of terror. She twined her hair and twined her hair, but did not step one step out of her place. Only her scalp seemed to have shrunk, dragging the features of her face towards her hair-line.

Anselm let each man and woman's curiosity work and work and work. And then he said, 'Of all the many beasts I've met in this last year of my life, this one outside is the most innocent. See for yourself.'

But he did not need to rely absolutely on the thrill of the dare. Because during the night he had sawn through the batons that secured the crossbar. Outside, Elshender had only to lean on the gates to burst them open. 'Stand very still,' said Anselm.

Everyone but Gwyne believed him. She gathered together the skirts of her shapeless nursing-robes and started up the steps – not running, but in big, masculine strides. Her lips were pursed together so tightly that she seemed to have no mouth at all. Anselm barred her way, curious to know what she would do. The rather grotesque weight of headcloths heaped on her head had collapsed like a pile of laundry down her back, and fell strewn, unregarded, on the sodden steps. Her coppery hair came suddenly to light as she wiped her face with fingers incredulous at the temerity of the rain.

And then she laughed and said to Anselm, quite conversationally, 'I have you, booby. You should have put your wits to better use.' She put her hands through his arm, like a lover endorsing the object of her affections. 'Look at your dragon. Did you suppose he would make a meal of me?' Anselm could feel her trembling with either fright or excitement, but outwardly nothing showed but contempt.

Elshender, on the other hand, was jibbering visibly. His

back legs staggered. His jaw gulped at the air, and a stream of urine splashed down on to the tail that was curled hard up between his legs. He did not come on into the yard: he even took a few steps back.

His size alone held the assembly in thrall, but it seemed simply to entertain the lady. She addressed the crowd. Even before she had spoken a sentence, serf and gentility alike were cowed by her voice. 'My brother Anselm is right. I did make this thing. Look at it and tell me I'm not a masterly breeder of beasts. What should I make next, pray? A pig, out of you? A tribe of frogs out of your children? *Bo!*' She clapped her hands at the shuddering dragon. 'Well, see how little Elshender's come back to eat me up. What a dread beast! Owow, what a fate's in store for me! Listen, Elshender. Horsey, horsey! I know what sugar-cake you want from me. You want your dear body back. Yes, I have the magic. Yes, I may use it – a month or a year from now, or when I'm chasing Grace on my death-bed. Yes, I can restore you. I can restore your sister, too, who's a fat fish wallowing in the sea.' The crowd sucked in a communal breath. 'But only if I'm living – and only if I choose. Patience, lizard. Perhaps next year. Perhaps if you do some little service for me – such as eating up this fool-fond uncle of yours. What couldn't I ask of you, Elshender, that you wouldn't do for me? What wouldn't you do to have your body back and your sister out of the sea? Fall down on your knees and worship me, you hulk-ballast you!'

She broadcast her seeds of destruction: 'Compare, good people! Consider your fortunes. This morning you've invested a fairy child. In time I'll confide in him all the secret magics of my art. And who knows but he'll be a tolerant, open-fisted little lord one day? See, your alternative. What? To be in feud to a worm? Pay fealty to a newt?

231

'Now, Prior, give me my son, and let everyone fall down and reverence him. On your faces, reverence him. And you, dragon, you'll be my scaly lap-dog . . . I'll tell you the way of it! For seven years' faithful service, I'll fetch back your sister from the sea, your fishy little Frideswide. It shall be like Jacob working for Laban, to earn a bride. And seven years after that . . . Prior, give me my child.'

The Prior, who had the baby under the folds of his cloak, examined his conscience and drew the cloak shut. 'Madam, I will not.'

'Sir, you will. Or what might I make of you?'

The Prior began to invoke God, in Latin, under his breath. Gwyne was lifting her hand, pointing her finger. The child struggled inside his clothing like a demon. He closed his eyes, but went on seeing the wavering white tip of Gwyne's finger dancing in front of his face. He pursed his lips as if, like a wasp, it might stray inside him and sting. Oh God! But to be made into a beast!

He felt the back of his cloak lift. So soon, the transformation? He clutched tighter to the child, shouting out loud with fright. He was changing: something was happening to his knee!

Once, twice, Leo's hand squeezed the Prior's knee, which was the only part of him within reach, then the hand dropped down again, exhausted. The Prior turned and stared down at him – into Leo's half-open mouth – then stooped and collected up the hand from where it lay like litter on the ground. 'What must I do, sir?' But Leo could not say.

Then Anselm dropped down off the edge of the staircase and wrapped the Prior in an embrace. And into the yard, in long strides, came the monk Alban, leading a horse. Face-down across the horse, his ankles tied, hung a man. Alban pulled back the hood which had flopped down to hide the man's head, and Bruno screwed up his eyes against the light and the sight of the dragon.

Anselm stood below Gwyne now, but her height gave her no advantage over him. She was merely the lightweight end of the scales. Her hands were at her mouth. Her feet made little steps, first one way then the other. Her hands were in her hair, dragging the wet strands out of her eyes the better to see Bruno. She called out to him. Her hands were in her breast, plucking at the edge of her robe and cramming it into her mouth to silence her own submission.

Anselm said, 'Your magic is in a liquor. Elshender has told us as much. It can only be forced on the weak or the willing. Not on such as the Prior here who's strong in health and secure in the Lord.' (The Prior's face was exultant. He clutched Leo's hand to him in rapture.) 'Elshender did not come here to rifle it from you, or to kill you out of childish desperation. You see, Jacob bested Laban in the end. And when you've freed Elshender from his toils and fetched back his sister from the sea, then we'll talk of who shall live and who shall prosper and who shall be meat for the dragon.'

Gwyne came down the steps and across the yard, pushing people aside. 'Out of my way. Out of my way!' But as she approached the horse, Elshender, though his body was racked with shivers at the smell of her, laid the tip of his snout on Bruno's back and let his tongue loll out over the man's breeches. Bruno began to sob. The crowd began to spit on Gwyne.

'*Please*, Elshender,' said Gwyne.

After the distillation dropped from a muslin bag into a funnel, it trickled down into a green glass phial and stained it a sulphurous yellow. There was staining to the brim of the phial, but no more than a layer of liquid in the base. In all the time they stood there beside it, the single brown drop that bulged through the muslin only swelled and shook, but did not drip down. It was as slow as the sweat of decomposure. Elshender's dragoning had used costly months of the ferment. The sweat of the cave to which Gwyne took them could not be excited, by labour or conjuring, to flow more liberally.

The rigid limbs of small, dead creatures stretched the muslin bag. The smell of herbs was so sweet it all but made honeycombs of a man's cheekbones. They drew off what little had accumulated, and diluted it with wine, the Prior intoning prayers to keep his hand from shaking.

A mile away, the Mardi Gras caravan of serfs and minor gentry were encamped in the rooms and outhouses of the castle, waiting for good news or bad, miracles or a demonic cataclysm. They had been invited to leave, but like flies on a carcase they only circled and returned, buzzing even louder.

'Will this be enough?' Anselm asked Gwyne.

'Maybe,' said Gwyne.

'Is it enough for all three?'

Gwyne shrugged. She was at the door of the cave, watching the dragon lick and toy with her lover. 'What do you want to make of Leo that he's not already? I've only starched him. He'll soften in the wash.'

'He'll recover?'

She shrugged again. How was she to know, who had never concerned herself with remedies? 'Give it to this mongrel out here; change Elshender back into the runt he was. So long as there's an heir. That's all you care about.' Elshender had just taken hold of Bruno's feet and was dragging him up and down, leaving dark furrows in the wet grass.

'And Frideswide?'

'Ah, give it, won't you? What's one pocky little maiden – even to Leo? Half the Hundred never even knew she was born. Here! Let me give it to him, if you won't!'

The Prior exulted in her show of remorse; she was so eager to undo her felony. Anselm stood by her in the doorway and watched the dragon play with Bruno like a cat with a bird, letting him start to break away, then fetching him down with paw or snout or tail.

'Frideswide too,' said Anselm.

'In time there'll be enough for the fish,' she said. 'There might be enough there.'

So Anselm looked around for a second container so as to divide the liquor: half for brother, half for sister. But they had brought only one. So small an oversight, it proved as big an impediment as forgetting the key to a door. 'Elshender!' called Anselm sharply. The dragon paid no heed, so engrossed was it in eating the clothing off Bruno as it held him down with one dextrous paw.

Brother Alban got up from beside a tree, the baby cradled on one arm. He went over to the dragon, trailing the ropes with which to rebind Bruno. 'Elshender!' he said, and the dragon broke off from its game and allowed itself to be drawn towards the cave by a hand in its jowl.

Anselm put the bowl of wine into Gwyne's hands and said, 'You must give it to him.'

'No! Don't trust her!' cried the Prior, so sharply that the wine slopped in the bowl and overran the rim.

Gwyne was panicked by more than the Prior's nervousness.

She mistrusted her own ability. 'I've not the feelings in me,' she said. 'I'm empty of the feelings. I must *want* the thing. Elshender – he's nothing. He stirs nothing in me. He's a . . . nothing.' She was plainly frightened. She was not asking to be spared the task, but she was afraid.

An awful inaction settled like a spell over the pack of them, and they stood and reflected, and imagined the appalling outcome of a partial restoration.

There was a sound of someone hot and weary climbing up the path from the castle. 'This way, madam. It was this way they came – though lord's brother Anselm had us on pain of death not to follow and make a crowd. Can you cope?'

Anselm went to cut off the sightseers – to turn them back down the hill and leave the stuff of magic to its private mysteries. God defend the general populace from witnessing the bungled reclamation of Elshender. God spare them, too, the peremptory executions of Gwyne and Bruno that would be forced on him then. It would be better for no one to return from the failure, and for folklore to supply an explanation. 'Mann, is that you? Go back down and take your customers with you! I told you . . .'

Mann's grinning face came up from below, then turned away as he gave a helping hand to the woman he was guiding. On the steep path, Elfleda had to choose her footholds carefully, and hold her skirts high up in one hand, exposing her legs to the knees. Her face was flushed with the exertion of the climb, and her hair, which had come unplaited, hung over one shoulder and split over the point of one breast. She was still smiling from the knowledge that Anselm was safe.

At the sight of him, she smiled more broadly and said, 'I

walked all the way from the house to tell you what a fearful bad day I've been passing this last while. I was going to rail at you for your slowness in coming home. But I hear you've been kept busy by matters of state, so I suppose . . .'

He ran and caught her up in his arms.

He was a mariner balanced on a yard-arm, in a black storm. Grabbing at a canvas full of spirited gusts and flurries of wind, he crammed it against his chest not just to reef it in but for lack of any other handhold. He went on until it stopped struggling in his frightened arms and was reefed, and he had safe hold, and the sky could no longer intervene to separate them.

By the time Anselm let Elfleda go, and readdressed himself to the dragon, he had travelled down many miles of thought and met with implications at every corner. He kissed her once more, told her to hold off at a distance, and insisted she cover her eyes against possible horror. Then he returned to Gwyne and took the bowl out of her hands. He said to her in a whisper, 'You say it would be as well for the magic to wish the thing . . . to wish Elshender more fearful than he is now.'

She nodded and reached out to take back the bowl. But Anselm turned and, with slow and careful steps to preserve every drop of the dangerous liquid, placed himself face to face with the dragon. He felt drunk, as if he had snuffed up too many of the fumes.

'Drink, Elshender,' he said. 'But leave half for your sister, if you care for her.'

The dragon turned its head side-on to look Anselm in the eye. It reached back, to scratch with its teeth an itch under its haunch – as if it might not have the opportunity later. Then it stuck its snout into the bowl and drank off most of the liquor, with a noise like ten pigs gorging.

237

19

REPARATIONS AND RESTITUTIONS

He did try to picture his sister: that girl who laughed and wept over trivia, who dressed up for no one, who talked ceaselessly about nothing.

He tried to imagine her tragedy, cut off from home and friends and possessions. And had it been winter, the thought of the terrible, remorseless, rolling cold of the sea might have helped him towards pity.

But with the sun beating down on his burned back, and the drink the first drink since dawn, and in it the promise of his body, Elshender ducked his head into the bowl and guzzled down most of the liquor. Pity is not a major characteristic of dragons.

He felt differently, lying in his flesh, when no one started towards him, when no one but hard-eyed men looked down on his brown and white nakedness. He would have liked Frideswide to be there, to fuss round him with sheets and embarrassment, to groan over his shiny red burns and shriek at the mesh of fine, shallow cuts on his chest, and to promise poultices for the various sores.

But Anselm – crazed Anselm who had tried to kill him – stood looking down into the bowl. And Gwyne was tending to the vile Bruno, pitying his wounds to the point of tears. And even Alban stood off at a distance, looking at a stranger he had never seen.

Alban looked, and said to himself, 'This was my dragon. Only a boy. He was my dragon just now. I should go to him.'

But Elshender was heir to a Hundred, doubtless full of disgust, revulsion for the thing he had been . . . not to be reminded. Besides, he could not be unaware – must still be aware – of the love that had existed between them. What hand laid on what part of Elshender in any gesture of comfort would make for a seemly act between them now? Alban found he could not countenance Elshender looking at him, and turned his head away.

It was left to the Prior to wrap Elshender in his cloak and ask him to speak if he was able.

'I'm weak,' said Elshender. 'I'm very tired and weak. And I itch.'

Then Elfleda came running out of the trees with feminine compassion and a gentle pair of hands to stroke his clarted hair. She even apologised for failing to know him – her own betrothed – when he had been wrapped in dragon. He saw how Anselm heard her, too. And some kind of an echoing shout down a long, dark corridor made Elshender sneer at his uncle while taking hold of Elfleda's head and holding it close.

Anselm turned and went back to Bruno, throwing Gwyne out of the way and lifting the man across his own shoulders. The Prior went back inside the cave to reinstate the green glass phial beneath the muslin bag. But whether his hand slipped, or his proper, lifelong values got the better of him, the distillation slipped and fell and smashed and scattered, and some of the oldest, mummified ingredients crumbled to sludgy dust on the floor. A castle dog ran off with something web-footed and dead in its mouth.

*

239

Armed men went with Anselm, Elshender and the rest to Worm Bay next day. No one could know for certain what change had overtaken the people who lived within the protection of their dragon-painted obelisks.

Having waited so long for retribution from the castle, the villagers were taken by surprise when it finally came. They thought that somehow they must have fallen through the grip of Leo's iron fist and been permitted to pursue their independent existence. Despite the poaching, the rustling, the disappearance of Brother Paul, they had begun to think themselves answerable only to the Seer. Perhaps because her rule was so binding, they had never felt anarchical or free.

Even when the streets and waterfront were crammed full of Anselm's levy of armed men, and villagers were herded together on the brink of the sea, with horses' heads wagging in their faces, their arrogance was almost intact. They were simply puzzled that the dragon, having gone inland, had left so many Christians as this uneaten.

Nothing interested Anselm but finding a boat and putting out to sea. Elshender, however, was among people who, a few days before, had worshipped him. He remembered them. And here he was, returning invested with his father's authority, and with the direction of forty men. The situation was novel.

He wished Alban had not come. He was ashamed of the memories they had in common. He was revolted by such memories as the sacrificial girl and the painted tablets. Surely that was the feeling in the pit of his stomach when he looked down into the villagers' upturned, sheep-placid faces? To look for a glint of recognition or awe in them – that would be almost perverted, wouldn't it? 'I need a boat,' he said, and was angry that his voice sounded so thin.

'And your Woman of Magic,' said Anselm.

'My lord Anselm, we must surely leave this in the hands of God!' protested the Prior, but he searched just as anxiously among the faces, in the hope that one might own some secret knowledge. He had, after all, broken the green phial. Frideswide's hopes were small.

The crowd parted. The Seer stood in the centre. They produced her like a bird out of a cuff, an egg out of a mouth, to conjure them out of their predicament. Her finery was grimy – a workaday regalia. The chalk on her face was haphazard.

'Are you a witch, woman?' snapped Elshender.

'No, sir!' said Mog. 'I just read the signs. The signs are there for all to see. There's some can read'm and there's some needs help reading'm.'

'Have the fish returned yet?' asked Anselm peaceably.

Mog hesitated each time before answering, looking for the trap that would fling her into the flames. It could probably not be avoided: she did not look for justice from such as Leo's kin. But she was not going to give them an easy blasphemy, nor one that would snare the whole village. Neither was she going to betray her season of glory. 'They been seen,' she said cautiously. 'Great shoals, close in. But we don't venture out on the sea no more. Not beyond the bar.'

'But the fish have come in over the bar, haven't they, Mother?' said a sharp, North Country voice. Alban, dressed in some of Anselm's clothes, his face shaven and his hair cut to shape and washed, spoke to Mog as if he knew her. And though he had never so much as glimpsed her, he did feel she was someone from the other end of a long rope he had once pulled on. 'When I was with the dragon, down on the beach, I saw a shoal there. Or was that the only time they came?'

Mog's composure slipped. 'You been with the Worm? Is it you? Is it the Worm's monk?' She tried to push forward to kiss his stirrup, but an armed man held a halberd to her throat. She was confused and excitable with hope. 'Not Christians, then? You know the Worm, all of you? You've come to worship the others – the ones in the sea! You're men o' the Worm!'

Elshender rode his horse forward into the woman so that she had to jump and clamber out of the way, and the halberd held across her body tore some of her regalia. Her browband slipped over her face. She looked up at him uncomprehendingly.

He suffered her to stare at him, thinking she must see him for what he was. Hadn't she recognised Alban? But she, of course, saw nothing but an acned youth with much of his hair burned off and his hollow chest packed out with aromatic flock wadding. She was eager only to get around him and touch the servant of the Worm.

'*I am the Dragon!*' The words roared unspoken around her blank, shovel-shaped face. Then Elshender reined away from her and gave an order to the halberdsman. 'Burn down the village.'

'Elshender, no!' cried Alban, and reached out and held his wrist. 'You're not your father yet,' said Anselm quickly, and restrained the halberdsman with a gesture.

Elshender looked into Alban's face.

'Please not,' said the monk.

'You, you heretic, you would defend blasphemers and witches,' he said. 'These pigs have abused their fealty. Now – all of you – burn it down.' And the halberdsman shrugged off Anselm's restraint, and followed his own inclination, setting a torch to the heathen sprawl.

242

Mog the Seer was bundled into the largest of the boats, and a crew was empressed, with offers of clemency. There were four for the oars, and a man at the tiller. But when they asked where to pull, they got no reply. Anselm, Alban, Elshender and the prisoner Gwyne boarded the boat, and the Prior blessed it as it pulled out from under the growing pall of smoke.

From beyond the bar, Worm Bay seemed fittingly named, with its outcrops of fire, its copses and spinneys of black timber, its low constellation of sparks, and the dour, beast-shaped cloud of smoke grazing over all.

No one explained to Mog the purpose of the boat trip, or what role she might serve, other than as hostage or scapegoat. She fully expected to be drowned in deep water. She could make nothing of their clownish behaviour.

The Lady Gwyne – all of a sudden a despised and man-handled creature, it would seem – crouched in the bottom of the boat with her arms clasped round her knees. Only once did she blurt out: 'If he dies I'll not help you. You can do as you like.' But though the others stopped peering over the side and stared at her blankly, it took Elshender to say, 'The strappado never killed a little runt like that.'

To which she replied, 'Lizard. I should have killed you at the very first.'

There was a dirty, broken swell running. Twice the Worm's monk pointed to a flurry of white water and shouted. The third time, Mog could not keep silent any more. 'Is it a catch of fish you're after, then?'

Alban looked round at her squatting in the stern by the tiller-man's knees, in her preposterous feathers and tear-streaked chalk. Her whole world was gone, and yet her curiosity far outweighed her despair. He was ashamed to be an

243

unwitting high priest in her foolish ceremonial. How could he fail to disappoint her now? He wished he could spare her the loss of her religion: it was not something he wished on anyone. 'Just the one fish,' he said, grinning at the absurdity of the thing. 'Just one particular fish out of the whole sea.'

'A dogfish,' said Elshender tartly.

They did not see how he could possibly know, but the way he said it forbade argument.

'A partic'lar dogfish,' said Mog, nodding her head.

'A female.'

'Ah, yes. I see. A partic'lar *female* dogfish,' she said, and exchanged a look with the helmsman which said that they were in the hands of madmen.

After half an hour, Elshender began to look green, and sat down low, with his head pressed back against the boards. The oarsmen stopped rowing, to spit on their hands, and since no one reviled them for it gave over the task of rowing, except to keep the boat head-on to the swell. It seemed that one place was as good as another to look for one particular female dogfish.

'A mackerel,' said Mog, without addressing any one person. 'It's mackerel to take nurse-hounds.'

'Ah, now we're saved,' said Alban drily. 'Now we have only to take a mackerel.'

'Look, you capon,' snapped Elshender, 'since you've no use for women, is my sister to rot in the sea? One more word and I'll throw you over to join her!'

Alban did not conceal his reaction, but it went unnoticed, for Mog had found her usefulness. She was assembling a fishing-line. Her costume was a miracle of concealment. With feathers from her headband and the fish-hooks that backed her abalone

244

buttons and twine that held up her skirt, she made up a jigging lure – a feathered rig which she ran over the side. It streamed out behind the boat. Even through the dirty water they could see the first few bright feathers dancing as she jerked the line. Nothing came.

'I suppose she warned them,' said Elshender under his breath. 'Put them wise to fishermen and hooks. She was a clever one, my sister.'

A moment later, the line took two fat fish. The success made the gentry slightly hysterical. They told Mog to let the mackerel trail, and stood up in the boat shouting, 'Frideswide! Frideswide! Daughter of Leo!'

'Oh my bones and blood,' said Mog, and sat down amidst her unfastened skirts.

'There!'

When the shoal was confirmed, even Gwyne got up out of the prow to watch the white fleece of spray come gliding in astern. Among an entourage of little leaping fish, two dark, cylindrical shapes rolled without breaking the surface themselves. Anselm jumped over Mog's legs, pushed the helmsman aside, and hauled up the string of hooks. The dogfish seemed to turn away.

'Look. Split'm. Like so,' said Mog, and clawed the guts out of one mackerel without detaching it from the hook. 'That's proper bait.'

'No. Give that to me.' Anselm unhooked the whole mackerel and threw it to Alban. 'Souse it in the liquor,' he said then called across the water, 'Frideswide?'

'It's her. I know it's her,' whimpered Elshender, and began to grow panicked by the recollection that he had drunk most of the liquor. He could hardly bring himself to look out to the pair of dogfish rolling in the wake. He simply kept saying, 'It's her. I know it's Frideswide. Poor little Frideswide!'

'You've scared 'em off with all that racket,' said Mog, when she lost sight of the big fish. 'Let that bait run out a bit, or you'll never take'm.'

Anselm snatched the trolling rig out of her hands and threw it all in the sea. 'We're not trying to hook her, you fool,' he said irritably.

Mog sat down again saying she had done trying to help. But Anselm squatted down in front of her with his hands on the bulwark to either side of her head. The look on his face was friendly, but his bulk was intimidating. 'Woman. Tell me, have you any kind of a *way* with sea creatures?'

'I don't rightly understand you, sir. I can catch fish, if the fish are there. If I got twine and hooks.'

'No, I mean can you . . . with your arts . . . can you make yourself *understood* to them?'

Mog gave a shriek and pushed him away. '*Talk* to 'em, you mean? You want me to jump in the fire my own self, don't you? You want to have me damn myself for a witch. Talk to fish!'

Anselm seemed on the verge of tears. 'That fish out there may be my niece – my brother's child – a poor girl not above fifteen. You can't though? It would be worth gold to you.'

After an age-long pause, Mog found one last shred of self-possession. 'I'll do't, sir – not for the money, sir, but as the mother of a dead child myself, and the widow of a man who's rolling in cold at the bottom of the sea. I'll try. But if you burn me for't after, sir – that would be a traitorous thing, now wouldn't it?'

So she stood up, with her top skirt round her feet, and Alban thrust the soused mackerel at her. 'What's this, then?' she asked, contemptuous of the pulpy thing in her hands.

'It's soaked in a liquor that might restore Frideswide. If she's once restored, she'll maybe thank you by keeping you from the hangman.'

'Maybe she will, maybe she won't,' said Mog, cheerful in her disbelief.

Elshender was crying quietly. He turned his face in towards Alban's chest and let himself be comforted.

'You hold my feet!' said Mog to the helmsman. 'And the Devil 'quit you if you drop me in on me head.'

She called across the water softly: 'Frideswide! Here child! Here girlie! There's some come to help you, darling. There's your uncle and your brother come with magic to fetch you back home. And there you'll be, with your pretty pink skin and hair all hanging down, and all those velvet robes still lying in your press. Come close, darling, and take this little fishy from me. Sweet as sherbet. And who'll be there to welcome you home, eh? Your father. And maybe a sweetheart or two?' In ducking up and down as the boat rolled, Mog caught sight of Alban shaking his head and signalling with an erasing motion of his hands that she was on dangerous ground.

The boat began to tilt, as the oarsmen shuffled along the thwart in the hope of seeing this wonder for themselves. The dogfish swimming astern moved gradually closer.

'You!' said Anselm to his sister-in-law. 'You must feed it to her!'

'I haven't the magic in me,' said Gwyne pleadingly. 'She has more than me! Let her do it!'

Mog turned back to the dogfish, her hand cupped round her ear.

'What's that you say, dearie? You're afeared of your step-mother? No need, darling. She's held fast. Look, we'll bind her and cast her over and drown her before your eyes, if that'll ease your mind.'

Gwyne began screaming, and Elshender wanted to know how Frideswide could make herself heard over such a racket.

'Well that's a fine, loving girl,' said Mog softly (though the distance between her and the fish would have needed strong lungs for hailing). 'I'm sure all your sins are forgiven, too, darling. Now gobble down this fish of mine and give me a pretty hand to pull you up out of the sea.'

Mog's big petticoated rump suddenly swayed, and she snatched her bait out of the water as she shrieked in surprise. One of the nurse-hounds came rushing towards her, its two dorsal fins directly in line.

It came so close that they could all see clearly the big black blotches down its rust-red body. It was close to five feet long, and rolled as it entered the lee of the boat, to show the intimate pallor of its soft white belly.

Elshender, fascinated, reached down to touch it.

'You'll cut yourself,' said Mog, and Elshender sucked in his breath. 'Told you. She's not for handling yet.' But the tone of Mog's voice was suddenly quite altered. Preposterous magic had taken a hand. She was ecstatic with amazement.

The dogfish turned on her back and showed them the crescent grin of her big mouth, opened and closed the flaps in her nostrils and let her ventral fins dandle on her belly. Then, with a flourish of the tail, she turned one large dark eye on the boat before swimming off.

The flurry of little fishes had subsided. There was only the other spotted dogfish, holding off at a greater distance than before, patrolling the surface layers while the wind scudded over his flank. As the female returned, she rolled in under him, and he reached out with splaying fins to rest on her back, and a pelvic hook to seize on her vent. A shudder sank them both out of sight. Elshender's spine stiffened, where he stood and gripped the bulwark. Gwyne crouched down as low as she could get in the bottom of the boat. Anselm felt himself blushing, and looked across to see the same colour in Alban's cheek.

'There you are! You hear that?' Mog clapped her hands in front of her face and laughed, almost convincingly. 'You've no call to worry yourself over the girl!'

'What?' said Elshender, who was suddenly green again. 'Why? What did she say?'

'That she's found herself a sweetheart among her own kind! The fishy kind, anyways. Didn't you see? She's mated. And she's well pleased with him, too. He's a prince among nurse-hounds!'

'But she was a virgin,' breathed Elshender, straining not to be sick.

'Wha' then! She was free to give herself away, eh! Where's the hurt in that? She's happy. She were free to choose, weren't she? Eh?'

Elshender saw his uncle spread one hand over his mouth and, though up until then he had seemed the seaworthy one, half heave himself over the side of the boat. Elshender righted himself with a smoothing of his hair, and straightened his clothes. He took the magic mackerel out of Mog's hands and flung it over the side. 'Let her go. She's happy. My little sister's content to my satisfaction. She *was* free to give herself, after all. Wasn't she, Uncle? Not like some others.'

Not until they were ashore, not until they had picked their way through the debris of Worm Bay to their horses, did Anselm or Elshender speak to one another. Seeing the ghosts of the huts in individual clouds of smoke, the burned-out hulls of boats like the smoking rib-cages of dead dragons, the eyes empty of hope, and the hands full of ash, Anselm was ashamed for Elshender. He pitied him the guilt he must be feeling for the spiteful act of firing the village. He felt he ought to say something reassuring. He said, 'They must have been expecting something of the kind. Leo might have done the same.'

But Elshender only jutted his chin and responded in a high, hinnying voice, 'I don't need Fa' to approve what I do. I mean, I don't wish the old man . . . I pray he gets better . . . But I've not much to thank him for while I've been . . . Or you, Uncle.'

"Shender! You surely don't hold us to blame for the hunting of you. Not Leo – not when he was innocent of what you were?'

Elshender half closed his eyes and sniffed. 'Not in the least, sir. But would you say he *protected my interests* while I was gone? Hardly. You'd be the first to admit, he was . . . quick to dispose of my chattels.'

Anselm's face turned brick-red, and a drop of sweat broke cover from his hair and ran for his beard. 'Leo disposed of nothing.'

'Then he let great advantage be taken of my absence.'

'Did you never hear it said, *What Man allows, God forbids*?'

Their voices had risen so much that the column of horses was jostled out of line by riders turning to stare. The two thwarted their eavesdropping with a long, agitated silence.

'What's that mean?' hissed Elshender, when he could no longer contain himself.

Anselm, who had been chewing on the border of his cloak, spat it out. He spoke with his eyes shut. 'Are you entirely ignorant of the facts, boy? Has it escaped you altogether that your "Brother" Alban is not in Orders – hasn't been since before he set foot in these parts? Has it missed your notice that there's not now and never *has* been a marriage? In ignorance . . . yes, in ignorance, I have done you a great mischief. But since there's no undoing it, I can only give you back what's left. And since what remains is a sweeter thing than most men ever aim at, I dare swear you'll take it and not despise it?'

The apoplectic agitation in his uncle's face excited Elshender into thoughtless retaliation. 'So-ho! You've drunk the wine and now you're offering me back the cup!' But then he slumped back in his saddle and into silent thought.

Anselm knew all the thoughts perching and preening and pecking in Elshender's head, for they had been in his own head since the first moment he learned of Elshender's condition. There was no impediment to a wedding, barring the waste that had been made of Elfleda's virginity. Deterrent enough, if it were not that widows marry.

And if he were to reject the offer of Elfleda, what other noble father would chance marrying his daughter to a man who had once been a dragon? There were scars on Elshender's body that would mark him out everlastingly for the boy who had worn dragon's flesh and stunk. Elfleda, on the other hand, was obligated to him legally: she had grown up anticipating the match – wanting it. No need to overcome revulsion or superstition. Just a sweet-faced, submissive girl, bound by bonds of betrothal to sweeten the lot of her much-abused lord.

Only one thought pecked on Anselm's brain that did not on Elshender's. The child in her was his. But if Elshender's marriage to her could be brought about quickly, no one need know. He must speak to Elfleda and persuade her of the need to keep silent . . . she would see the need herself.

Anselm wished he were in any doubt as to Elfleda's feelings. She would surely be overjoyed to recoup the marriage of her childhood dreams.

But he wished that the column of riders would increase its speed, the quicker to see her again, the quicker to reassure her of her future. He had left her that morning fully laden with the shameful knowledge that her marriage was no marriage. Bad enough that she had given up her maidenhead to escape the villagers' paganism. That she should have given it up to an old man not her husband forbade all mention. Anselm knew he could not bring himself to refer to it, but he still longed to reach the castle and see her again: to relieve her distress. He was impatient with the slow trot. He was impatient with Elshender for taking so long to reach an inevitable decision.

And yet suppose he did not? Suppose Elshender could not bring himself to forgive Elfleda's accidental shame, her innocent ruin? Suppose he could not forego the gratification of a virgin bride? Then there would be nothing for Anselm but to remarry his little Elfleda and continue the discreet miracle of his bliss into old age and death. Just suppose Elshender rejected her.

'I will. I'll do it!' shouted Elshender, with an edge to his voice as sharp as wire. 'I'll take her, if it's just to save her from your abuses, old man. You can pay me a hundred pounds' reparation for her maidenhead. And I'll have her to me tomorrow, and see if you got your money's worth! Was it worth a hundred pounds, Uncle? Well, was it?'

Anselm reined out of the column and galloped off at right-angles to it, sweeping round in a wide hoop until he was heading in the direction of the castle.

From a little way behind, Brother Alban said, in a voice not intended to reach the riders round about, 'Elshender, I loved you better when you were a dragon.'

20

CLAY SPARROWS

'We aren't married,' said Anselm again. 'We never were.' He took it for granted that she understood the implications.

'I realise that,' said Elfleda, smiling. He had fetched her away from tending Leo, helping him to a bowl of chicken jelly; she was anxious to get back indoors to him. Considering that he had arrived at the gallop, Anselm's movements and speech now were intolerably slow; they hung clogs on her quick, busy, cheerful excitement, so she protested, 'Anselm! We have no right to be gloomy! We should be celebrating! Elshender's saved. Leo's saved. The Hundred's rid of its dragon. Forgive me – I must be hardened in my sin – but I can't feel undone! Nothing I did was out of wicked intent! There must be a simple remedy!' And she clapped her hands in his face.

He tried not to flinch. 'Of course there is. Yes. Oh, yes. As usual, Elfleda, you make things easy. I'd thought you would be quicker to blame. I would to God I thought Elshender could match you in patience. I'm afraid he's too young . . . much younger than you in patience.'

'Patience? What should 'Shender be doing with patience at a time like this? Can you imagine how glad he must be to be a man again – in his rightful body?'

He could not pretend to be surprised by her happiness. He had to admit what a consolation Elshender would be for her humiliation. Now she could have the young husband she had wanted all along: a husband wearing that 'rightful body'. Instead of him.

She went chattering on. 'All morning I've been holding things – doing things – trying to imagine how it would be to be wrapped up in all that gross flesh and with no way of calling for help. I don't believe I'd have kept my wits. I hate myself for the way I treated that poor creature now. Don't you?'

'Naturally.'

'I mean, to want to kill a thing so much for its ugliness and its nature! Just because of its ugliness. And all the time the real monster was beautiful Gwyne and her pretty fellow. I'll never lay any trust in beauty again, will you 'Selm?'

'No, Elfleda. I suppose not.'

And where, without Elfleda, was the promise of beauty in Anselm's life? Not even the ugliness of his monstrous middle age could wrest the sympathy of this girl; she was so overjoyed at Elshender's recovery. He felt far uglier than any dragon as he stood in the angle of the wall and watched her rejoice at Elshender's recovery.

She began again, relentlessly. 'And imagine – your own kin come to kill you! Your own friends setting about you with . . .'

'Elfleda. Your imagination's better than mine. God knows, you're more feeling than I'll ever . . . But can I give you a piece of advice? First and last, I promise,' and he tried to laugh – to lessen the impression that he was an old and sterile irrelevance. But then since when did a girl of seventeen take notice of the advice of elderly relations on the eve of her wedding?

'What then, Bear? Be quick growling. I must get back to Leo.'

'Then don't tell Elshender about our child.' (He could not resist it one last time: our child.)

'But I've told Leo already! While I sat with him this morning. I don't see . . .'

'Leo won't speak – even supposing he could.'

'Oh but he can! Already he's speaking, 'Selm! He's that much mended! He's –'

'Leo won't speak of a child to Elshender. So long as I persuade him that I'll never lay claim to it. I'll go away, if need be. I think that would be best. I've been with Elshender, you see. I've seen how he feels towards me. He's not so generous or tender as you may . . . Blood! Why should he be? Just because he was a dragon, why should he be grateful to get back less than he lost? But he'll take you, for the blessing you are, I know it. Better I shouldn't be here after. I'm afraid his spite against me might flare up against you . . . And I suppose if I can't imagine what it is to be a dragon, I can still imagine how it would be to watch your wife grow big with another man's child. It's purest charity and pity to keep silent. Much the best if you could keep silent – make him believe that nothing . . . that I couldn't . . . that I didn't rob him of anything. But if that's not possible, at least keep silent about the child. I don't know how I'll rest, else, for fear of him hurting you.'

Behind his back, lumps of creeper were coming off the wall in his fists. He could hear the rootlets breaking in the crevices, like a million little blood-vessels bursting at the back of his head, and the mould showered down on him as if he were already dead.

'So,' she said. Her back was to him. She had slowed down now to his pace. 'I'm to marry Elshender and pass off on him your child.'

'Our . . . Yes. I realise how much you care for Elshender;

256

you won't want to deceive him. But if it's for his own happiness . . . If you had a mother, she'd tell you the same! And if you can hold to the secret all your life – no sudden breaking out when the boy does something gross and clumsy because of my blood in him . . .'

'A boy is it to be, then?' She still had her back turned. 'You might wish for a girl, rather. Your likeness in a boy would be hard to ignore. But then perhaps, since I saw the dragon, it will have the looks of a dragon. That should satisfy Elshender, I suppose.'

'Elfleda. Don't joke . . .'

She wiped her hands on her dress. 'No indeed. And life so laughless after all . . . I'm sorry, Anselm, but I really must go to your brother now. When exactly had you and Elshender set your hearts on for this wedding?'

Anselm was not slow any more. He had done his duty, and now he wanted to be gone. 'Oh. Tomorrow, Elshender said. Soon, eh? Yes, well . . . I suppose he's anxious to put some joy in place of all the suffering that's gone before. I can imagine how he feels, can't you?'

She turned her huge eyes on him for a long moment, and there was a little frown lodged like an inflection between their plainsong. 'You're wrong, Anselm. It's you who has the better imagination. I could only think as far as being a dragon.' And she ran back into the house, like some silken rabbit evading the hungry, slow old bear that slavered beside the wall, rending at the fruitless ivy until its pelt was filthy and no gleam remained.

Leo took dinner with them all that evening, and was well enough to nod smilingly at his son and draw dogfish with a stick of charcoal on the arm of his chair. Foolishly, no one sat in

Gwyne's place, and each time his eyes rested on her chair-back, a dismayed bewilderment twitched his face, and the charcoal splintered against the wood. Elshender took his cue from it.

'Father's right, of course. She must be burned. The man too.'

Alban's hands shook as he tore his bread in half, and he let it drop in the trencher. It was comfortably easy for the others to overlook Alban. Clean-shaven and with strands of hair combed over his scalp, the servile hunch of his shoulders relaxed with wine, and his big, labourer's joints concealed by linen, he was like some familiar but distant member of the family who had called over to hear its good news.

'Yes, but what about the child?' said the Prior. 'I would undertake to raise him inside the Order. But . . .' The Prior did not seem to have thought up the objection to his own suggestion. He relied on the others to find one.

'A little close to home,' said Anselm. 'Sooner or later the boy would find out his makings by hearsay.'

'Don't hurt him,' said Elfleda. 'He can't help his parentage.'

'My dear – ' The Prior began to furnish Elfleda with the sin which, theologically speaking, hung round the baby's neck, but Alban interrupted.

'I could take the child back to Northumberland. If you could supply a wet-nurse.' The others looked to Leo for signs of objection.

'What? To your old House? It would be years before they'd take him,' said the Prior scoffingly.

'Of course. I'd raise him till then.'

'And then what would you tell them?' said Anselm.

Alban shrugged. 'That he's my bastard. I'm an

258

excommunicant. No chance of marriage, see? Why wouldn't they believe it?'

The Prior shook his head superciliously: 'Lies, lies, lies.' Then he enjoyed what he thought was a flash of insight and jabbed an accusing finger at Alban. 'You think it would buy you back into your House. That's it, isn't it?'

Alban's face was blank. 'I hadn't thought of asking.' It was true. To look forwards beyond a space of six or eight years? He had only thought – and then in a flash – of the possibility of sharing a half-dozen years with a little creature as benighted as himself. There they would be, in the privacy of a hiding-place, and then somehow he would make a ladder of his own back for the child to scramble up, out of the miry Pit.

'I say we should burn it with its mother,' said Elshender.

'Oh for Jesus's sake . . .!'

It was the first blasphemy Alban had ever spoken, and the whole table was startled by the ferocity of it. They stared at him, and seeing their eyes on him, he blushed and threw down his mangled piece of bread. 'Well,' he said disgustedly. 'Well.'

'Well what?' demanded Elshender, half rising out of his chair.

Alban let his eyes travel up the length of Elshender's body to rest on his face as if he could not believe the need to argue. 'If you've outgrown the memory of standing in the fire,' he said, 'I haven't.'

Elshender put his fingers automatically to the burn on his shoulder. 'But I was innocent!'

'So is the child.'

'Gwyne and Bruno, then.'

'Not them and not the baby. If you're a Christian, you'll put no one in the fire. Leave it for the Devil on Judgement Day.'

Elshender continued to finger the padding under his clothes, and stared at the burns on Alban's face. Suddenly, there was no one else in the room, for either of them, such was the intensity of their staring. Elshender pulled open his doublet to show the wadding and said uncomprehendingly, 'But this is *exactly* why we've got to burn them!'

'For revenge? That's not a wholesome argument in law. Oh, Elshender! Why didn't you eat that poor bastard Bruno when you had him in your jaws? You bargained with Gwyne: his life for yours. I was party to the bargain. I'm heartily glad you tricked yourself back into your skin. But you'll not put a pitchfork in my hand and make me a party to a burning – or a broken promise. That poor wretch has more tooth-marks in him than a steak of meat, and you've tormented him till he's half-mad. You've marred his beauty more'n he's marred yours. Now let him go, and let the woman look after him. Since she fell for the sake of his body, let her spend the rest of her life on it. She'll get no delight from it now that you've chewed on'm.'

Anselm leaned forward and discreetly slid the eating-knife out of reach of his nephew's hand. Alban stood up, bowed to Leo and Elfleda, and faced for the door.

They all waited for the eruption of spleen, the flying fists, the obscenities. But Elshender had begun to shake and, wiping his mouth on his sleeve, he slid back into his chair and held his knees until they stopped bouncing and knocking together.

A growling noise from Leo's throat preceded the words, 'Put them in a boat. Let God decide. Put them in a boat. And give the child to the monk.'

First to bed, Elfleda found Alban sitting on the staircase. He jumped up when he saw her.

'No. Don't go, Alban. Please.'

'I can't look you in the face, madam.'

'Why, Alban?' She sat down beside him. 'You preserved me from marriage, didn't you? Until Elshender could come back.'

He had lost all the mannerisms of a monk. He sat with his knees splayed and his forearms resting on them, and he said flatly, 'I did that, madam. And that pleases you, does it? And there's me thinking . . .'

'Pleases? It's not for the likes of us to be pleased, Alban. Me, I'm an object of reparation. I'm Calais, to be ceded when there's a threat of war. Tell me, what did you do wrong to merit sitting on a staircase so far from home? Did you take a woman, or steal the poor-box?'

'Lady, I've been in Orders so long I wouldn't know what to do with either.'

She laughed. 'I like you, Alban. I really do.'

'And I wouldn't have ceded Calais, lady,' said Alban, reciprocating, 'if it'd been mine.'

'Ah, I ought to declare Calais a principality and give you dominion over it.'

'And be laid siege to by every lousy dragon in Christendom? No thank you, lady.'

She tucked her hands through his arms. 'Alban, whatever did you do to be cut off? I won't believe you deserved it.'

He looked down at her hands, and thought too of the child, and was profoundly content – but for the prospect of damnation. 'I denied the Despair of the Unpreached Heathen.'

'Whatever does it mean?'

261

His hands shuffled the major precepts into something she could handle. 'The idea is that those who lived before Christ, and those who've never heard the Gospel, can't hope for everlasting bliss. It's senseless. At least, it's unjust. You can't condemn a man for ignorance. It's like burning children.'

'Of course it is!' He looked at her doubtfully. 'Well, isn't it?' she asked.

'Probably.'

'Does your House suppose King David and Abraham aren't in Heaven?'

He shrugged. 'I suppose I'll not find that out now.'

'Till you reach Heaven.'

He threw her a look of undisguised reproach and took his arm away. She was uncontrite. 'D'you mean to say you believe the heathens are sinless but that you aren't, for defending them? Don't be ridiculous, Alban! Would the Almighty Judge pardon the prisoner and burn his advocate?'

'Ah, different. It's different.' He slid away from her down the tunnel of his own thoughts. 'I had a chance to believe obediently, see? Besides, there was the matter of the clay sparrows, too.'

'What clay sparrows?'

But he had broken off, and was laughing silently but hilariously, banging his hands on his knees as he rocked backwards and forwards. 'I said it made Christ less human . . . oh, you know the story – the one about the Christ-child making sparrows out of mud and them flying off. I said it weren't Scripture, and besides that it makes Christ less of a man – less human – to have Him tossing off tuppenny fairground miracles before His Ministry. He was a child, see. An ordinary child. That's what I said. Not a pocket magician.

262

And ordinary children don't make sparrows out of clay. Hah! Don't they? Don't they, though? Look at me! Perdition take me! What an ignorant Thomas! Don't they, though?' And he struggled drunkenly to his feet.

'Why? It's *not* in the Scriptures. I know it isn't! I never even heard it for a story!' protested Elfleda, tugging at the skirt of his doublet, feeling she should not let him go off to bed in such a state of excitement; wanting just then to see the comical side to anything.

His hands touched his shoulders and he flapped his elbows like wings. 'I'm clay, aren't I? You're clay! We're all clay. At least we were. Before. *How do I know? Because I've seen it!* Fool that I am. Anyone can do it! Even dragons. But chiefly children – most of all children. I know! I've got one into my keeping! Touch me. Go on, kiss me – like the child will!' and he thrust his head down towards hers and clapped her hands to either side of his shaven face.

She kissed him nervously on the forehead. 'Like that?'

'Like that! You see? You see? Clay into birds! Clay into birds! That's what children *do*. That's the purpose of 'em, almost!'

And he danced off to bed in big capering skips, flapping his arms and laughing and snorting with self-mockery and delight and saying, 'Clay sparrows! Sparrows out of clay!'

Elfleda sat for a while, and then went to bed.

Anselm, when he left the table an hour or so later, lingered outside her door for a long time, running his fingertips up and down the doorpost, before shaking himself and pressing on to the room he had allotted himself.

He dreamed that a dragon came and announced to him the

End of the World. It wagged its seven heads and scowled at him and said, 'Don't want *you*.' And when he woke up, he found it had been telling the truth. Here was the End of the World: the day of Elfleda's marriage.

His body's response was to stay asleep, to stuff up his head with a woolly pain resentful of daylight. In and out of sleep he sprawled, until he believed he must have slept the whole loathsome day away. When he finally sat up, it was only just dawn.

He would go and see his brother – ask his absence to be excused, so that he could leave before the event.

Leo was not in his bed, and only the narrow half to which marriage had accustomed him was creased by his restless night. There was a great plain of loneliness and regret there in that empty, undisturbed half. It would lie there, unbreached for ever, within reach of his sleeping hands. Pity condemned Anslem then and there to seeing the ceremony through. When he got back to his room, Elfleda was sitting on his bed.

Her face was muzzled with sore, red speckles and narrowed to half its width by two clumps of dishevelled hair.

'Elshender came to me last night,' she said, and a Caesarian misery ripped him in shreds.

'At least he came and stood at the foot of my bed. I thought he had come to . . . speak to me. And then I thought perhaps he had found too many objections . . . I thought perhaps, at dinner . . .'

'Who could have found objections to you at dinner, lady? No one.'

'And he said nothing? After I had gone to bed?'

Anselm hovered by the door. His awkwardness was making her awkward. 'He said a deal.'

'But not about me?'

'No. *No, no!* No.' She flinched, he was so emphatic. He saw at once how insulting a thing it was to say.

But how could he repeat any of the filthy, lewd things Elshender had said at dinner, after she went to bed? What woman had he been talking about? Anselm had tried to pretend it was not Elfleda. But finding this a roofless refuge, he had told himself instead that Elshender had been talking of some strange new field of science. Perhaps because Elshender was younger, he was hotter, more learned in foreign fashions, more ingenious by far. As a lover, hadn't Anselm sold short Elfleda with his lack of imagination, variety, bravura, ingenuity? This young man could bring arts to a marriage-bed from a newer, saucier world than the one in which Anselm had grown to dull manhood . . . But was it the same act – that one spewed up by Elshender in so many filthy words? Was it the same act as the one Anselm remembered as bliss?

'I won't see you married to him!' He cried out, all of a sudden.

She knelt up on the bed and tossed back her hair. 'No? Oh Anselm!' The look of relief in her face was dazzling.

It crushed his last hope of salvation. It was his cue to slink away to Outer Darkness. There now. She had not liked to say it, but she had been hoping against hope that he would go away and not discomfort her glorious day.

'No. Of course. I'd be a goblin. A blot. No, no. I never meant to be here. I never meant it. I'll pray for your joy – night and day – always. But I'll go now and do it at a distance.'

She fell forwards on to her hands, and her hair hid her expression. Without the spell of her face, he was free to go, and backed blindly out of the room, and fled towards the stairs.

'*Anselm!*' She only called once, or he might have stopped to wonder why. But he blundered on down the staircase to the stableyard. He would leave in secret and perhaps be clear of his own house, too, by nightfall. Nothing would persuade him to share the same Hundred with the dragon and his wife.

'No luck for the Damned,' he said to himself. The yard was full of people.

A peasant wet-nurse was sitting with her back to the stable wall, feeding Gwyne's baby. Alban, in coming and going, in and out of the stable, kept stopping to look at the baby and being reproached for it by Elshender who was single-handedly rigging a covered cart. Leo, half-dressed and leaning for support on Mann, was roaring at his son. 'How am I better off than before? You might as well have stayed a beast! Where shall I look for an heir now? *At least explain yourself!*'

But Elshender would not say a word in reply. At the sight of Anselm creeping down the rear staircase, Leo turned on him for help: 'Anselm, make him see reason. Make him speak, at least. Don't I merit an explanation?'

Anselm appraised the speed and aggression with which Elshender pushed the horses backwards into the shafts: the boy's head was tightly tucked down; he was a picture of obstinacy. Walking round Elshender, Anselm drew Alban aside, instead. 'What is this?'

'Think of Elfleda!' Leo was wailing. 'Think! A bride! If she's spoiled, we'll find you another!'

Alban made no success of concealing his happiness from Anselm. He did not even try to keep from smiling. 'Elshender has decided to go with me. To Saint Front. He's going to take Orders. He's going to be a Brother. He says he'll sue for me to be absolved and readmitted with the child when he's of an age.

I'm happy for you, my lord Anselm. I'm happy for Elshender too, of course. God knows, I'm happy for me. I'm happy for everyone – except your poor brother, of course,' and in glancing across at Leo he allowed a moment's guilt to hang on his face.

'But *why*, Alban? Why?'

They had moved right into the stable. It was entirely dark except where the sunlight in the doorway made a dazzling goldwork tapestry out of the straw on the floor. 'A man's vocation is private, sir. Only he knows.'

'But *you* know, don't you?' said Anselm impatiently. 'He's your dragon. You know what he's thinking well enough.'

'Yes, I know,' said Alban simply. He clasped his hands together over his lap and looked down: already Anselm could smell the cloisters on him. 'He came looking for me last night – agitated – oh agitated – more than this. I don't know where he'd come from, but he was jibbering cold. And he swore that he was ruined – said I must find a way to make him back into a dragon.'

'He was lousy with drink,' said Anselm.

'No,' said Alban peaceably. 'No, he was really . . . really . . . *lacking*.'

'Lacking what, for Jesu's sake?'

Alban spread his hands. His shoulders rose and fell helplessly. It seemed to Anselm that he knew well enough, but he said, 'I couldn't say, Lord Anselm sir.'

At the foot of Elfleda's bed, Elshender had taken up, as best he could, the same stance he had held outside the wall of de Rochfoll's house. It was easy, too, to balance on two legs, even on paltry pink feet. And it was easy to focus on Elfleda, even with his astigmatic sight.

He did not want her in terror of him, and after the initial shock of seeing him, she was not. No fear. And fear had given him an edge, somehow, male over female.

And the smell of her was less: there was no smell, or none that pierced his small, sore nose.

And she was not vulnerable – not when she could say so assuredly, 'Go back to bed, Elshender. Don't be foolish.'

It was her fault, then. It was her fault – the feeling that hourglass sand was running down into the lower half of his body. All evening he had tried to prick up his lust with every dirty word he could muster, all the pictorial words he had met like strangers on the lips of whores. Everything lewd he had ever guessed at. He had gored his defeated rival, Anselm, itemising every last joy conquest would bring him. But the sand had gone on running, burying his vital organs. It was Elfleda's fault, but all the dragony violence of lust had dwindled down to a human scale. Never very much at best.

All evening he had tried to prick up his anger with little acts of spite and suggestions of vengeance. But the sand had gone on running, burying his dragony spleen in human indifference.

There was no lust. There was no anger. At least. in comparison with the passions of the beast. He was a small, cold, twigged creature devoid of feeling. Except that in the grate of his ribs one smouldering feeling survived: an emotion born in his dragony days.

He had dismissed Elfleda with an expression of repugnance and a flick of his hand, and turned away from the end of her bed.

In the stable, Anselm was helpless to prise secrets out of the monk. This morning Alban did not even think of Elshender as unhappy. His dragon had found a way into the perfect tranquillity of a monastic life. Alban's happiness was impregnable.

Unexpectedly, Elshender came in and without looking at either man walked straight between them to fetch the harness off the wall. 'I had a lust for Elfleda a yard long,' he said loudly. 'Now she can't stir me to a span. You see how well suited I am to my Calling, Uncle? Are you coming, monk, or not?'

After he had gone, Alban was clearly anxious to go too. 'I must help now. He's ready. I'm needed.'

'There is one love he's kept, then,' said Anselm.

But Alban had already turned to go, and did not seem to hear.

'Spare a thought for his father!' shouted Anselm to fetch him back.

Alban turned in the doorway and looked unabashed. 'There'll be a nephew for heir.'

'And my w – Elfleda? Will he disappoint her and shame her a second time?'

'Are you serious, sir? Don't be foolish. She doesn't even like Elshender. Anyone with two eyes can see that.' And making a little leap in the air, Alban left. When Anselm came out of the stable, Alban had the baby in his arms and was sitting up on the driver's board, shoulder to shoulder with his dragon. The wet-nurse was waving a tearful goodbye to her parents, while Leo continued to shout and rage after his son, and Mann's old bones creaked under the strain of supporting him. There was no luggage to speak of.

21

CONSOLATION

There were two ways of saying it. He could shoulder his way into her room and say, 'There now. He's spurned you. Nothing for it but to take me.' Or he could offer her a discreet friendship and sympathy. In time she might come to think he was better than nothing.

Anselm did neither. He hid in a bedchamber, not daring to show himself, not wanting to see the preparations for the wedding dismantled, and not willing to go home with the matter unsettled.

In the end, Elfleda came to fetch him. She was dressed in a deep blue woollen dress of Gwyne's with flowers embroidered down the bodice, and her unbraided hair was covered with an unfastened square of lawn. 'Well?' she said. 'If you don't come now, we'll begin without you.'

'I'm not really hungry.'

'Good. The meal won't be ready for an hour or more.'

'What . . .?'

'The wedding, Anselm. We are waiting to begin the wedding.'

'Whose wedding?'

She lifted two little fists and let them fall again. 'Do you really intend that I should be let drop between the two of you? What objection do you have to me that wasn't there a week ago?'

'Oh, Elfleda!' His lunge stopped short of her: he did not know what part of her it was fitting to touch, what caress might crease the brave front she was wearing. 'I'm so sorry. Not to be Elshender! I'd be Elshender if I could, I swear it . . .'

'Would you? Much use we'd be to each other, then. For I'd not be in your heart and you'd not be in mine.' And he suddenly knew why she reminded him of Alban as he stood in the stable doorway: they had both been laughing at him.

'That's what Alban said . . . He wasn't right, though? Alban said you didn't care for Elshender. I mean, the fool.'

'There's no fool been talking to you, my lord. Except that fool Anselm. Was it he who persuaded you not to marry me? That bear?' She took his shirt collar out of his mouth, demanding an answer.

'No,' he said, declining to smile. 'You have to marry me. It's unavoidable. The first time, I took advantage of your fright. This time it's the child. All this forcing of young women into my bed – it's enough to risk my immortal soul. If I had one left to me.'

'And don't you have a soul?' she asked, putting her arms round his waist.

'No, I traded it last night for a miracle.'

'Oh! You too?' She breathed in awesomely. 'Anselm! I see a terrible dilemma! Two tenders for one miracle. Which of us was successful?'

They considered this for some time before Anselm reached a conclusion. 'Madam. At the Last, I'll speak in your defence if you'll speak in mine.'

'By all means.'

'But then I'm afraid we're obliged to stay in each other's

company until Judgement Day,' he said, and held her head against his chest.

There was less of an audience than there might have been for the casting-adrift of Gwyne and her lover. The people of Worm Bay had chosen not to rebuild, but to sail in a little flotilla round the coast in search of a new harbour. In fact it was difficult, because of that, to find a boat. There was not a man there but wondered why one hull remained on the foreshore. Why leave it behind – if it were sound? But no one chose to speak the question out loud.

A trader came in from Bruges, and its master was persuaded to tow the hull after him when he sailed, and let it go in mid-sea. Leo was not recovered sufficiently to be present on the beach. At least he stayed in his bed that day, and another too, because of the storm that blew up in the afternoon. It made for draughts round the castle. He was highly susceptible to the cold.

When he was better recovered, he often took a horse over to Worm Bay and the surrounding beaches. People said he was looking for wreckage, but he denied it.

Sometimes he met a mad old woman there in a moulted cape and browband of feathers. She had not sailed with the refugees of Worm Bay. She frequently confided in Leo (though he paid no attention) that she had sailed in a boat once with a man who had eaten her son. If she had known at the time, she said, she would have stuck a fish-hook in his throat. 'If I had my time again,' she would say. 'If I had my time again.'

A son was born to Anselm and Elfleda and was named as heir to the Hundred. It was Elfleda who named him Leo – always a thoughtful, imaginative woman. After the son was born, Lord Leo spent a long while more scuffing along the beaches at low water. He seemed to take pleasure in finding those dogfish egg-sacs known as mermaids' purses, in among the decomposing seaweed and the flies.

The Laily Worm

'I was but seven year auld
When my mither she did dee;
My father married the ae warst woman
The warld did ever see.

'For she has made me the laily worm,
That lies at the fit o' the tree,
An' my sister Masery she's made
The machrel of the sea.'

Also available in Minerva

JUAN PERUCHO

Natural History

Set in the Spain of the 1830s, this eerie, elegant novel of vampires and politics relates a young aristocrat's heroic triumph over a macabre adversary. Antoni de Montpalau, a believer in science and progress, is summoned to the aid of a village terrorized by a creature of darkness who can assume various shapes and guises. Through de Montpalau's pursuit and confrontation of his adversary, Perucho weaves an exquisitely witty, rich and poetic narrative, which transposes a figure of popular myth into a complex philosophical thriller. This is the first novel by Juan Perucho, the distinguished Catalan writer whose work was suppressed by the Franco regime, to be published outside Spain.

'Comparisons with Borges are easy to draw – the razor-sharp intellect toying with the fantastical' *Observer*

'Will intrigue those readers who willingly follow Italo Calvino into the implausible, and will appeal to the devotees of fantastical Latin American writing. They will be mystified, thrilled, intellectually ensnared, and left impatiently anticipating the next translation' *Preview*

'The book is beautifully written and constantly echoes that other vicious Civil War when Franco tried his best to destroy Catalan culture. It is one of the most entertaining novels of the year' Paul Pickering, *London Evening Standard*

JEANETTE WINTERSON

Boating For Beginners

'Winterson has re-written The Book of Genesis and turned it into a surreal Cecil B De Mille epic. Feminism and Twentieth Century kitchenware run riot in the ancient city of Ur; Noah is Howard Hughes crossed with Frankenstein – an eccentric overseer of thriving capitalism who makes "God" "by accident out of a piece of gâteau and a giant electric toaster."

'The result is a tetchy, omnipotent ice-cream cone who decides to drown all the decadence of Winterson's world (and, curiously, that world resembles Queensway) in a flood – out of which, of course, a more fitting myth can be born, ie that God is a benevolent old man with a white beard who loves us all.

'Occasionally, Winterson ceases to be a jester and seriously explores the power of myth ("they explain the universe while allowing the universe to go on being unexplained . . .") and of faith ("when the heart revolts it wants outrageous things that cannot possibly be factual . . ."). I could have done with a bit more of this and less jokes about fast food. But then I prefer depressing books, and Winterson has proved with *Oranges Are Not The Only Fruit* how popular her wit is'   Jane Solanas, *Time Out*

'If you find the Monty Python *Life of Brian* amusing, this is your comic book of revelations'
Andrew Sinclair, *The Times*

GERALDINE McCAUGHREAN

The Maypole

'Set in England, in a mythical and mystical Middle Ages, *The Maypole* is a bewitching love story, drawn from the old ballad tradition and lustily retold. It tells of a fated passion, of lovers betrayed and yet ultimately redeemed, of desire transfigured. Presented as a love story, pure and simple, there is a refreshing vigour in the telling, a disconcerting strangeness to the imagery that creates a novel both perverse and enchanting.

'A finely-crafted enthralling narrative of the redemptive power of love and friendship'
Oxford Times

'A superb novel of violence and love, earthy as Chaucer. A small masterpiece'
David Hughes, *Mail on Sunday*

KATHY PAGE

Island Paradise

'In a perfect society in which there are no wars and no fear, one woman finds herself struggling against the conformity of this not so brave new world. A superbly provocative read' *Elle*

'Set 100 years in the future, *Island Paradise* posits a world in which nuclear conflagration has been heroically averted, all weapons (supposedly) destroyed and a cult of peace established. Murder (Untimely Death) is so unspeakable that its very existence is denied. But the price for such peace is one that all citizens must pay – Timely Death. As her time grows nigh, narrator Laurie thinks back to the events 20 years ago on Island Paradise, a luxurious holiday resort: events which opened her eyes . . .' *Time Out*

'This is a remarkable novel, visionary in its descriptions of the future, psychologically and politically rich. Kathy Page's language has passages of striking beauty' Maggie Gee

'Kathy Page's *Island Paradise* represents a remarkable shift away from the moralism and towards the eroticism of the post-feminist novel . . . Page's voice is by turns lyrical and laconic, with a narrative dexterity which is reminiscent of Margaret Atwood at her very best' *City Limits*

'Kathy Page is a young writer to watch'
Financial Times

A Selected List of Titles Available from Minerva

While every effort is made to keep prices low, it is sometimes necessary to increase prices at short notice. Mandarin Paperbacks reserves the right to show new retail prices on covers which may differ from those previously advertised in the text or elsewhere.

The prices shown below were correct at the time of going to press.

Fiction

☐	7493 9026 3	**I Pass Like Night**	Jonathan Ames	£3.99	BX
☐	7493 9006 9	**The Tidewater Tales**	John Bath	£4.99	BX
☐	7493 9004 2	**A Casual Brutality**	Neil Blessondath	£4.50	BX
☐	7493 9028 2	**Interior**	Justin Cartwright	£3.99	BC
☐	7493 9002 6	**No Telephone to Heaven**	Michelle Cliff	£3.99	BX
☐	7493 9028 X	**Not Not While the Giro**	James Kelman	£4.50	BX
☐	7493 9011 5	**Parable of the Blind**	Gert Hofmann	£3.99	BC
☐	7493 9010 7	**The Inventor**	Jakov Lind	£3.99	BC
☐	7493 9003 4	**Fall of the Imam**	Nawal El Saadewi	£3.99	BC

Non-Fiction

☐	7493 9012 3	**Days in the Life**	Jonathon Green	£4.99	BC
☐	7493 9019 0	**In Search of J D Salinger**	Ian Hamilton	£4.99	BX
☐	7493 9023 9	**Stealing from a Deep Place**	Brian Hall	£3.99	BX
☐	7493 9005 0	**The Orton Diaries**	John Lahr	£5.99	BC
☐	7493 9014 X	**Nora**	Brenda Maddox	£6.99	BC

All these books are available at your bookshop or newsagent, or can be ordered direct from the publisher. Just tick the titles you want and fill in the form below. Available in:
BX: British Commonwealth excluding Canada
BC: British Commonwealth including Canada

Mandarin Paperbacks, Cash Sales Department, PO Box 11, Falmouth, Cornwall TR10 9EN.

Please send cheque or postal order, no currency, for purchase price quoted and allow the following for postage and packing:

UK   80p for the first book, 20p for each additional book ordered to a maximum charge of £2.00.

BFPO   80p for the first book, 20p for each additional book.

Overseas   £1.50 for the first book, £1.00 for the second and 30p for each additional book
including Eire   thereafter.

NAME (Block letters) ....

ADDRESS ....

....

....